A LOVE YOU MORE ROCK STAR ROMANCE

MORE JADE

Laura Pavlov

More Jade Playlist

If I had a gun ~ Neil Gallagher

Milestone ~ Matt Walden

Unsteady ~ X Ambassadors

Us ~ James Bay

One thing right ~ Marshmello & Kane Brown

Crossing a line ~ Mike Shinoda

Shining Star ~ Earth, Wind & Fire

I Found ~ Amber Run

To Greg, Chase & Hannah,
Thank you for always believing in me, supporting me and encouraging me to reach for the stars. You are the loves of my life! xo

*There is no
remedy for love,
but to love more.*

-Thoreau

Chapter One

JADE

I GAZED AROUND THE ROOM ONE LAST TIME, TAKING IT ALL IN. IT WASN'T like I was moving far away—but this was home. The only home I'd ever known. It was pancakes on Sunday mornings and Friday movie nights. Family gatherings, card games, and Monday night football with Dad and his friends. This thousand square foot space owned the happiest and saddest memories of my life thus far. Dad and I had lived in this apartment since the day he and Mom brought me home from the hospital.

I opened Mom's journal and found today's date. It was a ritual for me, reading along on the same day all these years later. It somehow made me feel connected to her. Like we were experiencing things together. Maybe in a way we were.

August 21st

Dear Journal,

Today is the first day of the rest of my life. I am about to walk to my first class at Northwestern. I feel like I've been preparing for this day for as long as I can remember. I went to my first official college party last night and met a boy named Jack. He doesn't even go here. He was with a group of high school friends that attend the university, and he came along to the party. We stayed up talking outside my dorm until almost 2 o'clock in the morning. He wants to be a firefighter. He doesn't live far, as he's from Bucktown. I like him. He's gorgeous, and smart, and funny. I'm meeting him for lunch after class, so I'll keep you posted.

I'm off to charge the tundra. Change the world. I'm so ready for this next adventure.

Ciao for now,
J.E.

"You ready, Jady bug?" Dad called out from downstairs. I closed Mom's journal and slipped it in my backpack.

"I'm going to college today. Don't you think it's time to drop the charming nickname?" I said as I made my way downstairs and into the kitchen. I dropped my backpack on the table and grabbed a bottle of water from the fridge.

"Ah, big college girl. What should I call you—*Dr. Moore*?"

"Dad," I moaned. "I'm an undergrad. How about you call me by my *actual* name."

"Jade? Nah, that's boring." He laughed.

My dad, Jack Moore, was the newly promoted captain of his firehouse in Chicago, a single dad, and my favorite person on the planet. He was a chronic jokester, ridiculously protective and fiercely loyal.

I tossed him a banana and tried to hide my smile. "News flash. You named me."

"News flash. Your mother named you." He grabbed his keys off the counter and scooped up my backpack. He already loaded everything in the back of his truck at oh-seventeen hundred hours, because the man functioned on no sleep.

"Well, she didn't name me *Jady bug*," I say.

He backed out of the driveway and I didn't miss the forced smile. It was still hard for him to travel down memory lane. Even after all these years. It was still raw. Jaqueline Marie Edington-Moore had been the love of his life, and for the short time I was with her, she was the love of mine too. My memories had faded, but her absence was always there. Like a big, black gaping hole. There had been a void in Dad's life ever since we lost her. I'd tried hard to fill it, but he missed his wife. He always would.

The guys at the firehouse all stepped up after Mom died. My grandparents picked up the slack when Dad had to work, as I was all they had left of their daughter. You know the saying *it takes a village*? Well, I was the epitome of that saying. I lost my mom unexpectedly at five years old to a rare congenital heart condition. Thankfully, Dad and I weren't alone with the support of my grandparents living nearby and a half dozen men that were more like family. They had worked with Dad at the station for the last eighteen years. And now, for the first time in my life, I was going to be living on my own. And so was Dad.

Northwestern University had been my dream school for as long as I could remember. Mom was a Wildcat and so was my grandfather. I'd always imagined that if I got in, I'd be commuting from our apartment to school each day. Dad and I lived in a two-bedroom walk-up in Bucktown, which was about thirty minutes from Evanston on a good day. With no traffic. Which never happened. Commuting more than an hour each way on public transportation was not ideal. So, when the university offered me not only an academic scholarship but room and board, it was a no brainer. Dad wanted me to have the whole college experience, but I worried about him. I worried about him all the time. I hated the thought of him being alone. But a part of me knew we both needed this. He needed to start living for something other than me. It was time for him to be selfish and do things for himself. And I needed to spread my wings and see where they took me. I would still see Dad often, just not daily.

"Are you nervous?" he asked as we moved fifteen miles an hour in traffic.

"No. Not really. I'm not going far," I said, but we both knew I was lying.

"Always so stoic." He reached over and rumpled my hair, which annoyed me. Obviously.

"I learned from the best," I said.

"You know I can be there in thirty minutes if you need me."

"I know, Dad. I'll be fine. Stop worrying."

"Uncle Jimmy can be there in half the time. You know that, right?"

He'd told me this more than a dozen times over the last twenty-four hours. Uncle Jimmy was Dad's best friend, and they worked at the firehouse together.

"I'll be fine. Don't be a helicopter parent. You know they frown upon that in college, right?" I said.

"Yeah, yeah, yeah. You've mentioned it. I'm sure Sam will be checking in on you often too."

Uncle Jimmy's son, Sam, was more like a brother to me, as we'd grown up together since birth basically. He was a year older than me, and our dads had been in the same firehouse our entire life. He attended an art school in the city, which was only an hour away. Last year sucked when he left for college, and I still had one more year at our uber small Catholic high school without him. Thankfully, I had a good group of girlfriends who I'd gone to school with since kindergarten, so I survived without him. I didn't know anyone attending Northwestern, so I'd actually be friendless until I met some people. My roommate Meagan seemed nice enough, at least from what I could tell over email. I didn't require much from a roommate, and I'd settle for *not crazy*. Sam loved to tell me all the insane horror stories that had gone on his first year in the dorms.

Meagan was from Michigan and she had a boyfriend of four years who was going to school out west. They were going to try the long-distance thing. She asked me to *help her stay in line*, whatever that entailed, I had no idea.

"Yep. He's just waiting until I get settled and he'll come visit. And I can always take the bus out to see him. It's only an hour away. You need to stop worrying."

"I'll try, Jady bug," he said, pulling into a front spot marked 'resident unloading area'.

"Are you trying to ensure I make no friends?" I whined when he called me by my nickname again before I hopped out of the truck.

"You've got plenty of friends already. You don't need more," Dad said when he met me at the back of the truck. I gave him a hard stare. He was familiar with the look.

"Alright. I'll stop. It's a big day, kiddo."

"Yep." I led him toward the dorm check-in.

The girl at the table asked me my name, and shuffled through some folders, pulling a file from the stack. She looked a few years older than me and appeared to be running the show.

"Here you are, Jade Moore. I'm actually the RA for the fifth floor, so we'll be seeing a lot of one another. I'm Dominique, but everyone calls me Dom." She reached over the table and shook my hand.

"Nice to meet you. This is my dad, Jack."

"Great to meet you both. I'm available for anything you need," she said.

Her blonde hair cascaded over her shoulders in perfect waves. Her makeup looked like she'd just come from a makeover at Sephora. She was stunning, and a reminder of how *not* put together I was. Insecurity reared its ugly head. My dark hair fell just past my shoulders, and of course I let it air dry this morning which left it looking disheveled.

Half straight, half wavy. Mostly hot mess.

This is how I usually wore it, but I wasn't normally surrounded by people who looked so put together daily, either. I subconsciously tucked my hair behind my ears. Dom pushed to stand, and I zoned in on her preppy navy pencil skirt, white button-up, and some sort of fancy name brand of flats I'd seen before, but never paid much attention to. Damn. My Chicago fire tee, skinny jeans, and white Chucks suddenly felt inappropriate.

She handed me a few items and talked a mile a minute. "These are your keys. The green one opens the main door, the yellow one opens your dorm room and the purple one is your mail key. You'll need to keep these with you at all times to get in the building."

"Okay. Thank you," I said, looking up at Dad. He put a hand on my shoulder because his bat senses always went off when I was anxious. He was far too intuitive for a man.

"Of course. We've got a crew over here to help unload your car. I can walk your dad over if you want to go check out your room. He can meet you up there with our awesome move-in team," Dom said.

Five minutes with her and it was easy to see that she was a leader. I tended to sit back and observe rather than taking charge of situations.

"Yeah, sure. Thank you," I said, trying to remember what key went where.

I found my way to the fifth floor. When I stepped off the elevator, there were signs pointing to the boys' and girls' wings of the floor. The guys' side was to the left. I made my way to the right. An odd odor lingered in the air. A mixture of stale beer, urine, and lemons. Obviously, they were trying to cover up the disgusting smell while students moved in and the parents were here. Lemons weren't a bad choice; however, they weren't strong enough for this particular situation.

I made my way down the hall and tried to calm my racing heart. My entire life had led up to this moment. I wanted to take it all in. Be present. It wasn't a strength of mine, but I was trying.

Enjoy this.

Don't think so far into the future.

I silently repeated the mantra in my head.

At the end of the long hallway, I found room five-fifteen and stared at my keys. *Yellow.* Yellow opened the door to my room. I shifted my backpack on my shoulder and tried the key. I had to jiggle it a little before I got the door open. Someone gasped loud enough to startle me, and I heard a guy mumble, "Oh shit," as I stood there stunned by the scene before me. I could only assume it was Meagan, my new roommate, down on her knees with her back to me fumbling about, while her boyfriend quickly adjusted himself while he sat on the bed. He pushed her head back from between his legs and she broke out in a fit of giggles.

Welcome to college, Jade.

I couldn't imagine being caught with my head between some guy's legs, and giggling. Not the best first impression. I mean, to each his own, but come on. She knew I'd be arriving this afternoon. And why is her boyfriend here when he goes to school on the west coast? I hoped this wasn't a preview of the upcoming year. I didn't want to have some strange dude sleeping in my room every day.

I turned around for a second to give them a moment. "Sorry about that."

Why the hell was I apologizing? Shouldn't she be the one apologizing to me? I just walked in on her giving her boyfriend a BJ, after all.

"Oh my god, oh my god, no. You must be Jade. I'm Meagan. I'm so excited we're rooming together. We're going to have the best year," she said, extending her hand to me. I smiled and nodded, pretending my hands were full holding the *one* backpack. I knew where those hands had just been.

No thanks.

"Nice to meet you." I dropped my bag on the empty bed and glanced over to find her boyfriend watching me. *Stalker much?* Maybe he's embarrassed and this was his coping mechanism. You know, to be super creepy and gawk at his girlfriend's roommate.

"Okay. You scared the bejesus out of me, and now I have to pee. This is Cruz. Cruz, Jade. I'll be right back," Meagan said as I processed the fact that I was ninety-nine percent sure she'd told me her boyfriend's name was Josh and this must not be him.

She left the room, and the creeper pushed to his feet. I said a silent prayer of thanks that Dad didn't witness this little welcome party going on in room five-fifteen. He would have tried to haul me back to Bucktown. To call him protective was an understatement.

The Cruz guy moved to stand beside me and reached for the welcome folder I had just dropped next to my backpack on my bed.

"*Jade Moore*," he said.

"Impressive. A college kid who can read."

"So, Jade Moore's a wiseass."

"Do you even go to school here?" I asked.

"It's your lucky day, because, yes, I'm a student here. I'm a junior. My friends and I just came over to visit the dorms and welcome all the new freshmen to Northwestern," he said.

I had to look up at him, so he had to be over six feet tall. He wore a backward baseball cap with dark blond scruffy hair poking out, a torn-up white T-shirt, and black skinny jeans. His gaze locked with mine. His eyes were an unusual color, one I'd never seen before. Although keep in mind, I hadn't been out of the state of Illinois. *Ever*. So, it wasn't saying much. They were a light honey-brown with orange and gold specks. He had a bit of scruff peppering his chin. He was definitely good looking, and he knew it. The boy oozed confidence.

"Ah, sorry to disappoint you, but no one else in this room is going to drop to their knees for the welcome wagon. Feel free to move along," I said, and made it clear that his ogling was not impressing me. The kid just zipped his pants up after having my roommate between his legs. Have some dignity, man. Instead he laughed. Loud. Like I just told a super funny joke. It's called rejection, bud. It wasn't supposed to be funny.

"Very witty, Jade Moore. I like that. Wouldn't mind seeing *more Jade*," he said with an arrogant smirk.

Ah, the play on words. Jade Moore. More Jade. Every once in a blue moon, someone got it and used it. He wasn't the first and he wouldn't be the last.

"That makes one of us," I said, turning my back to him just as Meagan threw the door open.

"Look who I found hanging out down the hall," she said as two guys followed her into our room.

"Jade, this is—" She paused and laughed, all while twirling a chunk of blonde hair around her finger. "I'm sorry, what are your names again?"

Someone, please stab me and put me out of my misery. I felt like I was trapped in a bad reality show.

"Hey, I'm Lennon and this is Adam," one kid said.

These guys actually appeared normal, unlike the jerk who just got caught with his pants down. Lennon was shorter than Cruz and Adam who were about the same height.

"Nice to meet you, I'm Jade." I smiled.

Thankfully, there was a loud ruckus and the door swung open again. It was Dad, along with four large guys carrying what looked to be everything in one shot. My dad had a huge box in front of his face, and I guided him over to my desk to set it down. The room was crowded, and I wished Meagan would say goodbye to her friends so Dad and I could get me moved in. Everyone was talking at the same time when Cruz sidled up next to me, grabbed my hand, and shoved something in it before I could tug it away. He closed my fingers around it. His nearness made me uncomfortable. My palms were sweaty and my mouth dry. No one was the wiser as Dad grabbed laundry baskets from two of the guys and stacked them on my bed. He insisted on filling these ridiculous baskets with clothing because I could load them up, empty them and he could take the empty baskets back home.

When I opened my fingers, I saw my pink and white panties which must have fallen out of one of the stupid laundry baskets. Dammit. This would have been a helpful tidbit to mention when I begged Dad to buy actual boxes. If he knew this boy just handed me my panties, he would have a conniption.

Cruz leaned close to my ear and said, "I thought you might need these, *more Jade.*"

I shoved the panties in the back pocket of my jeans and glared at him before turning to help Dad find a place for the TV.

We thanked the moving crew and Dad handed them a couple bucks before noticing the other three guys and Meagan who were standing around talking like they belonged there. They introduced themselves before heading for the door.

"You should come to the welcome thing tonight. I hear they've got a killer band playing," Lennon said, and they all laughed. Not sure what that meant, but I had no intention of going to anything tonight. I wanted to unpack and get organized.

"I wouldn't miss it," Meagan said. "Hey, can you guys show me where the mailroom is on your way out?"

The girl had no shame. You'd think she'd be horrified by what I walked in on, but she didn't seem to have a care in the world.

"Sure. See ya, Jade," Adam and Lennon said on their way out, with Meagan in tow.

Dad was under my desk trying to attach one of those multi-plug thingies and Cruz took his sweet time getting to the door.

"See you, *more Jade.*" He winked.

"I doubt it," I said with a forced smile as he turned to leave.

Finally, a moment of peace.

"They seem nice," Dad said.

"Sure."

If he only knew.

Chapter Two

CRUZ

WE BELTED OUT OUR LAST SONG, AND I WALKED BACKSTAGE AND SLAMMED a beer. The crowd was going wild for more, and Dex yelled for me to get ready to go back out there. Our band, Exiled, was growing in popularity. I could feel it in the air. The way you knew a storm was coming. The sky turned gray, the air cooled, and there was a shift in the universe—that's what was happening here. Whether the storm was going to be a good or bad thing, I didn't care. I'd been waiting for so long, it was inevitable. Almost like something greater than myself.

"Yeah, I'll be right there." I snubbed out my smoke and strode back on stage.

Bright lights blinded my vision, but I knew what was there, nonetheless. Screaming college kids, mainly chicks. Their boyfriends were bellied up to the bar getting toasted while their girls threw their bras on stage and danced all sexy and dirty below us. It was hot as hell until it got sloppy. Which it always did. There were always a few middle-aged women who dragged their friends here for a girls'-night-out to ogle young dudes who resembled their rebellious days. Exiled was an edgy alternative rock band comprised of me, my brother, Lennon, my best friend, Adam, and my sometimes friend, Dex. Dex was cool when he wasn't on my fucking nerves, which wasn't often.

We performed for another twenty minutes until my voice was raw and gravelly. I knew I'd have to kick smoking soon, because we were performing more often, and my vocals couldn't take the abuse. But damn if nothing beat a good drag after a set. I'd cross that bridge when I had to. The energy grew with each show. Security hustled us off stage to the back room. We had performed at this venue, The Dive, every week over the last two years, but the crowd was changing. Our following was growing at a rapid rate, and our manager, Luke, thought we'd outgrown The Dive. We liked it here and the owner gave us our first break, so we kept coming back. It was sort of where we got our start.

Lennon and I had known Adam since we were kids. My brother was a kickass guitarist. He was seriously skilled and passionate about music. Adam had been playing the drums since we were kids, so they started a band and made me the lead singer, mostly because no one else could sing. We met Dex in high school, and Lennon found out he played the electric keyboard, and history was made. Exiled was formed. We started out playing for fun, at least I did, but things had really taken off this past year.

Adam and I both attended Northwestern University, Lennon went to community college in the city, and no one knew what the fuck Dex did. He was a trust fund kid, and he lived for music. The dude jammed on the electric keyboard. He didn't see the point of any of us going to school, because he had no doubt that Exiled would make it big. He and my father were in the same camp. They couldn't fathom any other kind of life. Me? I wasn't sure what the fuck I wanted to be when I grew up. But I was interested in more than just music. I'd majored in Art history because I liked studying the architecture of different cultures and time periods. The guys made fun of me for it. Maybe it was all the traveling I'd done with my mom over the years, but I was drawn to the visual and physical characteristics of architecture as well as the range of different cultural practices. I was the opposite of Superman—I was a lead singer of a rock band on the outside and an art nerd beneath. I kept my inner Clark Kent hidden away whenever possible.

We finished the show and walked backstage.

"Cruz, my man, that was something tonight. You sounded good, brother." Luke pulled me in for one of those half dude hugs and clapped me on the shoulder.

"Yeah, everyone was on tonight," I said as Adam tossed me a beer.

We did our traditional cheers before we tipped our heads back and chugged.

"I don't know about you guys, but I need to get laid tonight," Dex said when he reached for another beer. The dude did everything large. He partied big. And he lived big. He went through chicks faster than most people could down a cup of coffee.

I sat back, lit a cigarette, and took a long, slow drag. Luke opened the door and in trickled a group of seven or eight girls. They were cute.

And drunk.

And loud.

And I wasn't in the mood.

I was by far the moodiest fucker in our band. Don't get me wrong, I liked to have a good time. I could drink whiskey with the best of them. And I enjoyed getting sucked off by a hot chick as much as the next guy. But not at the rate Dex did. And sometimes after a set, I just wanted to chill and take it in. Not numb myself through the whole process. I'd read enough articles about bands that ran themselves into the ground with the lifestyle that comes with it. We'd had a very small taste of it on a miniscule scale, and Dex had already shown signs of being a disaster of epic proportions. And my brother had the tendency to go off the rails as well, which was half the reason I was even here in the first place.

A blonde chick walked over to me. I squinted through the puff of smoke I'd just released to make out her face. Shit. It was the girl who dropped to her knees a few days ago when I looked in her direction. I couldn't remember her name, which was ironic because she never shut the fuck up during the few minutes I'd spent with her. I do, however, remember her roommate's name. *More Jade.* Now that one, I could handle dropping to her knees as often as she liked. She was unamused by me. Wholesome and natural looking. Apparently, that's my new thing, because I couldn't stop staring at her. There was something about her, but I couldn't put my finger on it. The girl was gorgeous sans makeup and all the extra shit most of these girls did. She didn't have a clue how fucking hot she was. Maybe that was the draw. She also didn't appear to give a shit what anyone thought of her. I wanted to run my fingers through her dark hair. Her eyes though — that's what did me in. They were jade green. Hell, maybe that was why they'd named her Jade. Plump kissable lips, and a small, rockin' body. She didn't need to do much to be the hottest girl in the room. Not like these girls that just walked in, all fake baked with big hair and big tits. They didn't hold a candle to her.

Mandy, or Candy, whatever her name was, dropped down on my lap. Fuck me. Not interested. I blew smoke in her direction and she tipped her head back and giggled. Why was that funny?

"Do you remember me, Cruz? I thought we could finish what we started the other day. You know, before my annoying roommate interrupted us."

I pushed to my feet, forcing her to stumble to stand. "Not tonight. I'm out."

Her lips turned down in a frown and she said, "Boo."

Literally, that's what she said. *Boo.* How the hell did this chick attend Northwestern? I was embarrassed for her, but Dex had a big grin on his face and opened his arms wide, winking at me over her shoulder when she walked into his arms. No one was off limits with him.

I was halfway down the hallway when Luke caught up to me.

"Cruz, your dad thinks AF studios may be interested in you guys."

I paused. "I talked to him this morning and he didn't say a word."

Luke laughed. "Yeah, he thinks your head isn't in the game with classes starting."

I had the only parent on the planet who discouraged their kid from getting an education. He did the same to Lennon, but my brother's desire to please my father was greater than his desire to please himself. That's where we differed. And it pissed me off. My dad, Steven Winslow, was a famous Hollywood producer. Lucky for me, he wasn't around much during my formative years. He commuted from Chicago to Los Angeles because my mom insisted on raising us here. Not sure why it was so important to her, because she was rarely home either. Dad needed Mom by his side, which meant we spent most of our time with nannies growing up. Dad didn't go to college. He was a self-made man. My father based success on two things. Fame and fortune.

He agreed to let me get an education as long as I continued to pursue music, which I agreed to do. It wasn't like I didn't love making music. I did. And I knew my brother would die without it, so quitting wasn't an option. At least not now. Besides, it had grown on me and it gave me a creative outlet. But I'd also like to have a fallback plan, something with a future when music ran its course. Most bands didn't make it in this business. But I had a powerful father with deep pockets, and he was determined for Exiled to be the next Rolling Stones. He paid for a manager for the band long before we earned money of our own. Dad wanted us to be famous a hell of a lot more than I did. I didn't mind jamming in small bars or practicing in basements and making good music. Hell, I loved it. Dad wanted so much more. My goal? Get my degree before he found someone to sign us and I had to leave Chicago.

"He's relentless. What parent gets upset that their kid is going to college?"

"Listen, you know I always have your back, and I'm proud of you for pursuing your education while we wait this out. But, having a dad in powerful places with unlimited funds is not the worst thing in the world. He just believes you're destined to make it big, and I do too," Luke said, dropping his smoke on the ground and stomping it out.

I rolled my eyes. How many other fuckers would be destined to make it big if their daddies had private jets and endless resources? All of them. I hated that my father's success forced me to question my talent at every turn. Getting a degree would mean that I'd call the shots on my future. Being dependent on my dad allowed him far too much power, and he flaunted it like a badge.

"All right, man. We'll be ready for next weekend. But I've got my first day of class tomorrow and I have fucking biology which I've put off for two years. Science is a bitch for me. But it's a required course, so I've got to be on my game this semester."

"You're a good man, Cruz Winslow."

He clapped me on the shoulder before I got in my car. I knew my dad paid him well to keep an eye on me. Not so much with Lennon, because my brother catered to our father. My dad preyed on Lennon's guilt and insecurity about his addiction, and Lennon kissed his ass. I, on the other hand, never knew who to trust, because everyone was on the Winslow payroll. It was hard to know who had your best interest at heart and who was just trying to make their next buck.

Wasn't that the million-dollar question?

Not only did I hate biology, but I fucking hated eight A.M. biology class. I didn't get home until two-thirty in the morning, and to say I was dragging was an understatement. I lit up a smoke as I trudged through campus toward Hampton Hall, already late to class. I was more than aware that smoking was no longer *politically correct*. But guess what? I didn't give a shit. Vaping was for preppy, wanna-be motherfuckers, and I wasn't one of them. The nicotine hit my system with a jolt.

I hadn't bought the book yet for bio, because well, I rarely bought the books for my classes. I'd never needed them. I'd always made As easily, with the exception of science. And, this class would probably fuck up my GPA, so I'd stop by the bookstore later and buy the damn book. I found a notebook and a pen in my car, so at least I looked the part. The lecture hall was packed.

Great.

Eager fucking freshman.

I searched the room for a seat, spotting one, up in the front row. Just my luck.

"Thank you for gracing us with your presence. I already finished taking roll," Professor Douche Canoe said. "Give me your name, and you can take the unoccupied seat up here."

"Cruz Winslow." I cleared my throat and made my way to the front row.

My gaze locked with mesmerizing green eyes. *More Jade.* Things were looking up. She quickly turned away and I dropped down in the chair beside her. Of course, she sat in the front row *by choice*. I glanced over at her spiral notebook, and she already had half a page of notes. Class started five minutes ago, and all he'd done is take attendance. She wrote with a pink pen, and there were three other pens lined up beside her notebook in green, purple, and blue. *Are you fucking kidding me?* The girl was Type A on steroids. The professor started speaking and my god-damn pen failed me.

Shit.

I leaned into Jade and whispered close to her ear. She smelled like peaches and coconut. A mix of sunshine and girl next door. "My pen doesn't work. Can I borrow one of your rainbow colors?"

With lips pursed, she rolled her eyes and reached in her backpack. Apparently, I wasn't getting a pretty color. She handed me a black pen before returning to write in her notebook with her pink pen. What the hell was she writing? He was literally still talking about what we were going to learn this semester. Nothing worthy of note taking.

I sat back in my seat and studied her movements. Her dark hair was pulled back in a knot at the nape of her neck. Her shoulders were stiff and rigid, and I kind of wanted to rip the elastic from her hair and give it a tug. You know, just for shits and giggles. She was very attractive, in the most understated way. She wasn't flashy or showy. She had that wholesome natural beauty thing going, which I'd never been drawn to. At least not before now. She was wearing a white T-shirt, dark skinny jeans and peach-colored Chucks. This must be her 'first day of school' outfit.

Kind of fucking adorable.

She must have sensed me staring, because her head turned, and she shot daggers in my direction. If looks could kill, I'd be a dead man. Lucky for me, they couldn't. Professor Lockhart might be the most boring instructor I'd ever encountered. I nearly dozed off the last few minutes of class, but Jade nudged me, and I straightened up. She flipped through her notebook and there were no less than eight pages of writing. With no spaces. I had exactly three lines of notes.

"Be sure to read the first two chapters by Wednesday, we're going to have a quiz on the material," he said in a monotone voice. Of course, she wrote this down in her notebook as if it would be difficult to remember that we had a quiz in two days. No other professor was asshole enough to assign a quiz the first week of school. She used her purple pen to jot down the date of the quiz. Obviously, there was a color code system that was way beyond my realm of knowledge.

I handed her the pen back, but she didn't take it. "Keep it. You'll probably need it for your next class. That is if you can stay awake."

I followed her out of the classroom and tucked the pen behind my ear. "Thanks. That wasn't judgment you were passing, was it?"

She stopped in the middle of the quad outside and looked at me. Damn, this girl was cute. "Maybe. I mean, you did come late, forgot a pen, and fell asleep in class. You make judging very easy."

"I didn't forget a pen. My pen broke. Big difference."

"Sure," she said, studying her schedule as her gaze ping-ponged from building to building.

"You can't judge me. You don't even know me," I said.

"Well, let's see. I know that you *aren't* my roommate's boyfriend, yet she was on her knees doing *God knows what,* the first time I met you. And now, you come to class completely unprepared. I'd say I know enough."

"You can't say it, can you?" I smirked.

"Say what?" She held her chin up like it was a shield for whatever I was going to throw her way.

"*Blow. Job.* God knows what—it's called a blow job. One I never got by the way because you burst in the room before she could get down to business."

"You're so crude."

"Why? Because I like blow jobs?" I laughed. "Who doesn't?"

A pink hue spread across her cheeks and she moved her hands to her hips. "She has a boyfriend, if you didn't know."

"No. I didn't know. There wasn't time for semantics. I welcomed her to school, and the girl yanked me in her room and dropped to her knees. I'm not the bad guy in this scenario."

She shook her head and rolled her eyes. "No, I suppose you're not. You're just the *gross guy.*"

"I can live with that," I said as she fiddled with the stupid schedule in her hand.

"What's your next class?" I snatched the paper from her, and our fingers brushed. And I got a goddamn boner. It wasn't like I didn't get them often, but from the brush of a hand—that was a first. Damn, this chick's got some kind of girl-next-door superpowers.

"Give that back," she said. She was even cuter when she was mad.

"Just relax. I'll show you where you're going. I have class one building over from yours."

She took her schedule back. "Fine. Thank you."

"Not a problem, I'm going that way anyway."

"So, why are you even in my bio class. I thought you were a junior?"

"Well, thanks for *not* making me feel like shit. I am a junior. I've put this class off until now. I hate fucking science."

"It's my favorite subject," she said with a big, stupid grin on her face.

I led the way. "Of course, it is. So, what's with all the colored pens for your notes?"

"There aren't *that* many colors. Pink is for notes. Purple for quizzes. Blue for tests. Green is for the extras. You know, study groups, or office hours."

I laughed. I'd never heard of such insanity. "Why can't it all be in one color?"

"Says the guy who falls asleep in class. The different colors help me remember things."

"So, what's your major, More Jade?"

"Will you stop calling me that? Just Jade, please. And it's human biology."

"Are you pre-med, Just Jade?"

Her head tipped back, and she laughed. And I fucking loved the sound of More Jade's laugh. It was sweet, and sexy, and genuine.

"Please call me Jade," she said with a shake of her head. "And, yes. I'm pre-med. That's the plan."

"Very cool. At least you know what you want to do," I said.

It was still warm in August, but a light breeze kept the air comfortable. Fall was around the corner, and the leaves on the trees were beginning to change color. Campus was buzzing with people making their way to class.

"What's your major? Is it music?" This was the first thing she had ever said to me that wasn't laced with sarcasm or annoyance.

"Nope. Art history."

"Oh. Meagan told me you're a singer. She said your band performed at the welcome party in the quad last week. I didn't make it, but everyone in the dorms was talking about how great it was," she said, tucking a loose piece of hair behind her ear.

"That's what they tell me." I laughed. "Are you a rock and roll girl? No, I'm guessing pop. Maybe a little rap?"

"Um, no. I like the classics."

"Like Beethoven and Mozart?"

She smirked. "No. Like Earth, Wind and Fire, and Barry Manilow."

I come to a stop. "You're fucking with me."

"No. That's what I listen to."

"What, are you, seventy? Barry. Fucking. Manilow. 'Oh, Mandy' and 'Copacabana'? You need to get out and live a little, More Jade."

With those words, she got pissy. "I get out plenty, thanks for your concern."

I stopped in front of the large building with big letters across the top spelling out Winslow. Yes, my family's name was everywhere in the state of Illinois, but it was here on campus because it was my grandfather's alma mater. He went to undergrad and medical school here, so this school was special to my mother, who also attended Northwestern for two years before she dropped out to marry my father. And, well, Dad had one soft spot in his life. *Mom.* Thankfully, Jade doesn't know the connection. People always acted different once they realized who my father was.

"You'll have to come hear us perform sometime if you can handle some alternative rock with a little R&B. We play every weekend at The Dive. This is you." I motioned to the building.

"Maybe. Thanks for showing me the way."

"Yeah, I'll see you around, More Jade." I couldn't see her face, but I knew she was smiling. And like a fucking lame ass, I smiled too.

Chapter Three

JADE

THE FIRST MONTH OF SCHOOL WAS A WHIRLWIND. THANKFULLY I MET Ariana, and we clicked. I avoided my roommate Meagan at all costs. I'd decided she was clinically insane. She cried to me about her boyfriend, Josh, daily. She suspected he was cheating on her. I made the mistake of mentioning what happened on the first day I met her and that maybe they both just wanted to test the waters a little. You know, sow their wild oats. My mention of the event sent her into a tirade. She claimed my interruption the day we met ruined everything, so nothing happened between her and Cruz, and now he wouldn't give her the time of day. Go figure. Meagan was needy, unstable, and immature. She woke me up at two o'clock in the morning to ask me why I didn't go out more. I pretended to be too sleepy to hear her, because I didn't want to deal with her type of crazy. Ariana and I had requested to live together second semester, so hopefully we'd be able to make the switch. My RA Dom was cool, and she said she'd do what she could to help us out.

Biology was my favorite class so far even though Cruz Winslow made the spot next to me his permanent seat. I just found out that the Winslow Building was named after his grandfather, a well-known doctor. Yet the kid hated science? At least he bought the book and actually managed to stay awake the entire class now. Professor Lockhart was brilliant, and we just had our first test.

There was a knock at the door, and I grabbed my backpack.

"Ready?" Ariana said as I pulled the door closed behind me.

"Yes. You have your calc test today, right?"

"Yep. I hope I'm ready. I've heard Professor Hamlin grades really tough. There's no curve."

"You're going to do great. You're a freaking math wiz," I said.

"We should celebrate. That cute guy in my class, Jace, told me to meet him at The Dive tonight. Exiled is playing, and it's going to be packed. I think we should do it."

"I would go with you, but I can't get in," I said, biting down on my bottom lip.

Not having a fake ID was becoming a problem, as everyone seemed to go to The Dive. I hadn't rushed a sorority, so it wasn't like I was going to frat parties.

"Yeah, we need to find you a fake. Maybe there's a way to sneak you in? Isn't that Cruz guy in your bio class? He's the lead singer of Exiled. I'm sure he could find a way to get you in." Her tone was desperate. I wanted to help her, but asking him for a favor was not high on my list.

"Yep. I can mention it. I don't think he'd help me though. He's not like that."

"Not like what? Didn't he show you where your class was the first day of school? He doesn't sound so bad."

"Well, yeah, I guess. We haven't really spoken since that day. But he does sit next to me. I just usually avoid him." And by avoid, I meant I ignore him.

He's the kind of guy you wanted to hate, but kind of liked, but you knew it was a bad idea. Cruz Winslow was definitely a bad idea.

"Please, please, please try. I'm not going without you, and I really want to go," Ari said, stopping and clasping her hands together like she was praying.

"Okay, I'll see what I can do. I'll meet you for lunch at noon."

"Yay. See you in a few hours."

I jogged up the steps and into the building, down the hall into room two twelve, and took my seat in the front row. Cruz walked in and settled next to me. He was consistently one of the last to arrive, which had been part of the reason we barely spoke. Class usually started right before he entered the room.

"Hey," he said.

"Hi. You're early."

"Am I?"

He was acting strange. Less cocky than usual.

"I hope we get our tests back today," I said, pulling my notebook and colored pens out.

"Yeah, I think we will."

"How do you think you did?" I asked.

"Not well. Which is going to blow. I have to pass this class. I can't take my upper division courses next semester until I complete bio."

He appeared genuinely stressed.

"I'm sure you did fine."

I wanted to bring up the show tonight, but I couldn't just randomly ask him for a favor. He was so good looking, I tried not to stare at him. His dark blond hair was shaggy and disheveled, but it worked for him. He had a striking face, and he made looking good seem effortless. He stretched his long legs out and leaned back in his chair.

Professor Lockhart and his two TAs started passing out our tests. When he placed mine down in front of me, I saw the one hundred percent on the top of my paper, and I wanted to burst. Yes, I had good grades in high school. But Northwestern was no joke and making it through this program would not be an easy task. Approximately sixty percent of the kids planning to become doctors would change their major by December. This quiz was a huge boost to my self-esteem. I pushed all the doubt and insecurity away. At least for today. I was going to enjoy this moment. I turned my paper over to keep my score private.

"The class average on this quiz was fifty-three percent, which is disappointing. I don't curve, I've made that perfectly clear in my syllabus. So, you need to decide if you're going to dig deep and turn it around, or you may want to consider dropping the course now while it's still an option to drop without it showing up on your transcripts. It is possible to do well. *One student* received a perfect score, and eight students scored above a ninety percent. It will take hard work. Refer to the syllabus for my office hours and take advantage of my availability. You can also consider getting a tutor," Professor Lockhart said.

Thomas, one of the TAs, handed Cruz his quiz. He stiffened beside me. I didn't want to look, but I couldn't help it. I saw the fifty-eight percent on his paper because he dropped it on the table and didn't flip it over.

"Fuck me," he said under his breath. It was barely audible, but I heard it.

My stomach twisted because I knew what it was like to be disappointed by a grade. I hated the feeling too.

"Hey, you can bring it up on the next test. You scored above the average. You can turn this around."

He scrubbed a hand over his face. "I don't know. I studied for this. Hell, I studied more than I ever have. And, I still fucking failed."

No one paid us any attention as several students stood and slowly walked out. They must be dropping the course. Over the next few minutes, more

21

than half the class left the auditorium. Cruz remained in his seat, and for some reason, I was relieved. I didn't want him to quit.

"You aren't far off. You have plenty of time to pull it up. You still have three tests and a final exam," I said just above a whisper.

He nodded, but it was obvious he was torn about what to do. Professor Lockhart began his lecture and didn't acknowledge the fact that so many students had abandoned their seats. Cruz sat beside me but didn't take notes or speak the rest of class. I didn't run off ahead of him like I usually did when we stood. I walked beside him, not saying a word, as we headed in the direction of our next class.

"You got the perfect score, didn't you?" he asked.

My heart raced. Should I tell him? I didn't want to rub it in his face. The only person I wanted to share the news with was Dad. He lived for this stuff. But telling someone who just failed a test that you got a hundred percent, seemed cruel. "I did okay."

"I saw your score before you flipped your paper over. It's impressive."

I tucked my hair behind my ear, unsure why I felt guilty about doing well. But I did. "Listen, you aren't far off. You can pass this class."

"Will you tutor me? I'll pay you."

Flecks of amber and gold sparkled in his honey-brown gaze where the sun hit his face, and he stared at me. He wasn't kidding. My instant reaction was to say no; however, I could use the money. I tried to stretch what Dad gave me, because I couldn't work and maintain my grades, but a tutoring gig wasn't a bad idea.

"You'd have to work around my class schedule." I bit down on my bottom lip. I didn't even know what a tutor got paid.

"That's not a problem. What about two days a week, an hour each time? I'll pay you a hundred bucks a session," he said.

"That's two hundred dollars a week. Eight hundred dollars a month."

His black skinny jeans were torn in the knees, and he wore a Rolling Stones T-shirt. I noticed a tattoo peeking out from one of his sleeves and I wondered what it said. People turned and stared at him as they walked by, like he was some kind of celebrity. It was weird. He didn't acknowledge it.

"Is that not enough? I don't know what tutors make. I've never had one."

"No," I said, waving my hands in front of me. "That's a lot of money. I didn't know if I heard you right. Are you sure you can afford that? I think it's too much."

"You might be the worst negotiator on the planet, More Jade. I can afford it. It's not a problem. So, what do you say?"

"I'll do it." What the hell. I could save a ton of money, and I'd technically be studying the material at the same time I was tutoring him.

"Can we start this weekend? I have a show tonight, but I can meet tomorrow or Sunday," he said. This side of Cruz was different. Vulnerable, maybe? I liked it.

The mention of his show reminded me of Ariana. I was so uncomfortable. I hated asking for things from people. "Yes, I can do either day. Um, I actually have a favor to ask you."

"Shoot."

"Well, I know Exiled is performing tonight at The Dive, and my friend Ariana really wants to go, but she won't go alone. She really likes this guy Jace, and he's going. And, well, she's begging me to go." *Oh my god.* This was painful. He watched me with a puzzled look, and for some reason, I couldn't stop rambling.

"So why don't you go with her?"

"I, um, I don't have a way to get in," I said. I hated the desperation in my voice.

A grin spread across his face. "You don't have a fake?"

"No. I'm saving up for one, so I should be able to get one soon. Especially with my new tutoring gig." I paused and winked for dramatic effect. "But I just haven't gotten that far yet. And, I know there probably isn't anything you can do, but I told Ariana I'd try—" My rambling was so uncomfortable, but I didn't know how to stop it. Thankfully, Cruz interrupted.

"I got you, More Jade. Give me your phone," he said, and I handed him my cell.

"You think you can get me in?"

He laughed. "Yeah. Text me when you and your friend get there. You don't have to wait in line. I'll come out and get you."

"Oh, okay. Thank you. And, just text me and let me know what day you want to start working on bio."

"Yep. See you tonight," he said, handing me my phone back before he walked away.

I went to my usual spot in Anatomy class and texted Ariana.

Me ~ Cruz thinks he can get me in tonight. I need to text him when we get there, and he will come out and bring us in. Hopefully we don't get in trouble.

Ariana ~ SHUT UP! Awesome. It's meant to be. We're finally acting
like college freshmen. We're going to have so much fun. Imagine
Meagan's surprise when she sees you out!

I couldn't believe I had found a job making eight hundred bucks a
month. And I got a hundred percent on my biology quiz. I texted Dad as
people started to stream into class. He may or may not get it depending on
his schedule at the firehouse.

Me ~ Hey! Got my Bio quiz back and I got 100%!

Dad ~ That's my girl! Couldn't be prouder, Jady bug. Just telling the
guys, and they are cheering, acting like idiots.

Me ~ Thanks, Dad. Tell everyone hi from me. Class is starting. Talk
to you later.

Things were coming together. I had an actual friend. A job. Classes were
going well. I was going out for the first time tonight. And I was looking
forward to it.

"Oh my god, it's so crowded," I said when Ari and I stepped out of our Uber.
    "Are you sure he said not to wait in line?"
    "Yeah, I think so. But, how are we going to sneak in if we're cutting this
huge line? That's not very inconspicuous." The line ran all the way down to
the far end of the block.
    "Maybe we should get in line, and then you can text him and see what
he says."
    "Okay. What if he doesn't respond? I mean, how is he going to get me in?
Look at this line, and those are some big bouncers. I think this is a bad plan,"
I said. My chest tightened, and I was having second thoughts about doing this.
    "Don't panic. Just text him. If he doesn't respond, we'll leave."
    "Okay."

Me ~ Hi, it's Jade Moore. I'm here, but the line is really long, so no
worries if it isn't going to work tonight. I can try another time.

I chewed on my thumbnail and watched the three little dots appear and then disappear. He didn't reply. My stomach twisted.

"He's not responding," I said as we both stared at my phone.

People were shouting up ahead, but I couldn't see over the tall guys in front of us.

"Maybe we should go," Ariana said.

"Okay."

We stepped out of line.

"Jade," someone called out from the crowd.

People continued to yell, and it took me a minute to realize they were calling out to Cruz. And he was yelling *my* name. Butterflies fluttered for some reason. Maybe it was the horror of all these people staring at me. He jogged toward us, and some girl screamed his name in the highest pitch causing everyone to laugh. I hadn't been to a concert before, but this seemed a little outrageous for a local band.

"Oh, hey. Thanks for coming out here. I don't think there's any way you're getting me in there tonight. Look at this place," I said, and Ari squeezed my hand beside me because we were both awkward freshmen and for some reason, this moment felt important.

He looked me up and down, taking a slow perusal of my body. I crossed my arms in front of my chest, suddenly self-conscious about my outfit. I was normally a jeans and baggy T-shirt girl. Tonight, Ari convinced me to wear her pink bodysuit, which was way too low cut for me, not that I had much to contain in the boobs department. I could easily be the president of the itty-bitty-titty-committee. But all the same, it was way sexier than anything I'd ever worn before. Top it off with my black ripped skinny jeans and Ari's black heel booties, and I was certain I looked like a skank.

He chuckled and grabbed my hand. *Yes, he grabbed my hand.* I'd never been a hand holder. Not even with people I actually dated. But I didn't push it away. "Grab your friend's hand and don't let go. Follow me."

I did as he said, and we made our way to the two super-sized bouncers. I prepared myself for rejection. Cruz asked Ari for her ID and he handed it to one of the large men. The guy fist bumped Cruz and stepped back so we could mosey on by. He tugged me through the crowd once we were inside, and I was thankful to have something to hold onto as we made our way across the room and down a hallway. He dropped my hand and Ari and I unhooked as well.

"Here you go, *Celine Regata from Atlanta*. This is yours to keep, so make sure you know the info." He handed me a driver's license. Celine Regata wasn't my doppelganger, but she was twenty-one and had the same color eyes and hair as me.

"You got me a fake ID. To keep?"

"It's yours," he said. I looked at Ari who beamed with excitement. This would make going out easier, not that I planned on going out all the time, but it would be nice to have the option.

"These are expensive. I can't believe you did this. Thank you."

"You worry too much, More Jade. I've got to get ready for the show, so you two have fun and be careful. It gets a little crazy out there."

He sauntered off, and I stood there watching him walk away for far too long.

"Holy hotness, Jade. He's totally into you. You didn't mention how good looking he was," Ari said.

"He's not *that* good looking." I fanned my face, because I always got hot when I tried to tell a lie. It was God's way of outing me.

She laughed. "Sure, he's not. And he even has a nickname for you."

"It's hardly a nickname. It's a play on words." I rolled my eyes, even though I thought it was cute he hadn't dropped it. But it would be wise to remember that I met him with my trashy roommate's head between his legs. Ari reached for my hand and tugged me to the bar. We ordered two beers. I wasn't much of a drinker, but I'd had a beer before. Once. I heard my father's voice in my head, because it was always there.

Pace yourself, kid. Be smart. Don't set your drink down. Don't take a drink from a stranger. Stay in control. Never let yourself be at the mercy of others.

Ari and I clinked our bottles in cheers. We made it into our first college bar. I officially had a fake ID, and we even sort of knew the main attraction. I tipped my head back and let the cool liquid make its way down my throat. I felt an instant buzz when I finished the beer and we decided to make our way to the dance floor as the band was getting ready to start.

"Jade?" I recognized Meagan's voice before I turned around, dreading the encounter with my roommate.

"Oh, hey."

"What are you doing here? I saw you cut the line with Cruz. How do you know him? I'm not getting this."

Meagan wore the shortest red dress I'd ever seen. I was one hundred percent certain if she sneezed, we'd all see her ass. Her boobs were barely covered and overflowing from the top of the dress. Nothing was left to the imagination. Her blonde hair was in a high ratted ponytail, and her makeup was dramatic and somewhat caked on. Not my favorite look, but guys sure seemed to love it.

"I don't know him all that well. We have a class together and we're study partners," I said, leaving out the tutor part because she struck me as the type of person who would throw it in his face.

"Ohhhhh. Of course. I knew there had to be a reason he'd hang out with you. I mean, no offense my *little nerdy roomie*." Her tone was condescending, and her smile just as fake. She gave *mean-girl* a whole new meaning.

And—there went my buzz. I was sober as a cucumber.

"Okay. Well, have fun," I said, turning my body away while Ari shot daggers at my roommate.

"What a bitch," Ari said.

I waved my hands. "I don't care what she thinks. I just want to have fun."

"Yes. We came to celebrate. And to find Jace," she said and we both scanned the room.

A voice came through the speaker and I looked up to see Cruz on stage. I was mesmerized. This was the reason I needed to pace myself with the cocktails. Sober Jade didn't get mesmerized. Hell, she didn't even get distracted. Cruz wore the exact same outfit he had on this morning, but somehow now, standing up there, he looked like a rock star.

"How's everyone doing tonight?" he said.

The cheers and screams were loud and startling.

Deafening.

"Sounds like you're ready."

There were three other guys on stage with him and I realized I met two of them the day I moved in. I was pretty sure it was Adam and Lennon. I didn't recognize the other guy. But the four of them moved like a fine-tuned machine. They didn't miss a beat. Cruz started singing, and his voice was smooth and sexy and nothing like I imagined. I closed my eyes, let my hips sway to the beat while I danced with Ariana, singing along as I caught on to the chorus. Jace found us out on the dance floor and introduced his two friends, Brayden and Cam. They seemed nice enough and offered to buy us beers. I insisted on going with them to the bar, because well, I promised Dad. I didn't tell them that I wanted to see the bartender open the bottle, because that would mean admitting I was afraid they might try to drug and kill me. Instead, I said I could use a break from the crowd. Ariana and Jace agreed to hold our place out on the dance floor, as we were pretty close to the stage and the bar was packed.

I took my beer and thanked Brayden before we made our way back to our friends. The song Cruz was singing got the crowd going. His voice was soulful and intoxicating. I didn't realize how much I liked alternative rock. He's so natural up there, commanding everyone's attention. The exact opposite of me. I'd never be comfortable being the center of attention. I admired his ability to manage the spotlight with such ease.

The second beer hit me fast. I had a good buzz and I swore my gaze locked with Cruz as he belted out a song about taking what you want. I could be hallucinating, but it felt like he was looking straight into my soul. I wondered if everyone felt that way. It certainly made for a good performer. I smiled and continued to sway my hips and even raised my arms above my head, moving with the music.

An arm wrapped around my waist from behind and I startled. Before I could even react, a bouncer appeared, moving the guy away from me. Wow. Dad would love this place. Security blocked guys from hitting on you. I was fine with it, because right now there was only one guy I was looking at. And obviously, he was off limits for a multitude of reasons—but for tonight, I was going to enjoy the show.

Chapter Four

CRUZ

CHRIST. THIS GIRL WAS TOO MUCH. JADE WAS SEXY AS SHIT, AND I COULDN'T stop watching her. She had her hands in the air, her hips were swaying, and her bodysuit fit like a second fucking skin. Her tight little body was driving me out of my mind. I scanned the crowd as I belted out the lyrics, but I kept coming back to her.

More Jade.

I laughed when the bouncer took it upon himself to keep every guy away from her. I never said a word to him, but I also never asked for a favor in the two years we'd been playing here. They knew she was someone special because I asked the owner to get her in. They provided her with an ID and decided to throw in security for the night. Some poor dude came up behind her and the bouncer pulled him out of the crowd. The guys in her group appeared harmless. At least they never put their hands on her. Must be friends of Ariana's.

Fucking Meagan made her way to the front of the crowd and threw her panties at me. Her dress barely covered her ass, and she danced around offering everyone a free show.

Not interested.

I ignored her, which caused her to pout and stalk away. Thank fucking Christ.

Another chick climbed up and made her way on stage. Adam was jamming on the drums and the girl came up behind me and started grinding on my ass. The crowd went nuts, and I played the part. Hey, it comes with the territory, right? I glanced over at Lennon. I loved seeing him on stage.

29

It was where he came alive. He wasn't a confident kid, never had been. But when he performed, he was king of the fucking world. He laughed when Luke sent someone out to escort the girl off stage.

We took a break. It was hot as hell and I needed a smoke. I downed a beer and took a few drags until the nicotine flowed. Leaning against the wall, I had the perfect view of Jade and her friends. She declined a beer from two different dudes and continued talking with her group. One of the guys was giving her his full attention. He probably wondered if he had a shot. Couldn't fault the dude, I was sitting here watching her too. But I wasn't a dumbass, so I wouldn't try to take a girl like Jade home. She was too good for that shit, and she was clueless about the attention she warranted, which made her even more appealing.

"Who are you looking at out there?" Lennon asked, moving to stand beside me.

"No one. Just seeing who's here tonight."

"Damn, dude. That chick from the dorms is a train wreck. Did you see her throw a hissy fit after you ignored her desperate panty toss?" Adam said.

"I'm pretty sure Dex banged her. Maybe she was aiming for him."

"Been there, done that. In the literal sense," Dex said with a cocky smirk as he stepped beside us. The dude had no shame.

"Who's the chick you got the ID for tonight? I saw you walk in with her. She's fucking hot. Something you want to tell us?" Dex dropped his smoke and snubbed it out with his foot.

"She's off limits, dude. No joke. Stay the fuck away from her. She's my biology tutor, and a nice girl. I don't need you to fuck things up."

They all laughed for some unknown reason. Luke walked up and told us it was time to get back out there. "What's so funny. What did I miss?"

"You missed our boy getting all worked up over his tutor. I think there's more to the story there," Dex said, tipping his head back for the last of his beer.

"Just stay the fuck away from her, dickhead." I led them back on stage and watched as Jade and Ariana walked out the door.

The three dudes were left in the dust, huddled and talking, probably whining about how they weren't taking either girl home. I liked that she left. She didn't get sloppy. She didn't leave with a dude. And I was more relaxed now because I didn't have to worry about anyone messing with her. Maybe it was because I got her in this place I felt an obligation to make sure she was okay. I wasn't sure why I cared, but I did.

We finished our set, and I was fucking beat. I wasn't in the mood for Dex's shit or hanging out with the chicks that he'd brought in the back room. There was something about a girl who could barely form a sentence because she was so wasted, that just didn't do it for me.

Adam and I took off first. Lennon and Dex stayed back to party with a bunch of random chicks. I didn't like when my brother hung out with Dex, but there wasn't much I could do about it. We all lived together, and Lennon was a grown-ass man. My dad bought a four-bedroom house for the band to rent out during our time here in Chicago. Another perk of having a rich daddy. I made my way to my room, dropped my keys on the end table and reached for my phone before settling on my bed. There were a few texts from Mom telling me she missed me, and she sent a funny picture of her and my aunt Kay. I pushed to sit up when I saw a text from Jade.

> More Jade ~ Hey. Thanks again for getting me in tonight and for the ID. Your band is really good. Almost as good as Barry Manilow.
> I can tutor tomorrow morning or Sunday afternoon.

I laughed and moved on to the next text when I realized she sent two.

> More Jade ~ Sorry for putting that in writing about the ID. I hope I don't get you in trouble.

Fuck me. This girl was too much. I shook my head before responding. She was probably asleep, but she would see it in the morning.

> Me ~ Shit, I just got my ass hauled in for questioning.

I saw the three little dots and reached for the water on my nightstand. Didn't expect her to be awake.

> More Jade ~ What? You're at the police station? Because of the ID?
> My dad is a fireman, I can call him and see if he can help.

Jesus Christ. I nearly dropped my water bottle trying to text her back before she did something stupid. Like confess to her dad that she had a fake ID.

Me ~ I was fucking kidding, More Jade.

Me ~ I'm home. The feds didn't come after me for getting an underage girl into a college bar that's packed with underage students. They have bigger fish to fry.

More Jade ~ Thank God.

Me ~ You do realize ninety percent of the people at The Dive are not 21, right?

More Jade ~ How old are you?

Me ~ 21 and we've been playing there for two years. We just weren't served until now. At least not out in the open.

More Jade ~ Oh. Got it. You guys are really good. I had a lot of fun.

Me ~ Thanks. You don't think I have better skills than Barry?

More Jade ~ LOL. Don't take it personal, it's hard to compete with Barry. Did you just get home? It's so late.

Me ~ Yep. You left hours ago. What are you doing up? Preparing lesson plans to tutor me?

I sent her two winky-face emojis so she'd know I was kidding. At least I thought I was.

More Jade ~ I'm studying. I have two tests this week.

Me ~ Two beers followed by hours of studying. Don't get too crazy, More Jade.

More Jade ~ How do you know I had two beers?

Shit. How did I answer her without sounding like a stalker?

Me ~ Did you really? I was kidding. Lucky guess.

More Jade ~ Oh. Yeah. I'm not a big drinker. Plus, I need to be on my game for my new job as a biology tutor. Do you want to meet tomorrow or Sunday?

I didn't want to wait until Sunday to see her again.

Me ~ I can meet tomorrow. Just let me know the time. Do you want to come over here? I have a house near campus. I'd rather not come to you. I'm afraid your roommate might assault me.

More Jade ~ I want to say you're being arrogant, but you're probably right. She was in line when you came out to get Ariana and I. She couldn't fathom why you would be talking to me. You don't want to meet at the library?

That pisses me off. Who the fuck did Meagan think she was putting Jade down?

Me ~ Fuck her. And, no. I hate libraries.

More Jade ~ Really? I love the library. I had my eighth birthday party at a library in Bucktown.

Me ~ That's awful. You can't talk in a library.

More Jade ~ You can whisper talk.

Me ~ I don't like being bothered by people.

More Jade ~ Hmm…Okay. I can come to your house. Send me your address. Does 10 work?

Me ~ a.m. or p.m.?

I knew that she meant morning, but I liked messing with her.

More Jade ~ A.M.! Who meets at 10 P.M.?

Me ~ Mobsters. Prostitutes. Drug dealers.

More Jade ~ Very funny. I can't do later in the day because my best friend, Sam, is coming tomorrow to visit me. I need to be done by noon. He's leaving Sunday morning, so I can do later in the day on Sunday if that's better.

Her best friend was a dude? Was that just code for boyfriend? Was he spending the night with her?

Me ~ No. 10 is fine. The rest of the house will be sleeping, so it'll be better.

More Jade ~ Okay. Text me the address. I'm going to sleep now. See you tomorrow.

Me ~ Good night, More Jade.

More Jade ~ It's not annoying at all that you keep calling me that.

Me ~ More Jade is so much better than less Jade.

She sent three emojis with the dude's tongue sticking out and the lop-sided eyes. She thought I was crazy. She was fucking right.

~♥~

Morning came fast. Especially when the two dickheads, Lennon and Dex, decided to come home at four in the morning with a couple chicks who were loud as hell. I checked the living room and thankfully no one was on the couch. Hadn't thought that out when I asked Jade to meet me here. Half-naked girls sprawled out in the living room would probably freak her out.

I collected a half dozen empty beer bottles and dumped them and the ashtray in the garbage. We had a no smoking rule in the house, but fucking

34

Dex broke it every time he got drunk. Which was the majority of his existence. I opened the door to air out the place and saw a pink beach bike with white flowers on the sides heading up the walk. Jade had her hair down and it blew back in the breeze. She was wearing black leggings and a gray firehouse T-shirt. Her backpack looked like it weighed more than she did, and her body leaned to the left from the weight. I assumed she had a car. That's what spoiled assholes did. They assumed everyone had what they had. I should have offered to pick her up.

"Hey," I said, jamming my hands in the pockets of my black joggers.

"Oh, hey. You're out here waiting for me? Am I late?"

"No. Just airing the place out. My roommate likes to smoke in the house when he's drunk," I said, lighting up a cigarette before we got started.

Her eyes bulged out. "You smoke?"

"There's that judgment again, More Jade." I turned my head to blow the smoke away from her face as she approached.

"How can I not judge? Who smokes in this day and age?"

"Hmmm… that's easy. Everyone I know."

"I don't know one person who smokes." She put her hands on her hips and fake coughed.

"Allergies?" I quirked a brow.

"I'm allergic to dumb choices."

"Well, prepare yourself, you're going to have a lot of allergies during our sessions, because I'm the king of dumb choices."

"You can't smoke around me. I'm not willing to die of second-hand smoke in order to help you pass biology," she said with a smirk.

"Are you always this fun?" I dropped my cigarette on the ground and snuffed it out with my foot. Of course, I picked it up and carried it inside, because I suspected she'd lecture me about littering next.

She followed me in the house, and I watched her gaze move around the room.

"Wow. This is your place? It's so nice."

"Thanks. We can set up at the table."

She put her backpack on one of the dining room chairs and started unpacking. She had a shit ton of stuff.

"You brought all those books for an hour session?" I said.

"Who's the judgmental one now? I'm going to the library after. Just the one book for you." She held up her biology book and shook it in my face like a dog treat. I must be the dog.

"I thought your boyfriend was coming at noon?" I used the word boyfriend on purpose because I was a nosy fucker when it came to More Jade. I wanted to know if she was dating someone so I could hate the lucky bastard.

Her cheeks pinked, and she dropped down in the chair. "I didn't say *boyfriend*, I said best friend. You better clean out your ears if you want to do well in this class."

"Ah, yes, a wax build-up must be the reason I'm failing biology. You said he was a dude, so I assumed he was your boyfriend. Why are you all flustered by the question?"

"I'm not flustered." She opened the book to the first chapter.

"So, your best friend is a dude?"

"Does that surprise you? Let me guess, you don't have any female friends because all the girls are too busy dropping to their knees when you walk in the room, *oh mighty one*."

I laughed. Loud. She was so snarky and full of judgment. I kind of loved it. Not many people in my life gave me shit.

"You bring up a valid point."

"Which is why I had to come here, right? Because you can't show your face at my dorm after what happened with my roommate?" She crossed her arms in front of her chest and raised a brow in question.

"You've got it all wrong. That chick is batshit crazy. I'm afraid she'll violate me. The girl doesn't take no for an answer."

"Like I said—I'm allergic to dumb choices. Let's get down to business so we don't have to add changing majors to the list."

I rolled my eyes and she placed the book between us. More Jade was an impressive teacher. She could give Professor Douche Canoe a run for his money. She went on and on about how cells were the basic building block of life, while explaining energy flow, heredity, and the chemical composition of a cell. She drew pictures and examples on a piece of paper. She explained it like she was teaching something basic, and she broke it down in such a simple way that it actually made sense.

We went back and forth for an hour, and I scribbled a few notes down. She pulled out her perfect scored quiz and handed it to me.

"I made a copy for you. You need to study this. The final will be cumulative, so you need to learn what you missed on this. But you should be ready for the quiz next week and we will meet two days a week so you're ready for the first test. Keep reviewing the material until we meet again."

"Thanks."

Noise came from down the hall and high-pitched giggles followed. *Speaking of Douche Canoes*, Dex made his way to the front room. There was a blonde flanking each side of him.

"Well, what do we have here?" Dex looked at Jade, and her eyes were big as saucers as she took in the scene. He wore nothing but white briefs that were a size too small and his junk was on full display. One of the girls wore a rhinestone bra and bootie shorts. *Classy.* The other wasn't in much more than a bathing suit.

"Leave. We're working." My words were harsh, but I didn't need him getting in my shit. Nor did I want the gory details about last night's orgy.

He made a tsking sound. "Cruz, I'm surprised to see you studying, so bright and early on a Saturday morning. Good boy. You must really like your tutor." He turned to face Jade. "I'm Dex."

He extended his hand to her, and it made my blood boil. The dude knew how to get under my skin. He was competitive and jealous and wanted what he couldn't have. I knew better than to let him know it bothered me when he spoke to her.

"Oh hey, I'm Jade."

The two girls waved in unison and giggled. They obviously shared one brain cell.

"Pretty name, prettier girl," Dex said, taking a slow perusal of Jade from head to toe. I swore to fucking Christ I had to stop myself from jumping over the table at him.

Jade and I would have to study in my room from now on. I wasn't exposing her to his antics. Everything was a game to this asshole.

"Okay, then," Jade said, catching Dex off guard when she rolled her eyes and turned back to face me. She didn't give the douchebag the time of day.

"Our Uber's here," one of the Playboy Barbies said, and they both took turns kissing him goodbye. Not a quick one—a full-blown make-out session. Tongue and all. The sound effects were over the top.

Jade's gaze locked with mine, and she didn't hide her discomfort. Maybe this was a bad idea. I should meet her at the library next time. Spare her the shady shit that went down at my house. Obviously, we lived in very different worlds. Mine was a shit show of a life. I gave Dex a hard stare after he returned from walking the girls out. He chuckled and made his way back down the hall.

"What was that?" Jade whispered.

"Just a regular Saturday morning at the homestead," I said. But in all honesty, this was my norm.

She laughed. "It's definitely entertaining around here."

"You have no idea."

She checked her phone. "Well, I better get going. I have a lot of work to do."

"We can meet at the library next time if you want. I won't make you come to the love shack."

I handed her a hundred-dollar bill and walked her to the door.

"I'm fine meeting here. It's not a big deal," she said before getting on her pink bike. She waved as she rode down the walkway.

"Have fun with your non-boyfriend."

"Always do," she said with a laugh.

I frowned when she pedaled down the street. I didn't like the idea of Jade having a boyfriend or a male best friend.

Because I knew that anyone who hung out with her would want More Jade.

Just like I did.

Chapter Five

JADE

"SAM AND JAY ARE SO NICE. SAM'S REALLY CUTE, TOO," ARIANA SAID.

I'm used to it. Everyone loved Sam. And apparently, he was really good looking. I never looked at him like that. He's family.

"Yeah, he's a great guy. And I've only met his roommate Jay a few times, but I like him."

"You and Sam have never dated? You seem so close," she said as we made our way to the dining hall.

"Oh, God no. He's like my brother. We took baths together when we were kids," I said with a laugh.

"Well, yeah, I guess that takes dating off the table. You never got to tell me about tutoring Cruz. How did it go? I swear he's into you."

"Not at all. We literally have nothing in common. His house is super nice. But one of the guys in his band, Dex, is a little, I don't know what the word is."

"Sexy?"

"No. Definitely not. More like, creepy? I don't know. He weirded me out. He came out of his bedroom with these two girls, and the way he looked at me made my skin crawl. Cruz seemed equally annoyed by him," I said as we flashed our dining cards and made our way to the food line at the dining hall.

"I've heard the name. He gets around."

"Sounds about right. I think they all do. But Cruz is nice enough. He's paying me well, and he did get me a fake ID, so I can't complain."

Ari chuckled. "Sam is so protective of you. He wasn't happy about you getting a fake ID. He's so funny."

"He's a complete hypocrite. He's had a fake ID since his senior year in high school. He gets that way. He grilled me about tutoring Cruz and doesn't think he's going to pay me. But so far, I've tutored him once and he paid me cash."

"What's he like? I mean, he has such a stage presence. Is he all hot and sexy when he's not performing?"

I sat across from her at the table we'd claimed as our own, three times a day for the last few weeks.

"He's actually pretty normal. I mean, he's really trying to grasp biology, so I'm sure it's humbling. He doesn't act all cocky and broody when he isn't on stage, I guess."

"I can't believe you get paid to sit with him twice a week. I need to find a hot guy to tutor."

I shook my head and laughed. "What happened with Jace? Has he texted you again?"

"Yes. He's texted me a few times. We're supposed to meet up again at The Dive later this week. Any chance I can persuade you to come again?"

"I can't go this week. I have three midterms coming up. But once I get through those, I promise I'll go out again with you."

I finished eating my grilled cheese sandwich and hurried off to the library. Between studying for three midterms, going to class and now tutoring, I barely had time to come up for air.

~*~

The smell of fall lingered in the air. It wasn't a specific scent—but you knew it was coming. The air was getting cooler, pumpkins were in the grocery store, and it got dark earlier. I survived three midterms and though I lacked sleep, I was feeling good. My biology midterm was tomorrow, and I was thankful it didn't fall at the same time as the others last week.

I pedaled up the walkway and Cruz was standing on the front porch smoking. We'd met several times, and he seemed to be grasping the concepts. I was learning as well, so I had a tinge of guilt about being paid as our tutoring sessions were more like a study group for both of us. And I didn't mind hanging out with him. He was smart and funny when he wasn't annoying me.

Dex hadn't been at the house the last few times we'd met, but Lennon and Adam had been there, and they were both very nice. I found out that Lennon was Cruz's younger brother by a year, and I could see a slight family resemblance. They appeared to be very close. Cruz didn't let them make small talk with me for long, and usually barked at them to leave. I saw him almost daily now because we had class together three days a week, and I tutored him the other two days.

"Don't give me that look. I'm taking a few drags before my drill sergeant makes me work."

He was leaning against the house with his long legs stretched out in front of him. He wore black joggers, a gray hoodie and a white baseball cap backward on his head. Dark blond hair peeked out the sides, and his defined cheekbones were even more prominent when he inhaled his cancer stick. Ari wasn't exaggerating when she said how hot he was. I saw it too. It was more than just good looks with Cruz. There was something about him. I didn't know what it was, but he had this confidence in the way he carried himself. He was everything you pictured when you thought of a rock star, yet he was easy to talk to and he actually cared about his grades. I reminded myself that he was off limits, but it didn't mean I couldn't look.

"Let me guess—I'm said drill sergeant?" I parked my bike on the front porch and followed him inside.

"Yes, you are, More Jade."

I rolled my eyes. He usually just called me Jade, but once in a while, he referenced the silly name.

"Are you ready for tomorrow?"

"I don't know. Am I?" he asked as he studied me.

"I think you're more than ready. You've totally got this. I wanted to talk to you about that. I feel bad taking your money when you don't really need me to tutor you. At this point, we're just studying together."

His brows pinched together. "I thought you needed the money. You don't want to do it anymore?"

Cruz Winslow was beautiful on a regular day, but splash in a little vulnerability and the guy was even sexier. We had nothing in common and he wasn't my type, but there was no arguing he was a twelve on a scale of one to ten.

"Of course, I can use the money. I just feel bad taking it. I don't know that I'm really earning it, though. It's completely up to you."

"This is why the world needs *more Jade*. You worry about things most people would be excited to get away with. Trust me, you're earning it," he said.

"Okay. Let's see how the test goes."

We got down to business, as there was a lot to review before tomorrow.

"Fuck. It's so much material," he said as we wrapped up the final chapter.

I intertwined my fingers and rested my hands on the modern glass tabletop. This house must have been decorated professionally because it was not typical for college kids to live like this. Two black leather couches sat in the family room with an industrial-looking metal coffee table. There were contemporary bookcases beside the couch, lamps, and paintings on the walls.

"Yeah, I agree. But remember, you'll have multiple-choice questions. The essays are going to be on the bigger concepts, which you've got down."

"Okay. How are you feeling? Are you ready?"

"Yep. I mean, I'll study the rest of today and tonight," I said.

"Of course, you will."

"It doesn't come easy for me either. I just work my ass off," I said. I load everything in my bookbag as we went well over an hour.

"You do work hard. I'll give you that. But you're also selling yourself short. It comes easier to you than most. I'll bet you were the valedictorian of your high school."

My cheeks heated. I didn't know why I always got embarrassed when this topic came up, but I did. I didn't like the attention, nor did I like talking about myself.

"I did fine."

"I did fine? Come on, say it."

"Say what?" I asked, raising my hands in question.

"Say, '*I was the fucking valedictorian of my high school because I'm a badass chick.*'"

I laughed. He was insane. He quirked a brow and waited.

"I'm not saying that."

"Why?"

"Because it's conceited and unnecessary."

"Jade."

"Yes?"

"Were you the valedictorian of your high school?"

"Yes," I said, exasperation flooded my tone.

"Say, '*I was the fucking valedictorian of my high school*' and I'll drop the other part."

I finished taking a drink from my water bottle and replaced the lid before looking up to meet his honey-colored gaze.

"Fine. I was the fucking valedictorian of my high school," I groaned.

A smile spread across his face, showing off his pearly whites.

"Was that so bad?"

"It was awful," I said.

"You're the opposite of most people. You sell yourself short, while the rest of the world fakes it till they make it."

"And what about you? Do you fake it till you make it?" I asked.

"Most of the time, yeah."

"I disagree. You aren't faking all the work you've done for this bio test. You aren't faking it when you're performing either. I saw it for myself."

"What'd you see, More Jade?" He watched me, and his smile caused a swarm of butterflies to flutter in my stomach.

"Passion and talent. You can't fake those."

He leaned back in his chair, watching me intently. "What are you passionate about? I mean, besides school?"

"Family. Becoming a doctor."

"You always knew you wanted to be a doctor?"

I squirmed in my seat. Not the way I saw this conversation going. "Yeah. Since I was a little kid."

"You just played doctor one day and then knew what you wanted to be?" He chuckled. I didn't.

"My mom died when I was five. A few years later, I decided I'd make a difference someday. You know, make a contribution to the medical field. Save someone else's mom, or dad, or loved one."

Cruz's gaze softened, and for a minute, I thought he was going to reach for my hand. He closed his fist and knocked on the table instead. "I'm sorry. That must have been really hard."

"Yeah. I mean, my dad overcompensates," I said, desperate to change the subject.

"You and your dad are really close, huh? I could tell the day he moved you in the dorms."

"Yeah. We are. How about you? Where do your parents live?"

"We have a home here, in the suburbs, but they spend most of their time in Los Angeles because that's technically where my dad works. I'm closer with my mom than I am with my dad. He's fine. I mean, he talks to my manager more than he speaks to me, but that's the way I grew up. We were raised by nannies. We get together with my parents for vacations a couple times a year."

I couldn't wrap my head around what he said, and I wanted to know more. "What do your parents do for a living?"

43

"My dad has a production company, he's in the movie industry, and my mom doesn't work. She was a model before they got married."

"She's a stay at home mom, but you had nannies?" I didn't mean for it to sound judgmental, but it does.

He laughed. "Yeah. It wasn't really up to her. Being a wife to my dad is a full-time job. You know, they're always entertaining. They travel constantly. Their lifestyle is not the most conducive for raising kids. Sometimes I think they had two kids so we would have one another."

My chest tightened. "So, you and Lennon are close?"

"Yes. He used to cry when Mom would leave for weeks at a time. I became a parent to him in a sense. How about you, do you have siblings?"

"Nope. My parents planned on having more kids, but my mom got sick, so it never happened."

"Hence your best friend, Sam. Friends become family, right?" he said.

I'm shocked that he remembered Sam's name. "Yep. We were raised together."

His phone vibrated on the table and I startled. He pulled two hundred-dollar bills from his wallet and handed them to me before sending his call to voicemail. "Sorry, I kept you way over today."

I tossed one of the bills back. I wasn't even comfortable taking one, I certainly wasn't taking two hundred dollars for studying with Cruz.

"Absolutely not. The second hour wasn't work," I said, smiling as I pushed to my feet.

The truth was, neither hour was work. I looked forward to my sessions with Cruz. And somehow, learning that his life wasn't perfect either, made me feel a small connection to him. Because whether or not someone you love passed away or chose not to spend time with you—loneliness was loneliness. And just like certain objects were drawn together by a gravitational force, wounded souls tended to seek comfort in one another. It was human nature. And Cruz Winslow may look like perfection on the outside—but he was just as bruised on the inside as I was.

Chapter Six

CRUZ

I WAS A CONFIDENT GUY. ALWAYS HAD BEEN. I KNEW IF I WANTED SOME-thing—I had the resources to make it happen. I had a badass house, a budding music career, and I was attending one of the most prestigious universities in the country. If I wanted a chick, I usually got her. And yeah, I was a good-looking dude. My mom was a model and my dad's a handsome motherfucker, so go fucking figure. Things had worked in my favor. But as I sat here waiting for the TA to hand me my bio test, I didn't have a fucking clue. I didn't know if I failed it or nailed it. It could go either way. For the first time in my life, I was working really hard at something. I was invested. And I felt like a ticking time bomb was going to detonate in my body. If I failed again, it would be even more challeng-ing to pass this class.

Professor Lockhart handed Jade her test. She flipped it over quickly, which pissed me off. If anyone in this class deserved to hold their test up and shove it in everyone's face, it was her. She worked her ass off. She was so disciplined. She had a reason and a purpose that drove her. I respected the shit out of her. I turned her paper over, and I kid you fucking not—I was happy to see she got a ninety-eight percent. Probably the highest score in the class. It was a hell of a test. She deserved it. I almost forgot I was still waiting for my own score because I was having an out of body Hallmark-movie-moment, being caught up in someone else's success. It was not a common occurrence for me. Aside from my brother, I usually looked out for number one. The TA handed me my test.

Eighty-seven percent was scribbled across the top.

Fuck, yeah.

My internal cheerleader did some serious high kicks when Jade shouted out, "Yes."

Everyone laughed, including the professor, but they didn't even know the best part. She was staring at *my* test, not hers. The girl with the near-perfect score was celebrating my subpar score in comparison to hers. And it was genuine. Hence the nickname, More Jade. I couldn't get enough.

Maybe this was a form of Stockholm syndrome. She'd sucked me into her nerdy little world, and now I wanted more. Like a psychological phenomenon, I'd developed positive feelings for my captor. A girl I had nothing in common with. Nada. Zilch. She would despise my world. She was sunshine and rainbows and I was booze and sex. Speaking of sex—wouldn't mind having some with my captor. Something about her goodness screamed virgin, which was not something I ever wanted to mess around with. There were girls who took that shit seriously, and many who didn't. I tended to stick with the latter. She was probably saving herself for something or someone special. That was definitely not me. But I guarantee if I spent one night with her, I'd want to tattoo More Jade across my body. After I rocked her fucking world, of course.

"You did it." She beamed. The girl literally beamed. Her face flushed, and those jade eyes were brighter than I'd ever seen them.

"Thanks to you. This is why you aren't allowed to quit on me. I'm going to need to suck some of that intelligence from your oversized brain for the rest of the semester," I said.

"We can figure that out later. Today you need to celebrate. This is huge."

Professor Lockhart handed back the last exam to someone in the back row and said something about watching a *riveting* movie about cells. Was there such a thing?

"Celebrate? You mean get drunk because I passed the test?" I asked, studying her.

"First off, you didn't just pass. You nearly aced this test. And if getting drunk is your thing, more power to you. Just seems like a terrible plan. You'll wake up hungover and miserable. What's the point?"

"Says the girl who's probably never gotten drunk nor had a hangover. FYI, they're usually worth it," I said.

She turned her body to face the front of the room. "Suit yourself."

Was she mad? Did she want to celebrate with me? I could think of a million ways I'd like to celebrate with more Jade. And getting drunk wasn't one of them.

"How do you celebrate?" I whispered close to her ear, and it took all my strength not to take a nibble. Her scent was intoxicating. She smelled like sunshine. And goodness. With a side of snark.

"My dad and I do this thing. I can't really explain it," she said, biting down on her full bottom lip as she stared straight ahead at the movie screen.

"Try. I'm curious."

"I can show you. What time are you done with class?" she asked.

"Four o'clock."

"Can you pick me up at four fifteen?" she whispered, her gaze searched mine. I wondered if she felt the pull between us, or if it was a figment of my imagination.

"Yep. I'll be there."

A grin spread across her face. "You'll never go back to just getting drunk once you get a taste of Jack and Jade Moore's celebration ritual."

I couldn't agree more. Minus the part about her dad. If I got a taste of More Jade, there'd be no turning back.

I texted her when I pulled in front of her dorm, a.k.a. Fort Knox. She came jogging out wearing distressed skinny jeans and a purple Northwestern hooded sweatshirt. She carried a black fleece blanket and a portable speaker. What the hell was she up to?

"Thanks for picking me up. Are you ready?"

"I can barely contain my excitement," I said. Sarcasm dripped from my tone, and she laughed.

I loved messing with her, and I actually couldn't wait to see how she celebrated. She navigated as I drove, because she wouldn't tell me where we were going. But we were headed in the direction of the city. She insisted I stop in front of a little hole in the wall pizza place, and she ran in while I waited in the car. She came out with a large pizza and two waters, and we drove a bit farther downtown.

"Pull in up here on the right. Go all the way down to the end of the parking lot. It's private down there," she said.

"Oak Street Beach? I've heard of it, but I've never been."

Holy shit. Maybe we were going to play seven minutes of heaven on a private beach and she'd rock my world? If so, hell yes, I was down.

"It's my favorite place," she said, looking out the window.

I walked beside her down the sandy beach, and she spread the blanket out close to the water. I set the pizza and drinks down and settled beside her on the blanket. She rolled her jeans up at the ankles, which led me to believe sex was not on the table. The jeans should be coming off, not rolling up. It was cooler beside the lake, but Jade was unfazed. She turned on the speaker and did something to her phone before pushing to stand.

"Okay, Cruz Winslow. Are you ready to see how I celebrate?"

I laughed. "More ready than you know."

"Normally you would join in. And, being a musician, you should catch on quick. So just jump in any time."

I didn't know what she was talking about, but I nodded.

"Okay."

Jade hit play on her phone and stepped a few feet in front of me, she was ankle deep in the cold water, and music boomed through the speaker beside me. I glanced around. She was right. No one was down on this end of the beach. I recognized the acoustics to "Shining Star" by Earth, Wind and Fire right away.

Holy.

Shit.

More Jade started belting out the lyrics right along with the soulful voice coming through the speaker. Her hand was a make-shift microphone, and she was in full-blown performance mode as she twirled and danced with her feet in the water.

"When you wish upon a star, your dreams will take you very far, yeah." She walked toward me, pointing her finger my way. "When you wish upon a dream, life ain't always what it seems, oh yeah. What'd you see on a night so clear, in the sky so very dear."

She did it all. She sang lead and did her own back-up vocals. It was ridiculous and fucking amazing at the same time. She started doing some sort of chorus line dance moves, shaking her hands in the air. Her voice was kickass. Her dance moves—were not, but it made her all the more appealing. It was the best fucking thing I'd ever seen. And I'd seen a lot.

"You're a shining star, no matter who you are. Shining bright to see, what you can truly be. What you can truly be."

She missed the high note and just laughed at herself. She spun in circles and clapped during the instrumental portion of the show, and then did some sort of wannabe Michael Jackson dance move before playing air guitar. I was completely mesmerized.

Now she stormed toward me all serious, still singing into her hand. Her hair was blowing back in the breeze and her face flushed.

"Shining star come into view. Shine its watchful light on you. Give you strength to carry on." She flexed her arms like a heavyweight wrestler would, and made her voice ridiculously deep, like a little girl imitating Santa, "Make your body big and strong."

I laughed hysterically, and she reached for my hands and pulled me to my feet. Her little hands were in mine, and then she released them. She jumped and sang, and the shallow water splashed around our ankles. I didn't sing along with her, because I wasn't taking one ounce of her light. Instead, I was reveling in it.

In her.

She broke out in the chorus again, dancing and laughing, and fuck if I didn't enjoy it. She collapsed on the blanket, and she was panting. I was thankful I wore joggers and a long windbreaker as I watched her gasping on the blanket so she didn't see the reaction I had to her. I was a typical dude, I reacted to naked women. But a girl dancing to Earth, Wind and Fire at Oak Street Beach shouldn't draw this type of reaction. It was like I'd just watched the best porn of my life.

She caught her breath and sat forward. We locked gazes, and I was sure she didn't miss the heat in mine.

"Fucking awesome, More Jade."

"Why do you call me that?"

"This is a perfect example. Watching you perform made me want even *more Jade*." My tone was all tease, and her cheeks pinked.

She fell back in laughter. "Next time you have to join in. You'll feel great. Although, I guess you perform all the time. But there's something freeing about singing 'Shining Star' at the beach."

"I'll join in next time. But today I wanted to just enjoy the show. Thank you. And you're right. It was much better than getting drunk." I lit up a smoke, because I needed a couple drags to calm down my raging boner.

She opened the pizza box and took out a few napkins. Once I snubbed out my smoke, she handed me a slice of pizza and she took a bite of hers.

"Damn. This is some good pizza."

"It's the best," she said.

The breeze swept through and her hair moved around her face. I wanted to brush it back with my fingers, but I didn't dare touch her. I was in uncharted territory. I didn't know what we were. I'd never had a close female friend, and I'd never hung out with a chick this long and not hooked up with her. Ever. I leaned forward and grabbed another piece of pizza just as she did, and our faces were close enough for me to feel her warm breath on my cheek. I wanted to kiss her. But I sensed her hesitation, so I pulled away. Hooking up with More Jade was a bad idea.

Her phone buzzed from her bag, and she reached over. "Oh. I have three missed calls from Sam. Do you mind if I call him back? It's not like him to call so many times."

Yes, I mind. But instead, I said, "Of course not."

I watched as she talked to him. I could only hear one end of the conversation, but I was already annoyed.

"You are? You're here? No way," she said, gathering her hair in one hand to keep it from blowing around.

"I'm not at my dorm. Cruz did so good on the test. We came to Oak Street Beach to celebrate," she said. It might not be a date, but Sam didn't know that. The dude should bow out. Bro code. "Of course. Sure. Come meet us. Yes, there's plenty of pizza."

Dick.

She ended the call and made no apologies for Sam crashing our party. After all, we were just friends.

"Sam drove in for the night. He and his girlfriend Cara broke up a week ago and I think he's having a hard time."

"He doesn't just want to drink it off?" My voice was all tease, but I was completely fucking serious. *Get a bottle and get over yourself, asshole.*

"He probably already did that," she said. "So, did you phone your parents to tell them about your test?"

A loud laugh escaped me. "No. That's not really their thing."

"They don't care about your grades?"

"My mom thinks it's cool I want to get my degree, but she's wrapped up in Dad's world. My dad wants me to pursue music, so he doesn't even want me to attend school at all. He's pushing for the band to sign with a label and go on tour."

"Before you graduate?" The expression on her face was sad. Like I just told her I ran over her puppy.

"I hope not."

Someone shouted in the distance. Jade was on her feet and jogging toward the dude. He hugged her and spun her around, and it felt like I was in the midst of a romcom gone bad. I hated him already.

"Sam, this is Cruz, the biology prodigy." She flashed me a smile, and all I saw was those full, kissable lips.

I stood and extended an arm. "Nice to meet you. She's tutoring me in bio, so I'm far from a star student."

The dude didn't smile. He just stared at me. I sat back down on the blanket beside Jade.

"Yeah, she mentioned that. You're paying her an awful lot of money." Sam quirked a brow like we were having a fatherly chat.

"He got an eighty-seven on the test. The class average was a fifty-eight. He got one of the top scores in the class," Jade said. This must be what it was like to have proud parents. Someone who wanted to talk you up.

"What did you get, J-bird?" he said.

J-bird? What was with the stupid fucking nickname? At least More Jade had a purpose, because I actually wanted more Jade. J-bird? Like coo-coo bird? What was the fucking point?

She didn't answer, instead she scowled at him. Of course, Jade didn't want him to rain on my parade, but what she didn't get was that I only came here to hang out with her. I wasn't big on celebrations. I just wanted to pass the class. I came here for her.

"She got a ninety-eight. Highest score in the class," I said, taking a swig of water.

"What's in the bottle, chief?" the pompous ass asked.

I screwed the lid on slowly and looked up at him. "It's water, *chief*."

"Ah, good to know. I know how easy it is to hide booze in water bottles, and seeing as you got J-bird a fake ID, I'm just making sure you aren't bringing her out here to get her drunk." Sam chuckled, trying to act like he was kidding. But he wasn't. He was pissing all over his turf and acting like a little bitch.

"Well, seeing as I'm twenty-one, I don't need to hide liquor in a water bottle, because I can go to a store and buy it. Legally. But, thanks for your concern." I stared at him hard.

"Sam, stop it. I'm the one who invited Cruz here. This was my idea. I wanted to show him how Dad and I celebrate."

"Wow. You got the live version of 'Shining Star?' I had to wait eighteen years to finally see it," Sam said, his tone cautious as he glared at me.

That's right you J-Crew looking motherfucker. I sure as shit got the live version. And I fucking loved every minute of it.

"Yeah, it was something," I said, because things just got way fucking awkward.

Jade looked puzzled, but they were obviously close enough that she could tell something was up. "Okay, well, it's getting cold out here. Should we pack up?"

I pushed to my feet. I wasn't sure who Jade was riding with. I didn't want to end our conversation, but I couldn't do another minute with this dude looking like he wanted to pounce me.

We walked toward the parking lot and Jade broke the silence. "I can't remember if I told you Cruz is the lead singer of Exiled. They're amazing. Have you heard of them?"

"Nope. Can't say I have," Sam said with a smirk.

Asshole.

We got to my car and there was an uncomfortable pause. I finally said, "Do you need a ride back?"

Jade looked between us, shifting the pizza box in her hands. "Ummm…"

"Ride with me, J-bird. I'm going to stay the night, so I'm heading to your dorm anyway." Sam stood behind Jade, and I couldn't figure out if he was trying to be her father or her boyfriend.

Jade didn't look happy about him telling her what to do. She turned back to look at him, handing him the pizza box and the blanket. "I'll meet you at the car. Give me a minute."

There was no tease in her voice, and he took the hint.

"I'm sorry. I don't know what his problem is. He's never like that. I think he's upset about Cara, but he shouldn't have been so rude."

"Don't worry about it. I have practice with the band anyway. Thanks though. You definitely know how to celebrate," I said.

"Well, Sam's leaving tomorrow if you want to, um, study or anything."

She didn't want this to end either. I needed to be careful. Jade wouldn't last a minute in my world, and I'd probably want to abandon mine if I spent even a day in hers. If she were mine, I fucking knew I'd never let her go. And there was no room in my life for that kind of attachment.

"The little drill sergeant is already making me study for the next test?"

"You can never start too early," she said. A loud honk came from Sam's car, and Jade gasped. "Oh my god."

"You better get going. Your male best friend is awfully needy. Text me tomorrow if you want to meet."

She smiled and turned to leave. Just before I got in the car, she called out, "Cruz."

I met her gaze. "Yeah?"

"Good job. I'm proud of you."

As I pulled out on the road, I thought about her dancing in the water and I laughed. I looked in my rearview mirror and Sam was right behind me. He looked like he was talking a mile a minute to her. Probably trying to smooth over what a dick he was. The more I knew her, the more I liked her. But we didn't fit. She knew it and I knew it. And I was pretty fucking sure Sam knew it too. He was your typical boy scout leader, while I was sneaking underage college kids into nightclubs.

I couldn't cross the line with this girl. She was the one person I actually didn't want to disappoint. And the quickest way to get a chick out of your system—find another one. I was too infatuated with Jade. Nothing a quick hook up couldn't fix. Tonight's goal—bang a random chick and focus on *less Jade*.

JADE

"THANKS FOR COMING, EVEN IF YOU WERE A TOTAL ASS AT THE BEACH," I said as I walked Sam to his car.

"I'm sorry. I don't trust him. He sneaks you into bars and gets you a fake ID, what's next, prison time?"

"You're such a hypocrite. Come on. He's a normal college guy. I asked him to get me into *one* bar. He's not pushing me to drink or taking me to the dark side. And nothing is going on between us anyway. I'm his *tutor*. We're friends," I said, but even as the words left my mouth, I knew I was lying. Something shifted yesterday, and I didn't want it to end.

"Trust me, he doesn't think of you as a friend. It's a dude thing. I can tell. I didn't mean to mess things up for you though. You know his dad is some big time Hollywood dude. I think they have buildings named after them here. He's a rich kid who's used to getting what he wants."

"I don't know much about his family, but it doesn't matter. He's a nice guy and we're friends."

"I know. I need to mind my own business. I was pissed about Cara. I'm sorry for being an asshole." Sam kissed my forehead and got in the car.

I checked my phone. No texts from Cruz. We never said if we were for sure meeting today. And he didn't know how late Sam would be here. I wanted to see him. I never texted guys first, so I was going out on a limb. But it was for tutoring, right?

Me ~ Hey, do you still want to meet today?

Cruz ~ Sure. You can come over now.

Me ~ Okay. See you soon.

Cruz lived about a mile from my dorm, and since I could cut through campus and take a few shortcuts, it was probably even closer. I pedaled up the walkway in front of his house and parked my bike. It was a chilly fall morning, and orange and yellow leaves decorated the oversized oak tree in Cruz's front yard. I loved this time of year. I was so ready for all things pumpkin flavored. He wasn't out on the front porch sneaking in a smoke, but it was still fairly early, so he was probably moving slow. I barely knocked on the door when it opened. My least favorite person stood on the other side.

"Sexy Jade, good morning," Dex said.

His rust colored skinny jeans barely stayed up on his lean hips, and he wasn't wearing a shirt. He bordered on too skinny and looked like he needed to detox and eat a balanced meal.

Somebody needed to get this guy some cucumber juice and a shot of vitamin C.

How would he hold up if they went on tour? He looked like he was burning the candle at both ends and they just performed locally right now.

"Hey, is Cruz here?"

"Yes, come in. He said to go on back. He's in his room."

I walked through the living room and Dex put his hands on my shoulders from behind and massaged them. I shook him off and gave him my infamous death glare. Dad claimed it could freeze people in their tracks. I didn't like how close he stood to me, or the fact that he thought he could touch me whenever he felt like it. He was in for a rude awakening if he tried that a second time.

He laughed as I moved down the hall. I'd only been in Cruz's room once, when the guys had people over last week, and we couldn't work in the dining room. The door was closed now, which made me uncomfortable.

I knocked lightly and it swung open. My jaw hit the floor. A girl with long blonde hair and a full face of makeup, stood there—naked.

Stark. Freaking. Naked.

She didn't even flinch as she played with her hair over one shoulder. "Is there a reason you're knocking on the door this early in the morning?"

"Oh. Um, I was supposed to meet Cruz here. I'm so sorry," I said.

I scanned the room and met his gaze when he sat up in bed, looking completely disoriented and rubbing at his eyes.

"What the fuck?" he said, and I couldn't get out of there quick enough.

I hurried down the hall toward the front door. Dex laughed from behind me and I didn't stop to look at him. I pedaled back to the dorms as fast as I could, and for the life of me I couldn't figure out why I was crying. I didn't cry. Not very often at least, and not over ridiculous things. And never in public. Why did I care if Cruz Winslow had a girl in his bed? Of course, he slept around. This wasn't a secret. And I didn't care what he did. I was his tutor. For God's sake, I met the kid with my roommate between his thighs. What did I expect? Dad always said that people show you who they are. We just need to believe them.

Had I actually developed a crush on this kid? How the hell did that happen? Yes, he was beautiful, and smart, and I had fun with him. But we had zero in common. Example, exhibit A—naked girl in his room. Big red flag. He smoked and drank and lived a wild lifestyle that I didn't relate to. I swiped at my cheek as I parked my bike in front of the dorm, feeling like a fool for wasting my tears on any guy. Especially Cruz Winslow. I hated that I walked in on him and his skanky girlfriend. She looked at me like I was the shit beneath her shoes. And his stupid roommate laughed as I fled the scene. Did Dex know someone was in there when he told me to go back? Most importantly, why in the world would Cruz tell me to come over when he was with someone? Just to be cruel? Maybe this was his sick idea of humor. Did he know I had a crush on him, and this was his way of letting me know nothing would ever happen? Either way, he was a douchebag. I wanted no part of it. In fact, I was done going to his house. If he wanted me to tutor him, he could meet me at the library. End of story. Maybe the naked skank could tutor him. She probably knew a thing or two about human anatomy.

I slid my key in the door to enter the building and heard my name being called in the distance. Cruz Winslow was jogging my way. He donned navy sweatpants and a white T-shirt. Part of me wanted to flip him off and walk inside, which would be pretty juvenile. I had no valid reason for being *this* pissed off, other than him wasting my time and inviting me over for a free show. He didn't know I actually liked hanging out with him. That was on me. Stupid, pathetic me.

"Hey, listen. I don't know what just happened," he said, sounding a little breathless. He shoved his hands in his pockets when he stopped in front of me.

"Yeah, it's fine." I waved my hands in front of my face because I didn't want to talk about it.

"What were you doing there? I didn't know we set a time to meet?" His sandy blond hair was a disheveled mess. I wanted to spit in my palm and press it down, because it looked like *after-sex* hair, and it pissed me off, as did his words. He was the one who told me to come over. Now he wanted to act like I was some desperate stalker.

"Excuse me? You texted me to come over. This is on you." I poked my finger hard in his chest. I didn't know why I was doing it. My anger wasn't justified. Sure, it was an embarrassing scene, but come on, Jade, pull yourself together.

He shook his head and stared at me with his stupid honey-colored gaze. "I don't know what you're talking about."

I rolled my eyes and pulled my phone from my back pocket and shoved it in his face. "Does this not look familiar to you?"

He looked genuinely confused. "I didn't write this. I don't even have my phone."

I didn't know what to make of it, so I said nothing.

"Fuck. It was probably Dex. He's such a dick," he said.

My disgust reached an all-time high. "That's not normal. Why would he do that?"

"I honestly don't know."

"Whatever. I'm over it. I don't want to tutor at your house anymore. Dex makes me uncomfortable. So, if you want my services, you'll have to come to the library. Period. Not negotiable." I was really laying it on, and he just stared at the ground.

"That's not a problem. I'm sorry you got dragged into this."

"Yep," I said, and turned on my heels and put my key in the door.

"Jade."

I paused. I was happy he didn't use his annoying little nickname, because I would probably throat punch him right now. His presence was infuriating me because I hated how I felt about him.

"What?"

"I didn't sleep with her." He looked up to meet my gaze.

I chuckled. It was a maniacal laugh that I didn't even know I was capable of. What the hell was happening to me? "I don't care what you do with your personal life, Cruz. Just don't waste my time, please."

I slammed the door hard and marched down the hall before stopping at Ari's room.

"I thought you went to meet Cruz?" she said as I stormed past her and dropped down on her bed. Thankfully, her roommate wasn't there, so we could talk.

"So did I. Turns out he didn't text me. His psycho roommate, Dex did. When I knocked on Cruz's bedroom door, some skanky, naked girl opened it and looked very annoyed to see me. It was mortifying."

Ari chuckled and then covered her mouth and sat down beside me on the bed. "Oh my god, I'm sorry. It's so crazy it's almost comical. What did you do?"

"What could I do? I got the hell out of there. I told him I'm not tutoring him at his house anymore. He'll have to meet me at the library from now on, or I'm done."

"You talked to him? At the house?"

"No. I biked home and he must have driven over. He caught up to me in the parking lot." I shrugged.

"What did he say?"

"He apologized and said he didn't send the text and that Dex must have done it. *Blah, blah, blah.* He also told me he didn't sleep with her."

Ari's brows pinched together, and she shook her head. "Why would he tell you that? He obviously likes you if he raced after you to tell you he didn't sleep with her."

"Are you kidding me right now? If he liked me, he wouldn't have brought another girl home. And I don't believe him for one second. She was naked in his bedroom. He also claimed I interrupted him and Meagan when I walked in on them that first day I met him. Now he's insisting he didn't sleep with the naked, hot chick in his bedroom? It's ridiculous."

"Jade Moore, you just might be the ultimate cock-blocker," Ari said, breaking out in a fit of giggles.

"Ewww... you're so crude. It doesn't matter. I may have had a little crush on him, but it's over now. I'm his tutor and nothing more."

"Sure, you are. I have an idea. Let's go out tonight. Jace said he and a few friends are going to The Dive. Exiled is playing. What better way to show Cruz you don't care than to go dance your ass off with a bunch of hot guys. You've got your ID, so you don't need him to get in. What do you say?"

It was childish. But I kind of wanted to show him that I didn't care. It wasn't a terrible idea.

"I'm in. But I need to go to the library for a few hours today if I want to go out tonight," I said.

"I'll come with you. I need to study too. And then we can have fun tonight."

"Sounds like a plan."

〜♥〜

"I can't believe you talked me into wearing this shirt. It's completely see-through," I said, looking down at my lacy bralette through the mesh fabric.

Ari tucked her shoulder-length blonde hair behind her ear and laughed. "You look hot. You can thank me later."

"These jeans are way too tight."

"They are not. They fit you perfectly and they show off your cute little bootie," she said. Ari had amazing style. She wore black skinny jeans and a white crop top. She was taller than me and she had curves.

The music blared outside where we stood on the sidewalk, and we finally made it to the front of the line. I was shivering because apparently a hoodie would have ruined my outfit, and Ari promised we wouldn't be outside long. The bouncer eyed me and read my ID. He didn't say anything, but I wondered if he remembered that this was the ID Cruz gave me. I assumed I was allowed to use it whenever I wanted. He did give it to me after all.

Ari and I walked inside, and it was packed. She got a text from Jace telling her they had a table for us. She led the way and we found them not far from the stage. I quickly scanned the area and there was no sign of Cruz. Not that I planned on seeing him or speaking to him tonight. I just wanted to make sure he knew I wasn't affected by what happened this morning. This was kind of a *save-face mission*. I didn't want to look like the sad little freshman who got her feelings hurt.

Brayden and Cam were there and Jace introduced us to his friend Lucas and his girlfriend, Mila. We made small talk, and everyone was having a good time. Jace was a sophomore, and so were his friends.

Mila pulled her chair close to mine, as it was hard to talk over the music and the individual conversations going on at our table.

"Are you from Chicago, Jade?"

"Yes. I grew up not too far from here, in Bucktown. How about you?"

"Nope. I'm from Colorado. It took me a while to get used to being so far from home last year, but now I love it."

"Yeah, I haven't been home yet, but I like knowing I can go see my dad if I want to. He's come here to take me to dinner a few times though," I said.

"That's nice. You guys must be close." Mila was stunning. Tall and lean, with long black hair and dark eyes. I already liked her.

A voice came over the speaker. "How's everyone doing tonight? Hope you're ready for a good show."

Butterflies fluttered in my belly. *Really, Jade?* I internally lectured myself when I looked up to meet his stare and looked away immediately.

"Shots?" Jace asked, and everyone cheered.

I opted out and started with a beer. I didn't want to get sloppy and I'd never had a shot. Jace's friend Brayden offered me a compromise and asked for an empty shot glass. He poured some beer in the shot glass and winked at me when we all raised our glasses. He was cute and preppy.

"Here's to a great night," Cam said.

Turned out shots of beer were a fabulous idea. I got buzzed quick, and it was my new favorite drink. I downed three beers fast. We were all laughing and having fun. Brayden tugged me out to dance in the crowd. He was flirty and nice, and I wasn't fighting it.

"I'm glad you actually agreed to dance with me tonight," he said.

"Of course. Why wouldn't I?"

"I don't know. The last time we were out, I kept trying to talk to you, but you didn't give me the time of day." He laughed.

Really? I didn't remember that.

"I'm sorry. I didn't realize you were trying to talk to me."

"It's okay. I just assumed you had a boyfriend. But if not, I'm very happy about that." His lips grazed my ear and though I didn't feel butterflies, I definitely thought he was good looking and nice.

"Nope. I'm single."

"That's good to know, Jade."

I probably ignored him last time because Cruz had a way of taking all my attention. But not anymore. It was time I put myself out there. We were dancing close, and I glanced up on stage and Cruz's angry gaze locked with mine. I wanted to flip him off and tell him that Karma's a bitch, but that would be a little too obvious. Instead, I looked away and I was happy he got a glimpse of me with someone else.

I turned in a circle to try to put a little space between Brayden and me, because even though I was glad Cruz was watching this little show, I felt a little suffocated at the same time. Brayden moved behind me, and he started to grind against my backside, and I didn't like it. I spun around quickly to meet his stare.

"You're fucking beautiful, Jade." He smiled down at me.

"Thank you," I said, and I got the feeling he was about to kiss me, so I stepped back a bit again.

He leaned in to go in for the kiss, and I put my hands on his chest to stop him. Someone grabbed him from behind.

The giant bouncer pulled him back and pointed his finger in his face. "Hands off, or you're out."

"Dude, I didn't touch her. We're dancing," Brayden said, shock in his tone. His words slurred a bit.

"It's fine. I've got him. We're going to go get a water," I said to the bouncer who looked like he was ready to throw Brayden out.

Ari hurried over to me. "What was that all about?"

"I have no idea."

Jace laughed. "That may be a sign it's time to get out of here."

Ari leaned close to me again. "Did he do something to you?"

"No. He was just dancing. It wasn't a big deal. I don't know why the bouncer came out there."

We decided to call it a night, as clearly everyone had had more than enough to drink. I glanced back at the stage just before I walked out the door, and Cruz's honeyed gaze locked with mine. I held his stare before I turned to leave.

"If he didn't do anything, why did the bouncer come out and pull him away from you?" Ari asked once we settled in our Uber.

"I have no idea. I mean, I think he was going to kiss me, and I wasn't really feeling it. But he didn't do anything to warrant the bouncer coming out and grabbing him. I don't know why the guy came out and did that. I would think people would complain if these bouncers think they can decide who dances with who," I said, feeling a little outraged at the whole thing.

"I don't think they do that with anyone else though. I made out with Jace last week when we were dancing. I think they're doing it because Cruz doesn't like you with anyone else."

I rolled my eyes. It was ludicrous. "You're insane. Cruz was with a girl *last night*. Why would he care if I danced with Brayden?"

"I don't know, but I caught him staring at you, multiple times. Regardless of his actions, there's something there."

I waved my hand at her to stop and leaned against her shoulder. "Thanks for tonight. I had fun."

"Me too. And I'm glad you turned me on to those beer shots. I would have been sick if I drank all that tequila."

"Stick with me, kid. I know how to have a good time," I said with a laugh.

Ari and I say goodnight and I went to my room and washed my face before bed. Thankfully, Meagan was out. I saw her at The Dive, but we didn't acknowledge one another. I couldn't wait to move out of this room. I climbed into bed and my phone vibrated.

Cruz ~ Can we meet tomorrow at the library? I want to start studying for the next test.

Wasn't he still out?

Me ~ How do I know this is you and not Dex?

Cruz ~ It's me, More Jade. Did you have fun tonight?

Me ~ Yes. Until that bouncer ruined all the fun.

I stared at the three little dots. I wanted to know if he had anything to do with it.

Cruz ~ Gus only gets involved when he needs to. You should be thanking him for pulling that douchebag off you.

For some reason, I smiled. I wanted it to bother him. But I was also annoyed that he thought he could tell me who I could hang out with.

Me ~ Brayden is not a douchebag. He's a nice guy. Maybe I didn't want him pulled off me.

I said it on purpose even though it wasn't true. I didn't want Brayden to kiss me, but I didn't have to tell Cruz that.

Cruz ~ Take it from me, you didn't look like you were enjoying it.

Me ~ You have no idea what I enjoy. I think you should take care of yourself.

Cruz ~ I know more about you than you think I do. Got to go back on stage. See you tomorrow. Goodnight, More Jade.

I didn't respond. I climbed into bed and pulled the covers up. The room was cold, and I tried to get warm under my comforter. I lay my head on my pillow and drifted away. And my dreams were haunted by a sandy blond haired rock star who liked to mess with my head.

Chapter Eight

CRUZ

"GOING TO STUDY WITH YOUR HOT LITTLE TUTOR?" DEX ASKED WHEN I grabbed my backpack.

"Shut the fuck up," I said. Technically, I wasn't speaking to him. Adam and Lennon were pissed at him for what he did to Jade too, and we all agreed Dex is out of control. I had it out with him after I got home from apologizing to her. The look on her face when Sabrina opened the door stark fucking naked did something to me. She looked hurt. Dex thought it was funny. I wasn't surprised, asshole loved a good joke at someone else's expense. He was a mean-spirited dickhead. I used to be intimidated by him, but over the years, I learned to accept him for who he was. A kickass musician, and a selfish prick. I was sort of tied to the dude at this point, so there wasn't much I could do about it.

Sabrina was someone I'd hooked up with a couple times in the past. She was hanging out during rehearsals and I took her home the night I'd been at the beach with Jade. I thought I could just bang another chick and get Jade out of my head. Not the case. Sabrina and I made out when we got back to my place, but she smelled like smoke and tasted like tequila. It was a turn-off. How fucked up is that? I pretended to be too drunk to take things further, and thought if I passed out, she'd take the hint and leave. Apparently, getting naked and spending the night in my bed was more her speed. My plan backfired. And the following day when Jade ran out of the house—it felt like I lost something. Something valuable. I told her I didn't sleep with Sabrina which probably sounded crazy considering Jade and I weren't even dating. We weren't anything. Yet it felt like—everything. How fucked up was it that I felt like I cheated on a girl I wasn't even dating?

And that I took home a girl I didn't even like to try to get the one I did like out of my head. We'd never discussed the attraction between us, because I didn't know if she was even aware of it. It was for the better. Crossing the line with Jade would be a mistake. I'd just fuck it up. But seeing that dude rubbing himself against her last night—I nearly jumped off the stage. I was glad Gus read my mind. He gave me a look, and I nodded and within seconds, he had that piece of shit away from her. Thankfully Dex didn't notice. Lennon asked me about it after the show and he laughed when I said it was nothing. Jesus. What was this chick doing to me?

The library wasn't too crowded yet, but it was Saturday morning, so most college kids were still in bed. Normally I would be too. But instead, I was jumping through hoops to make sure my non-girlfriend wasn't mad at me for hooking up with someone else.

"Hey," I said, dropping into the chair across from her.

She barely looked up. "Hi. I'll be done in a minute and we can get started."

I doubted I'd be getting any more live performances of "Shining Star." Jade was cold as ice right now.

She closed her book and pulled out her bio notebook. "Are you ready?"

"You want to talk about it?"

"Talk about what?" She tilted her head to the side with a straight fucking face.

"Why you're being so hostile?"

"I'm not being hostile. I'm busy, and I'm just trying to get everything done," she said before flipping the book over and pointing to the vocab words in the right margin.

Her phone buzzed and she read the text before she set it back down. While she turned to dig in her backpack for a pencil, I glanced at the message.

Unknown number ~ Hey Jade, it's Brayden. I hope it's okay I got your number from Ariana. I wanted to apologize if I offended you at all last night. I'd love to meet for coffee this afternoon so I can apologize face to face.

Jesus. What a boy scout. You said your apology. Move on, man. Now he wanted to meet her?

"Are you seriously reading my text? You know that's an invasion of privacy," she said. She was angry, which told me she was as frustrated as I was.

"What if I am? Maybe I'm looking out for you. You shouldn't meet random dudes alone. Who knows what he's capable of?"

"You're insane. He's a super nice guy. He didn't even do anything. Your bully of a bouncer made it into a big thing and now he feels terrible."

"My bully of a bouncer? He saved your ass. And he was doing me a favor, so you're welcome," I said, dropping my book on the table.

"I knew you were behind it. Have you always been a hypocrite, or is this new for you?"

I laughed. She was fucking hilarious. "I think *always* is safe."

"You had a naked girl in your room yesterday. Why do you care who I talk to?"

Her dark brown hair fell just past her shoulders and the layers flipped up at the ends. Her complexion was fair with hardly a stitch of makeup. Fucking beautiful. She had just a little pink on her cheeks and bright green eyes the color of jade. Her full pouty lips were driving me mad, and she had a little beauty mark above her top lip. I wanted to kiss her. Everywhere. Anywhere she'd let me.

"I don't know." It was the truth.

"Wow. What a great answer. Let me know when you figure it out. Can we get to work? I have a friend to meet for coffee at noon." She gave me a fake smile and responded to the douchebag.

We worked for the next hour, and she even laughed a few times at my jokes. When she closed her book, I tried to stretch things out. I didn't want her to leave. I didn't fucking know why, but I didn't.

"Did Sam head back to school?"

"Yeah. He actually apologized for being rude to you," she said as she loaded her backpack.

"He wasn't that bad."

"You're right. He wasn't. See ya," she said as she strode right past me. She didn't look back either. She'd never been so cold or short with me. I hated it.

I walked out of the library and my phone buzzed. My dad's name flashed across the screen. Could this day get any worse?

"Hey."

"Cruz. What's the down-low?" My father believed he was younger and hipper than he actually was.

I stopped to sit on a bench in the quad and lit up a smoke. "Not much. Just leaving the library."

"You should be at the studio, not the library," he said, and then laughed so loud I had to hold the phone away from my ear.

"We have a show tonight, so there's no need to go to the studio."

"Right, I talked to Luke this morning. He thought I should be the one to tell you that AF Records is interested. They want a fresh demo, and they're planning to come out in a few months and see you guys perform. There are several people who they need to get on board, but I think things are looking good, son." He only called me this when he wanted something. Which was the only time he called.

"Alright. I'll let the guys know." My tone was flat.

"When you're not performing, you need to be in the studio practicing. Lennon needs to tighten things up, and he'll follow your lead."

I rolled my eyes. "Lennon's fine. He's balancing school and the band. You should be proud of him."

"He goes to fucking community college. Exiled is all he has going for him and you know it. Why he insists on even taking classes is a joke."

"How do you berate your kid for getting an education? You have a gift for making him feel like shit. He's going to try to transfer to Northwestern next year. They take a ton of kids out of community college."

"He's wasting his time. You guys will be signed before next year rolls around. And community college is not going to pay Lennon's bills. Music is. Until then, I call the shots."

"You sure do. What's the plan for Thanksgiving?" I changed the subject because I wanted to irritate him because he bothered the fuck out of me.

"How the hell would I know? Isn't that a few months away? Your mom will be in touch."

"Thanksgiving is next month." It was only the first of October, so technically, it wasn't really a month away, but he didn't know that.

"Jesus, Cruz. I'll have her get it on the schedule. I need to know that between now and then you're going to put your head down and work your ass off to tighten things up with the band. I spoke to Dex yesterday and he told me you and Adam are bogged down with your studies and Lennon's not focused. If that's the case, you need to take a leave of absence from school and focus on your career. Do you understand me?"

Fucking Dex. My patience was wearing thin with him.

"Why the fuck are you talking to Dex? He doesn't have a fucking clue what I'm doing, or what Adam and Lennon are up to. You have two sons in this band, why are you going to that asshole?" I asked, running a hand through my hair.

"Because he checks in with me more often than you and Lennon do. You're too fucking busy with your classes. I told you from the beginning, if it interferes with your music, you're done."

I shook my head. "I got it, Dad. Everything is fine. Don't talk to Dex about me. The guy is an asshole."

"If I agree not to talk to him, will you agree to increase your studio time?"

Always the negotiator. My disdain for this man at times was difficult to manage. He was selfish and detached. I didn't know how my mom tolerated him.

"Yes."

"Okay. That's what I like to hear. We'll be in touch soon."

Dad disconnected the call. *We'll be in touch soon?* Was that something a father says to his son? He didn't know how to turn off work mode. He never had.

I lit up another smoke and walked to my car. The only thing that sounded good right now was Jade dancing on the beach. But she hated me at the moment, so I'd settle for the next best thing—a date with a bottle of tequila.

The next few weeks went by, and Jade and I were back to our routine. Whatever that meant. She wasn't as angry at me, and I was still fantasizing about her every day. I called it my new normal. We spent more time together than I'd ever spent with anyone, aside from my brother. Between biology class, tutoring, and now studying with her daily, she was improving my grades considerably. But I didn't spend hours with her in the library at night because I liked studying. I did it because I liked Jade. So, I faked it. But ultimately, it paid off. She hadn't been back to The Dive since the douchebag pawed all over her. She tried to act like she was dating him for all of one week. It drove me fucking crazy. One day she had rushed out of the library to meet him for dinner. I texted her twenty-two times that night with bullshit biology questions, which pissed her off. In the end, she admitted they were just friends.

Jade took up all the space in my head. I definitely liked this girl. But for now, friendship would have to do. She was cautious of me, and she should be. However, I hadn't touched another chick since my night with Sabrina, where not much happened anyway. So, to say I was uncomfortable was a fucking understatement. If you looked up blue balls in the dictionary, Merriam-Webster would have an eight by ten glossy of me.

"Hey," I said as I took the seat beside her in class. We had our second exam today, and I was feeling pretty good.

"Hi. Are you ready?"

She set her phone down and pulled out two pencils. Like it was completely normal for this girl to take care of me. I didn't know how it happened, but it did. We talked about everything—but the elephant in the room. That I wanted to do things to her that she couldn't even fathom. She hadn't brought up another dude since boy scout Brayden, so I didn't think she was dating. It would be tough with all the time we spent together. She didn't ask if I was. Or if I was hooking up with anyone either. Which I wasn't. And I wanted to tell her.

"Yeah, I think so. How are we going to celebrate this time around?" I asked. If I got another shot at the beach with her, we wouldn't be interrupted, and I could talk to her.

"I don't know. I figured you'd celebrate with a naked girl again." She tilted her head to the side and raised a brow. She deserved an explanation for what happened that night.

"That hasn't happened again, and I don't want it to."

"Is that so?"

"It is."

"Hmmm… so then how would you like to celebrate?"

"There's only one way to properly celebrate. What do you say about a repeat performance?"

"Let's see how you do first. Don't put the cart before the horse," she said.

Professor Lockhart passed out the exams and I spent the next hour and a half focusing on something other than the girl next to me.

I waited for her outside, because of course she was the last one to finish. She probably used the full amount of time to go back and check her work.

"Thanks. You didn't have to wait for me," she said.

"I don't mind. Had time to kill before my next class. How do you feel?"

"Good. How about you?"

"Same," I said, surprising us both. I laughed. Who'd have ever fucking thought I'd feel confident after a biology exam.

"That's awesome. He said he'll have them graded by Friday," she said.

The air was crisp, and Jade zipped up her jacket. Her cheeks were pink from the wind, and her sleeves were long enough to tuck her hands inside.

"Jade," an annoying voice from behind us called out.

We both stopped and turned around. "Oh, hey Brayden. This is Cruz."

"Nice to meet you." He extended his hand and I wanted to crush it when I thought of how he tried to put his hands all over her.

"Hey." I kept it short. I didn't like him.

"I was going to text you. Jace is going to talk to Ariana about getting a group together to go to The Dive on Halloween," he said, looking at Jade.

"Oh, really? I haven't been out in weeks. I've been pretty bogged down with schoolwork. You guys are playing that night, aren't you?" she asked, bringing her attention back to me.

"Yeah, we are. But it gets crazy on Halloween. The crowds always a little rowdier," I said before scowling at the dude standing too close to her. I moved forward, which forced him to step back.

"Well, I'm happy to keep an eye on her," Brayden said, and I wanted to punch him in the face. The way he looked at her and spoke to her. I fucking hated him.

"Thanks, but I can take care of myself." Jade's tone was light, but she was serious. And she meant it.

"I know you can, but I'll be your backup," Brayden said.

Jesus. Grow some balls, dude. Now he offered to be her back up? He was the one she needed protecting from. A growl escaped me, and Jade's head spun in my direction.

"I'll talk to Ari and text you later." She waved goodbye, and we continued walking again once the annoying intruder left.

"I don't like him," I said when we paused at her building.

She laughed. "You don't say? I think the growl was a dead giveaway."

"It was a warning. You don't like him either."

"I actually went out with him twice. We're friends," she said.

"You were fake dating him. You don't even like that dude," I said.

She studied me, and I cupped my hands over my mouth and blew into them because it was fucking freezing. "I don't hang out with people I don't like. But I wasn't attracted to him, so it didn't work out."

"Of course you weren't. He tried to dry hump you on the dance floor. I should have kicked his ass." I shook my head in disgust.

"What is your problem? You had a naked girl in your room. She slept in your bed for God's sake, and you're mad that Brayden danced too close to me. Listen to yourself."

"I told you, nothing happened with her," I said, crossing my arms in front of my chest, and invading her space with my body.

"Then why was she there?"

"You want the truth?" I asked. I was done with this bullshit. Done depriving myself of something I wanted so fucking bad.

"No. Please lie to me." She smirked.

"I brought her home with me because I thought that if I banged her, I'd stop thinking about you," I said. There. The truth was out.

She didn't speak. She studied my face like she was searching for something. But who the fuck would admit what I just did if they weren't being truthful?

"So, you brought her home, fully intending to sleep with her, I mean *bang her*, and all for the sole purpose of not thinking about me? But then you didn't do it?"

"Correct."

"You really are the king of bad choices," she said, tucking her hair behind one ear.

"No argument there."

"Let me digest this, okay?" She glanced down at the time on her phone.

"Okay. I better go. You want to grab dinner and study tonight?"

"Study what? We're done for a little bit."

"I thought you'd want to get started for the next one." I chuckled.

"Even I believe in an occasional day off."

"Okay. I guess I'll study on my own," I said. She knew there was no way in hell I was going to study on my own. I rumpled her hair and walked away.

"Cruz."

I turned around as people moved in both directions around me. I pulled my collar up around my neck as the wind whipped around. "Yeah?"

"We both still have to eat."

She was coming around.

"I'll pick you up at six."

Chapter Nine

JADE

"IS IT A DATE? ARE YOU SEEING HIM?" ARI BOUNCED ON MY BED WHILE I got dressed.

"No. I don't think he dates. He's never tried to kiss me or anything, so I honestly don't know. But I told you all the stuff he said about why he brought that Sabrina girl home. So, I don't know what to think," I said, because I was completely puzzled by all things Cruz Winslow.

"Friends with benefits?" She wriggled her eyebrows.

"No way. We're the opposite. It's like we're dating with no benefits."

We both laughed.

"But you like him?"

"I wish I didn't. My gut tells me it's not going to end well for me. But I don't know. I can't *not* like him, if that makes sense."

"It does. And sometimes you just have to live on the edge and go for it. You know what they say, if you don't take a risk there's no reward," Ari said.

"I'll bet they also say if you don't take risk you won't get hurt."

"You're young. He's a hot bad-boy, rock star. It doesn't get any sexier than that. Poor Brayden though. I think he really likes you."

"We went to dinner twice, and there just wasn't any spark. We're friends. He's a super nice guy," I said, pulling yet another sweater off and tossing it on my bed. "Ugh. I hate everything I try on."

"Let me help. I think those all scream, *virgin tomboy*, you seem to have a lot of clothing that falls into that category." She laughed. "Come on, you're young, you have a fab body, don't be afraid to show it off a little."

"You're insane. First of all, these are cute sweaters. Secondly, maybe they scream virgin tomboy because *I am* a virgin and a tomboy. Lastly,

I don't want to look like I'm trying too hard. It's not a date. Cruz isn't like that. It'll scare him off if I seem desperate to date him. Look at his track record."

"I hear you. How about this?" Ari placed my dark skinny jeans on the bed and paired them with a black fitted turtleneck sweater. "You can wear my black heel booties to dress it up a little."

"Wow. You should be a stylist. I like this." I slipped the turtleneck over my head. "Are you sure it isn't too tight?"

"I'm positive. You're wearing a turtleneck, for God's sake. But at least it shows off your cute shape. Man, I'd love to have your boobs," she said, staring at my chest and smiling.

I laughed. "Are you crazy? You've got the big knockers. Everyone wants those. I've got nothing going on upstairs."

"Yours are perky and perfect. Mine are big and annoying." Ari chuckled, and I shook my head.

"What's happening with Jace?" I asked as I pulled my hair into a messy knot at the nape of my neck and pulled a few loose strands out to frame my face. I applied a bit of bronzer, mascara, and a little shimmery lip gloss.

"He's great. I think he's officially my boyfriend as of lunch today. We don't want to see other people, and I really like him."

I turned around to face her. "Why'd you wait till now to tell me? I'm so happy for you. You two are adorable together."

"Well, I know things are a little weird for you with Cruz. I didn't want to come in singing about having a boyfriend when I know you like him."

"Don't be ridiculous. I don't need a boyfriend to be happy for you."

"I know. I'm excited about it. He wants us to all go to The Dive on Halloween. Exiled will be playing and apparently the place goes off that night. Are you down to go?"

My stomach twisted at the mention of Halloween. It was my least favorite day of the year. But I was all about expanding my horizons this year, so I shook it off.

"Yeah, Brayden mentioned it today. I've never been a big Halloween person, but I think it sounds fun. I don't have a costume, but I'll find one," I said, looking down at my phone when it buzzed.

Cruz ~ I'm outside.

"We'll go together this weekend. We can get matching costumes."

"Deal. Okay, he's here. I've got to go."

I followed Ari down the hall to her room and slipped on her black booties.

"You look amazing. Have fun. Ah, my little girl is all grown up."

She held her hands to her chest and closed her eyes like a proud mama. I gave her a hug and headed to the elevators, pushing away the butterflies and reminding myself this probably wasn't even a date.

"Hey," I said when I found him standing in front of his car.

Cruz drove an Audi, which wasn't a typical college kids' car, but nothing about him was typical. He took me in, a slow perusal starting at my face and moving slowly down my body. I lost my ability to breathe. He looked different. He wore distressed jeans, a black fitted sweater, and black leather tennis shoes. His hair was still disheveled, but it looked like it was intentional. It was sexy and messy and I wanted to run my fingers through it. Never in my life had I wanted to run my fingers through a guy's messy hair. But here I was.

Hello. My name is Jade Moore, and I'm addicted to Cruz Winslow.
"You look nice."

"Thanks," I said when I got in the car. "Where are we going?"

"How does Italian sound?" he asked.

"Amazing. My dad makes the best spaghetti and I've been missing it."

His hands were on the wheel and he glanced over at me before turning his attention back to the road. "You and your dad are really close, huh?"

"Very."

"He never remarried after you lost your mom?"

I glanced out the window before I spoke. Not because I was uncomfortable talking about my family with him. I wasn't. But opening up to him made me feel vulnerable. We were crossing a line, and I wanted to be cautious because I had no doubt that Cruz could shatter me pretty easily. I'd witnessed how casual he was about intimate relationships, and it made me cautious about entering into anything with him.

"No. My mom was the love of his life. They were really sweet together. I've heard so many stories about them over the years from friends and family. He believes everyone has one true match and she was his."

"What do you think?" he asked, pulling into a parking space in front of La Trattoria.

"About having one true match?"

"Yeah." His tone was serious, and he turned to face me.

"I don't know. I like the idea that there's one person for everyone, I guess. You know, like having a soulmate. But what if it doesn't work out with that person, like my parents. My mom died, and now my dad's alone. So, I guess I believe in it, but I also think it's okay to find someone else if things don't work out the way you hoped. You know? My dad could meet someone wonderful, and yeah, she won't be my mom, but she could still be great. He deserves to be happy."

"I like how you see the world," he said.

"Why do you say that?"

"Because you don't talk out of your ass. You're one of the rare few. You don't say what people want to hear. You say what you think. I like it." He unbuckled his seat belt and stepped out of the car.

When he opened my door, I started to think this might actually be a date. He'd never done that. We'd never gone to a restaurant like this before. Sure, we'd shared tacos and pizza, but it was different. The owner of the restaurant introduced himself to me and hugged Cruz. Obviously, he came here often. He seated us in the back at a table overlooking a gorgeous court-yard with twinkle lights.

"Do you come here a lot?"

"Nope. I've been here three times."

"Oh. The guy seems like he knows you," I said, placing my napkin in my lap.

"It's my name. Or my father's name, at least. They like to say he comes here when he's in town. And he has. But he won't remember the guy. He's not like that. I don't want to be like him, so I make it a point to remember people."

I tore off a piece of bread and Cruz ordered a bottle of wine. I assumed they wouldn't serve me because I wasn't twenty-one.

"You and your dad aren't close? What about your mom?"

The waiter opened a bottle of red and Cruz sampled it. He didn't ask me for my ID, he just poured two glasses, one for each of us. We placed our orders and we were alone again. I was anxious to hear his answer.

"My family is not a traditional All-American family. I don't know how to explain it."

"What makes them different?" I asked. I wanted to know more about him and how he grew up.

"For starters, money. We have a shit ton of it, and my dad wields it around like a powerful sword. Lennon and I didn't grow up spending time with our parents. Not the way you did, at least. I'm not close with my dad. He pretends we are. You know, in the press and in front of others. But he knows very little about me or Lennon. I'm closer to my mom, but she lives her life under my dad's thumb. He's an intimidating guy," he said before popping a piece of bread in his mouth, like he just told me it was cold outside and not that his parents suck.

"When you say you didn't spend time with them when you were young, what do you mean?"

"My parents spent more time on the west coast than at home with us when we were young. We stayed in Chicago with Clara and Sabine. Lennon and I each had our own nanny. When we vacationed, the nannies went along with us, you know, so Mom and Dad could go out at night. But, once a year, my mom would take Lennon and I each on a one on one trip anywhere we wanted to go. I loved it. One week alone with my mom. It's my favorite childhood memory, aside from worrying about my brother when I was gone."

I tried to hide my shock when I responded, "Why would you worry about him? You were afraid your dad wouldn't look after him?"

He chuckled. "No. My father didn't stay with the kid who didn't go on the trip with Mom. We stayed with our nanny. But Lennon, he was a shy kid. He always cried when Mom was gone for more than a few weeks, and I became his safety blanket. So, when I'd have my week with her, I felt guilty knowing he was home alone and sad."

My stomach twisted thinking of Cruz as a little boy, especially one who tried to be there for his brother.

"You have a much bigger heart than you show people," I said.

"Only to the people I care about, which isn't many."

I don't believe him, so I smiled and shook my head. "So, your mom would take you anywhere in the world you wanted to go? Where did you go?"

"Well, keep in mind we vacationed in places my father would pick as a family, so I'd been to more than a dozen countries before I was seven. So, I would choose something new like Alaska or Canada, places we hadn't gone as a family."

"That's amazing. I've never been out of the state of Illinois," I said with a laugh.

He stared at me for a few seconds before speaking. "Really? You've never been on an airplane?"

"Nope. I mean, Dad and I would do things, like camping or go out on my uncle's boat. But we didn't go far."

"Is there somewhere you always wanted to go?" he asked.

"I mean, I'd like to see the world at some point in my life. But if I had to pick somewhere—" I pause because my answer was somewhat mortifying.

"Tell me."

"I've always wanted to go to Disneyland or Disney World."

He smiled. It was genuine. He didn't laugh at what I'd said, which to someone who had been everywhere, it probably sounded stupid. But if he thought it, he didn't show it.

"I've actually never been there either. I mean, I've been to California and Florida, but not to the theme park. My dad thinks they're stupid, so we never went."

"Would you spend the holidays with your family growing up?"

"When we were young, we'd travel with our nannies to meet my parents, and occasionally my grandparents. They never came home for Thanksgiving or Christmas because my dad doesn't like the cold. As Lennon and I got older, we'd fly on our own, or sometimes we'd spend the holidays with friends here."

"Oh. Thanksgiving is one of my favorite holidays. I guess they all are, really. But Dad and I start cooking the day before and we have a few families from the firehouse over. Everyone comes and watches football and then we eat and play board games. It's one of my favorite days of the year."

"That's cool. Our holidays aren't like that. My parents like to entertain, so they hire caterers and turn it into a big party. That's why I don't like to go much anymore because it isn't good for Lennon. He struggles with being around that shit."

"What shit?" I asked.

Cruz's laughter boomed around me. "I love when you say *shit*."

I rolled my eyes and waved him on to continue.

"My dad runs in a fast crowd. My parents' get-togethers are not football and board games. There's a lot of drinking, drugs, things like that. My brother was exposed to that lifestyle far too young, and he's struggled with it."

"Struggled how?"

"He got caught up with drugs early on. Uses alcohol and drugs to numb himself when he can't deal with life, which is often. But when we started Exiled, things turned around for him. Music is his passion and it's given him something to work for. My father doesn't acknowledge drugs as a problem for Lennon because he's been numbing himself for years, so admitting Lennon has a problem would be admitting he has one too. So yeah, that's my family situation."

"You're a good brother. I'm sure it's hard to watch him struggle, especially when your dad doesn't support you. Can I ask you something?"

"Yes."

"Do you do drugs?" I needed to know, because it was a deal breaker for me. I wasn't going down a path that ended in a dead end.

He coughed and set his wine glass aside before tilting his head to meet my gaze. His smile made my stomach flutter.

"No. I drink too much and I smoke cigarettes, which I know is stupid. But I don't mess around with drugs. How about you?" he chuckled.

"No. I've never done any drugs."

"I was kidding. I know that. I like it. I envy it. My dad has tried to introduce me to almost every drug out there. I didn't try them because I knew he wanted me to."

"Does your mom do drugs too?"

"Yes, sometimes. She's not as strong-willed as I am. Even if she doesn't want to do something, she won't say no to him. She wants to please him. Her poison is prescription drugs, so she sleeps a lot. It's a shame."

"What's your dad like?" I asked, taking a sip of wine.

"He's charming, selfish, sloppy, and powerful. That about sums him up. What's your dad like?"

I smiled. It was impossible not to when I spoke of him. "He's great. He's loyal and kind. Fiercely protective, smart, and lots of fun."

"What would he think of me taking you out tonight?"

I released a ragged breath. "Is this a date?"

He laughed. "Yeah. I thought it was. You don't?"

"Yes. I just wasn't sure. I got the feeling you don't date."

"I don't. I mean, I've never liked anyone enough to want to."

"And you like me enough?" I asked, raising my brow in question.

His smile grew wide. "I do."

"What does that mean?"

"I don't have a fucking clue," he said, and we both laughed.

The waiter set our food down, and it smelled delicious. But my mind was elsewhere. Were we *dating*? Was this just a one-time thing?

"Wait until you try this. It's the best Italian in town," he said.

I twirled the noodles around my fork. Jack Moore style.

"How many girls have you slept with?" I mean, if we were even considering dating, this was something I should know, right?

He chewed slowly and wiped his mouth with his napkin. "I haven't counted."

I rolled my eyes. "More than you can count on both hands?"

"Yes."

Ewww. More than I thought. Restrain judgment, Jade.

"Less than one hundred?"

He laughed. "Yes, definitely. How about you?"

"Zero."

He looked up and his smile stole the air from my lungs. "So less than you can count on two hands?"

I continued chewing and took a minute to process this new information. "So, you've never had a serious girlfriend?"

"Nope. Never felt the need to."

"Do you feel the need to now?" I asked.

"Yes, *More Jade.*"

I rolled my eyes and chuckled. "Why?"

"Because I want more of you."

"No one wants *more of me*. I'm not that exciting."

"I disagree. I find you *riveting*," he said. His voice was all tease, and I couldn't look away from him. He was beautiful.

"Riveting, huh?"

"Yes. Smart and beautiful. Kind and snarky all at the same time. What's not to like?"

My stomach flipped and fluttered.

"Trust me. There's plenty."

"Doubtful. Have you had many boyfriends?"

"Two. Nothing super serious. But I dated Charlie my junior year of high school and Damon my senior year for a few months."

"Charlie sounds like a putz and Damon shared a name with the Devil— enough said. They didn't try to sleep with you?"

I laughed, and I couldn't stop. The wine was getting to me. I was drinking water the rest of the night so I kept my wits about me. "I didn't say no one ever tried. I said I haven't done it."

"Waiting for someone special?"

"Something like that, I guess. Waiting until I love someone."

His eyes grew wide and he coughed. "Wow. You're really holding out."

"I guess."

"You don't have to be in love with someone to kiss them, do you?"

I shook my head and smiled. "Nope."

"Ah, good to know."

We continued talking about our childhoods and I learned that Cruz played soccer all through high school and was offered an athletic scholarship to a few out-of-state schools. He didn't consider leaving Lennon who was still a junior. He knew he couldn't play sports and be in the band, so he chose the band. He chose his brother. We've lived such different lives, yet somehow, I felt like we got each other. Maybe that was how every girl who liked someone felt.

"You ready to get out of here?" he asked.

I didn't want the night to end, but we couldn't sit here forever. The place was empty, and everyone probably wanted to go home.

"Yeah, sure."

"You want to stop by the beach before we go home? I won't make you sing, but I brought some blankets and a few coats because I know it's your favorite place."

My heart raced. He remembered me telling him I loved Oak Street Beach. "I'd like that."

Once we got there, he spread out a blanket and handed me an oversized navy winter jacket, and he slipped on the black one. We huddled together on the blanket and he pulled me close, rubbing my arms to warm me up.

"I feel like a giant marshmallow," I said, leaning into him.

He turned me to face him and tucked the loose hair behind my ear. He was so close, his warm breath tickled my cheek. There was a breeze moving around us, but I wasn't cold anymore.

"You're a cute marshmallow." His voice was gruff.

His thumb moved back and forth across my bottom lip, and I was putty in his hand. I'd kissed a few guys, but nothing compared to this moment. I was practically panting for him to kiss me.

He moved closer, and his lips grazed mine, teasing and torturing me.

"Please," I whispered.

His mouth moved over mine, slowly. He was gentle, and sweet. My fingers tangled in his hair, the way they'd been dying to for the last two and a half months. His hand caressed my cheek, and he tilted my head back for better access. My lips parted and his tongue found mine. I moved onto his lap, placing one leg on each side of him. I'd never straddled a guy before, but I couldn't stop myself. His hands weren't traveling anywhere they weren't invited, they remained on my face and neck. Cruz moaned into my mouth and my body started moving against his on instinct. I felt his desire beneath me, and it stirred something inside me I'd never experienced before. I felt wanted and powerful. And I liked it. Maybe more than I should. Because when he pulled away, I whimpered.

"I like kissing you, More Jade," he said, and his gaze locked with mine. I saw the heat and desire there and I smiled.

"I like kissing you too. Why'd you stop?"

"Because if you keep grinding up against me, things could get very embarrassing for me."

"Is that so?" I pressed myself against his hardness and laughed.

He flipped me on my back and settled just above me. "Do you have any idea how long I've wanted to kiss you?"

"Tell me."

"Since the day I met you. How about you?"

"Well, not that day," I tease. "I was slightly disgusted by you the first time we met. But, like a fungus, you've grown on me."

He burst out in hysterics and then leaned down and kissed me hard. I never wanted him to stop. But he pushed to his feet and offered me a hand up. "Come on. Let me take you home."

I pouted and stood. "Party pooper."

He wrapped one arm around me and led me back to the car. "We've got plenty of time. I think we should take it slow."

For the first time in my life, I didn't want to take it slow. I didn't want to be safe.

I wanted to be reckless. And wild.

With Cruz.

Chapter Ten

CRUZ

ONE WEEK. I'D BEEN MAKING OUT WITH MORE JADE FOR ONE WEEK. AND I couldn't get enough. I'd never made out with a chick for a week. Hell, I'd never made out with a chick for an hour, if I was being honest. It always went to the next level. But not with this girl. That's the thing about her—the simple things are so much better than the big things with other people. Studying wasn't even bad, and I hated studying. But kissing Jade. Unparalleled. I've traveled all over the world, I want for nothing, and yet nothing has come close to being as good as kissing this girl.

She tasted like peaches. It must be her lip gloss, or she used some kick-ass toothpaste. She made these sweet little sounds that drove me fucking crazy. And she had rules. I'd always hated rules. But not Jade's rules. I don't even fucking mind them.

1. No hooking up with anyone else. No fucking problem. I only wanted her, and I'd want to beat the shit out of any dude that dared to touch her.

2. We could make out as often as we wanted, and for as long as we wanted, but nothing more for now. Fucking fine with me. Making out with Jade was better than sex with anyone else. Sure, I wanted more eventually, but I didn't want to rush her. That's how fucking crazy I was over this chick. I was happy to put her needs before my own.

3. There was no number three. Because she was fucking adorable and she only had two rules. And they were both doable. For now.

"Where the fuck have you been?" Dex asked when I walked into the studio for practice.

"I've been busy. What's your problem?"

"Don't ask. He's been a dick for days. You and Lennon are lucky you've been MIA," Adam said.

I hadn't been MIA. I slept at the house every night, but I was gone most of the day. I had class, the library, and I liked hanging out with my girl. At the beach. At the library. Hell, I'd hang out with her at a cemetery if she asked me to. We hadn't had practice in almost a week because Luke was out of town, negotiating on our behalf. And well, we were lazy assholes when he was gone.

"Where have you been?" I asked Lennon.

"Hanging out with Evie. She's Australian, gorgeous and cool as shit."

"You two are such wankers. How many pussy whipped rock stars do you know?" Dex snatched his electric guitar and rolled his eyes.

"Shut the fuck up," I said.

Luke walked in and broke the tension.

"AF Records liked your demo. They asked me to send over a few more things and then they'll fly out and watch you guys perform. Things are looking good. You're going to have a guy out here from SKY Records watching you on Friday night. You know Halloween is always a big night for the college crowd. It's a great night for him to be here. So, let's put on a great show."

"Fuck yeah. We need to take our shit on the road before these assholes knock someone up," Dex said as he slipped on his shoulder strap.

We all ignore him. Our distance was becoming a problem.

"Let's get our heads out of our asses and get down to business," Luke said.

"It's a great opportunity, Cruz," my art history professor said on my way out of class.

"Yeah, thanks for thinking of me."

I dropped the brochure in the passenger seat of my car and headed to pick up Jade.

"What's this?" she asked as she got in the car.

"Nothing. How was class?" I leaned forward and kissed her sweet mouth.

"Fine. I have a ton of homework though."

She buckled up and I pulled away from the curb, heading to my house. She flipped through the pamphlet even though I told her it wasn't anything important.

"This is cool. It's in the Czech Republic?"

"Yep. It's in Prague."

"Wow, it looks amazing. Are you thinking of studying abroad?" she asked.

"Nope. My professor recommended the summer program to me."

"Who? Professor Stein?"

"Yeah," I said as I pulled into the driveway in front of my house.

"It says here they only accept a few kids a year. He obviously recommended you because he thinks you'd be a good fit. You did get the highest grade on that big project. Why not consider it?"

"I'm in a band, Jade. I can't just pack up and leave for three months," I said. I'm irritated and it wasn't her fault. This was on me. I am at a crossroads in my life, and I wanted to veer one way, but I knew I couldn't. Not without hurting Lennon. I needed to stay the course.

"You're in a band, but that doesn't mean it's your only passion. Exiled isn't on tour yet. Don't you deserve to do what you want sometimes?"

How the hell did she know me so well already? There was a bond between us that I had never shared with anyone before. She always had my back. My best interest in mind. I'd never had a relationship with anyone that looked out for me. I wasn't sure how I felt about it. Most of the time, I was more comfortable brooding over my shitty life than trying to make a change. Jade challenged my entire foundation.

"My dad would lose his shit. He doesn't even want me attending college. Adding a summer program is going to push him over the edge. Lennon will freak out that I'm pulling away from the band. It's not worth the hassle," I said, and I meant every word.

"The best things in life aren't always challenge free. You just have to decide if you want it bad enough to put yourself through it."

"You sure didn't come hassle-free, but I'm glad I didn't give up on you, More Jade," I said, pulling her closer to me.

"You know you were the reason for that, you stubborn ass." Her head tipped back, and she laughed. "You must have wanted me pretty bad, then, huh?"

"No doubt about it," I said, pushing her hair back from her face.

"What else do you want?"

"*More Jade.*"

She sucked in a strained breath. "Don't distract me, Winslow. It's okay to want things for your life. It's okay to be selfish sometimes."

"What do you want for your life?" I asked her.

"I want to be a doctor. Make an impact in the medical field in whatever way I can. I want to have a family of my own someday. I'd like to be a mom. I want to travel and see new places. I'm not afraid to say what I want. But I understand if you're afraid to want things."

I studied her pretty face. Her gaze locked with mine. "Why would I be afraid to want things?"

"Because when you admit what you want, you have something to lose. You can't lose anything if you don't care about it, right?"

I leaned forward and kissed her mouth. She was right, but I didn't want to talk about it anymore. Instead I kissed her hard.

"You can't kiss me every time I have a question that you don't want to answer," she said, against my mouth.

"It kind of works though, doesn't it, *ol' breathless one.*"

She punched my arm and laughed. "Tell me three things you want. Really want. I won't tell anyone, I promise," she teased. "But I'm not kissing you again until you give me something."

I leaned back against the driver's seat. "Three things, huh?"

She climbed across the seat and settled on my lap. The girl was a little spider monkey. She took my face in each of her hands. "Speak. It's not that hard."

I thought about it. No one had ever asked me that question, nor had anyone ever cared.

"Well, More Jade is number one." I laughed, and she rolled her eyes.

"Waiting," she said.

"I think it would be cool to be a professor and teach art. I'd like to have a family someday. A normal family that lives in the same house and doesn't just vacation together."

Her entire face lit up, and her lips turned up at the sides. "Well done, Professor. Was that so difficult?"

"Painfully so," I said before she leaned forward and kissed me.

The horn sounded, startling us both as her back pressed into the steering wheel. We laughed, but I didn't miss the heat in her gaze. She climbed off my lap and back into the passenger seat before opening her door to get out. And for just a minute, I wondered what it would be like to keep More Jade forever.

"You better quit smoking, Winslow, or I might actually beat you one of these days," Adam said as he took a shot. He missed. Adam was a kickass musician, but basketball was not his thing.

"I could smoke you with a cigarette in my mouth, while blindfolded." I stole the ball and took a shot. Swoosh. "Two points, sucker."

He leaned forward to catch his breath and then held up his two hands and made a T to signal a time out. He dropped to sit and lifted his T-shirt to wipe his forehead. The dude sweat like an animal.

"You're spending a lot of time with Jade, huh? She's a cool chick. It's getting serious?"

"I like hanging out with her," I said.

Adam always had a girlfriend. He was a relationship guy. I'd never understood wanting to be with the same girl over and over, until now.

"I don't think I've ever heard you say that. I like her even more now."

"Did you bring me here to talk about my dating status?" I chugged my water.

"Always such an asshole," he said with a laugh. Adam and I could always be straight with one another. I trusted him. Always had. "Nah, man. I wanted to see how you feel about talk of Exiled going on tour. It used to feel like a pipe dream, but shit's getting real."

I nodded. "Yeah. Steven Winslow never stops pushing. I'm sure his ass is on the phone talking us up non-stop."

"How would you feel about that? I mean, you were hesitant from the start to do this. But playing locally and going on tour aren't the same thing."

"I don't know. It's not something I'm looking forward to. I like playing locally and going to school. Making this a full-time thing means leaving school, leaving Chicago—"

"I get it. I want to graduate too. But I can see myself playing music for the rest of my life. Can you?" Adam said.

"Hell no. I'm not even a great singer, dude. I only did it because you and Lennon convinced me to. But fuck, I know what it means to you and I know what it means to Lennon."

"What about Dex? You don't think he's all in?"

"No, I do. I just don't give a fuck about Dex," I said, and we both laughed.

"Listen, Cruz. You're a good guy. You may act like an asshole, but I know who you are. If there comes a point that you want out, you know I'll support you, right, brother?"

"Yeah. But what happens to the band if I want out? I can't shit on you and Lennon," I said, and I ran my hand down my face.

"We need to find a lead singer. There's a lot of talented dudes out there that want to tour and do this shit. I think you've sacrificed a lot to make this happen for your brother, and hell, even for me. But I know you don't love it, Cruz."

"And what happens to Lennon?"

"Lennon is a grown-ass man. You can't babysit him his whole life. You know I'll always look out for him, but at some point, he's going to need to look out for himself," he said.

"Yeah. I'm just glad he's in school. I want him to have a back-up plan, you know?"

"You can't control him, Cruz. He's not you. He doesn't like school and he's set on playing music the rest of his life."

"And being controlled by my father? He'll never be free," I said, pushing to my feet.

"Maybe he doesn't want to be."

The thought made my chest tighten. I offered him a hand and pulled him to his feet. Because the truth was, I was never going to turn my back on my brother, at least not until he grew the fuck up. And I didn't see that happening anytime soon.

Chapter Eleven

JADE

I HATED HALLOWEEN. IT WAS TECHNICALLY THE DAY DESIGNATED TO remember the dead. How fitting, right? My mom died on the evening of October thirty-first, thirteen years ago tomorrow. I had a vague memory of sitting at the hospital in a bumblebee costume while I colored with my grandparents in the waiting room. The tulle skirt was itchy and irritating, but somehow, I knew what was happening was bigger than the discomfort of my costume. Sadness simmered in the air, and my worst fear came true. I said goodbye to the best mom on the planet and a piece of my heart floated away with her. Yet, every year when this day came around, I'd watch kids go door to door collecting candy, dressed up in silly costumes. I hadn't dressed up since I was five years old. Dad never pushed me to trick or treat or wear a costume again. Sure, he'd always offer, but I'd end up in bed with a tummy ache. I was making a conscious effort to shed some of the sadness that still attached itself to me this time of year. I was dressing up and going to a party. I hadn't told Cruz or Ari that Halloween was the day my mom passed away, because for the first time in my life, I wasn't surrounded by people who knew what happened on October thirty-first, and I liked it. Maybe it would pass by just like any other day. Maybe I'd even learn to enjoy it like the rest of the world.

"I like these. We could be hot fire-women." Ari wriggled her eyebrows. We'd been at the costume store for thirty minutes and had yet to find anything we agreed on.

"They're cute. But it's a little sacrilege with my dad being a fireman," I said.

"Ah, fair enough. But I don't care what you say, Jade. I'm not wearing those goofy dinosaur costumes you picked out. We want to look hot, not like we're making an appearance at the *Jurassic Park* movie premiere."

I laughed, and my gaze landed on a bumblebee costume on the other side of the aisle. Mom had made my costume and I remembered thinking I would never take it off. It was the best costume on the block. I never laid eyes on it again after that night.

"Earth to Jade. Come on, you have to like something else."

"Fine. What about these? You can be the Mother of Dragons and I can be Arya Stark. She's such a badass."

"No way. I told you I didn't get into that show," Ari said.

I covered my ears because her words weren't in my realm of understanding. My obsession with GOT was not normal. "Maybe you just didn't give it enough time. You're far too cool to hate on *Game of Thrones.*"

She gasped. "What about these? I can be a devil and you can be an angel. It's pretty fitting, don't you think?"

"Not really. You're an angel outside of your lack of interest in GOT."

"Well, red is my color and you look great in white. Look how sexy these are? We're going to turn some heads," Ari said.

My phone vibrated and Cruz's name flashed across the screen.

Cruz ~ How long does it take to find a costume? I miss you.

Me ~ Almost done. You want me to come over? I can have Ari drop me off.

Cruz ~ Yes. Hurry. I need More Jade.

I smiled and shook my head at the phone. I'd been over to his house a few times, but Dex hadn't been there. Cruz said he wouldn't mess with me again, because now we were together. I still didn't like being around him.

"Okay, let's do it. These will work," I said.

She squealed and led me to the register.

When we pulled in front of Cruz's house, he was sitting on the front porch having a smoke. I hated the habit, and I let him know it every time we were together. He didn't do it in front of me very often.

"Damn, your boyfriend is so sexy in that rock star Justin Bieber kind of way," Ari said.

"Don't say *boyfriend*, it's not that serious. This is new for both of us, so we're taking it slow."

"What do you call it then?" she asked, shaking her head with a big smile.

"I'd say we're seeing each other. I don't know, but I don't want to freak him out," I said, stepping out of the car.

She put her window down and shouted past me, "Hey Cruz."

"Hey, did you guys find costumes?" He walked toward the car and wrapped his arms around my middle, resting his head on my shoulder.

"Yes, I'm going to be a devil. I know, shocker. And this one's going to be an angel." Ari thrust her thumb in my direction.

"Very fitting," Cruz said, and I knew he was smiling without looking over my shoulder to see.

"Okay, see you guys later." Ari pulled down the street and I turned to face him.

"How was your day?"

"Fine. My dad's all over my ass about this guy coming tomorrow to watch us perform. He's from some label, and of course my father is salivating over the possibilities," he said, leading me into the house.

No one else was home, and we walked back to his room and dropped down on the bed.

"How do you feel about that?"

We faced one another and he brushed the hair back from my face. He was so gentle. Never pushy. I was enjoying this phase as we got to know one another. I liked him more than I'd ever liked anyone. More than I ever thought I could.

"I don't know. I want to finish school. But we've worked our asses off and it would be cool to get some validation, you know. And Lennon, Christ, he'd lose his shit. This is what he's always wanted."

I traced the bridge of his nose with my finger.

"What about what you want?" I asked.

He rolled me on my back and settled above me. "I want more Jade."

I laughed and rolled my eyes. This had become our shtick. "Why do you want more of me?"

"Because you're perfect."

I ran my hand down his back and he pressed himself into me. And wow. He'd never been shy about how much he wanted me, but he'd never pushed for more. Our make-out sessions got pretty heated, but he always cut things off before we got carried away.

I wanted more. I wanted more of him. His mouth moved over mine and we spent the next few hours talking, and laughing, and kissing. It was becoming more challenging to stop. I'd never spent the night at his house because I didn't think I'd be able to sleep beside him and not want more. And I didn't know if we were ready for that right now.

— ⅋ ⌒

I knew as soon as I woke up that it was going to be a crappy day. There was a heaviness in the air. I already regretted getting out of bed. I didn't know if it was just the fact that I was changing what I always did on this day, or if it was my instinct warning me to be cautious.

When my phone rang, I knew who it was before I looked at the screen.

"Hey, Dad. How are you?"

"I'm good. Working today. You sure you don't want to come home this weekend?"

"Nope. I'm actually going to a party tonight. Wearing a costume and all," I said, leaving out the part about going to a bar. My dad was not naive, but he'd probably rather not be filled in on the fake ID and the alcohol.

"I'm glad to hear it, sweetie. You know I'm here if you need me."

"Same here. I love you."

"Love you, Jady bug."

I disconnected the call and swiped the single tear rolling down my cheek. I met Ari out in the hall to start our day.

"Happy Halloween," she said, bouncing up and down as we made our way to the dining commons.

I'm in a foul mood. "Yeah, good morning."

"Someone's grumpy. This is a first."

"Sorry. I didn't sleep well."

"I think you're sexually frustrated because your boyfriend is a hot, sexy rock star, and you're so hell bent on taking things slow."

I laughed. "I think that devil costume may be more suited for you than I originally thought."

"I hope you're right," Ari said, wriggling her brows.

Ari and I said our goodbyes and I made my way to biology. Cruz came in just as Professor Lockhart started the lecture. His hand rested on the table beside mine and his pinky finger hooked around mine. My stomach dipped. I didn't know why. I'd made out with him more times than I could count. But this felt intimate, somehow. And we were in class. I tucked my hair behind my ear and glanced his way. He was studying me.

"What?" I whispered.

"Nothing. You seem off. Everything okay?"

"Yeah. I didn't sleep well." I didn't want to tell him about my mom. He had a big day with the record label coming to watch the show. And I didn't want him to feel sorry for me. Everyone always did, and I hated the pity.

"It's sexual frustration," he whispered. His breath tickled my ear and goosebumps spread across my arms.

"How can I be frustrated about something I've never experienced?"

"Because you think about it all the time, just like I do." Cruz smiled and my stomach did little flips. I rolled my eyes, but I knew he was right. I did think about it. Often.

After we left class, a wave of nausea settled in my stomach. "I'm really not feeling well. I'm going to skip class and go lie down."

His eyes bulged out of his head like I'd just told him I was going to rob a bank. He rested the back of his hand against my forehead.

"You don't feel hot. Maybe you're just tired?"

"Yeah." We came to a stop in the quad because I was going to go to my dorm and skip class.

"Come to my house. You won't have Meagan bothering you. I've got a ton of work to do, so you can sleep, and I'll get my shit done at the house."

The idea of sleeping in Cruz's bed comforted me.

"Okay."

He looked over at me several times in the car, as I leaned against the door. I was physically ill. Whether I was tired or sad, I didn't know. But I didn't feel right. We drove in silence and his hand rested on my thigh. I dozed off on the short drive, thankful that I didn't have to talk or think.

Cruz led me inside, and I fell right into his bed.

He sat beside me on the edge of the mattress. "You sure you don't need anything?"

I nodded and closed my eyes.

"Hey," Cruz said, just above a whisper. He brushed the hair back from my face and his fingers stroked my cheek. My chest was heavy, and my stomach queasy.

"Hi. What time is it?"

"It's five-thirty. You've been out all day. I ordered pizza, if you're hungry?"

"I'm not hungry. I can't believe how late it is."

"Do you feel any better? Maybe you should stay in tonight. You can stay here if you want? It'll be quiet."

I pushed to sit up. "No. I'm fine. I promised Ari I would go out. And it's a big night for you. I want to support you," I said.

Cruz and I hadn't really said what we were, so I wasn't really sure if we would be hanging out in public at The Dive anyway. The only person I'd told about us was Ari, and Sam knew that I liked Cruz, but that it was nothing serious or official yet. My roommate Meagan would probably have a meltdown if she knew anything was going on.

"I'm going to be on stage all night. Don't feel pressure to go."

His words rubbed me wrong, but in all fairness, anything he said right now was bound to rub me wrong. I was off, and I didn't know how to snap myself out of this funk.

"I wasn't suggesting that you need to hang out with me, if that's what you're worried about." My tone was snippy, and he looked surprised.

"Jade. Come on. That's not what I meant."

"It's fine. Whatever. I'm just tired. Do you mind giving me a ride home? I don't have my bike."

"Of course," he said. We were quiet on the drive over to the dorms.

"Thanks for letting me nap at your place, and thanks for the ride." I pushed the door open, but he reached for my hand and stopped me.

"Go to the front of the line. I'll let Gus know to let you and your friends in."

My teeth sunk into my bottom lip. "Okay. I hate cutting, but if the line is long, I'll do it."

"The line will be long tonight. Wait for me after the show?"

"Sure. I'll see you tonight. Good luck," I said, and he leaned forward and kissed me. It was quick but sweet. I pushed the door open and waved at him as I walked away.

"You look so hot," Ari said as she attached the halo to my head, stabbing me repeatedly with bobby pins. I'd never worn loose waves, but apparently my hair could hold a curl according to my fashionista bestie.

"Thanks for doing this. My makeup and hair, and everything."

"Of course. I can't believe you slept all day. I was texting you like a crazy person. You sure you're alright?"

I stood up and looked in the full-length mirror. I was barely recognizable. I looked like some sort of stripper angel. I had big hair and smoky eyes. I'd never been so made up before. The costume was ridiculously small, but thankfully the angel wings were long enough to cover my butt, because this leotard wasn't covering much. We grabbed our things and headed out when my phone vibrated.

Dad ~ What's up kid?

Me ~ All good, Dad. I promise. Ariana and I are getting ready to go.

I sent him a selfie of Ari and I, of just our faces because Dad would not approve of the tiny outfit I was wearing. As predicted, the line was wrapped around the building. Ari and I got dropped off in our Uber near the front so everyone wouldn't see us walking past them. Thankfully, no one noticed, and Gus winked at me and stepped back.

"An angel and a devil. Sounds like trouble."

"Thank you, Gus," I said as we slipped inside.

"Perks of dating the lead singer," Ari said in a whisper-shout. The Dive was going off tonight. Energy crackled in the air around us.

"Did you ask Jace to make sure Brayden knows I'm sort of seeing someone?" I took in the crowd, scanning the room.

"Yes. But I said you were *dating him.*" She wriggled her brows.

Jace, Brayden, Cam, Lucas, and Mila had a table. I had no idea how they pulled it off, but I wasn't complaining. The place was packed and booming with club music. I took in our surroundings. The costumes were outrageous. Ari and I looked tame compared to everyone else. We all hugged and said our hellos. Mila was dressed as a sexy police officer and Lucas was her prisoner. They looked adorable. I started to relax because everyone was having fun. I still had a sick feeling in my stomach, but at this point, it could be due to the fact that I hadn't eaten much today.

"Sorry we don't have any beer shots for you out here yet, Jade. But we've got these tequila shots for whoever's ready." Cam paused when he looked at me and passed out the shots. I decided to give tequila a try. There was a first time for everything.

"Bottoms up," Jace said.

I tipped my head back and gagged once it went down.

"Not bad, right?" Mila said, wrapping an arm around me.

Cruz made his way onto the stage and the crowd roared. The place was packed making it hard to move. Jace and Brayden maneuvered through the crowd to get more drinks, and they came back with tequila shots and beers. I tipped my head back and felt the chilled tequila roll down my throat with ease. It was the best I'd felt today. I was relaxed. I looked up at the stage, and my gaze locked with Cruz's. Even in this crowd, his honeyed eyes always found me. His smile was stiff, and his brow furrowed. Maybe he didn't like me taking tequila shots, or maybe he was nervous about the guy that came to watch them tonight. I scanned the room and tried to find the man from the label, but in this crowd, it was impossible. And my head was fuzzy, which wasn't helping at all.

Mila and Lucas came back with another round of tequila, because guess what? This was how college kids did Halloween. The heavy weight on my chest melted away after my third shot. I laughed before polishing off another beer.

"Pace yourself, girl," Ari said, studying me. Her gaze filled with concern. "Why don't we grab some waters."

"I'm fine. I promise."

"Okay. No more shots for a while."

"Deal," I slurred.

I'd never heard my words slurred before. I couldn't even make out the people around me, because the lights were flashing, and the music was blaring. Faces were hazy and blurred together, looking more like a watercolor painting. I swore I felt *nothing*. I wasn't sad. Or depressed. Or grieving. It was just a regular day, and I was totally fine.

The guys didn't feel like dancing, so Ari, Mila, and I hit the dance floor. I swayed to the music, and it felt good not to think for a little while. I was having fun. I loved the sound of Cruz's voice, the way it soothed and settled me. Mila hugged me and we spun around, and Ari jumped around us. The music slowed and I put my hands in the air and closed my eyes, swaying to the melody.

A hand wrapped around my wrist and tugged me back. My eyes flew open and I struggled to make out who it was.

"What the hell, Jade," a familiar voice shouted in my ear.

"Sam?" I pushed against his shoulders and tried to focus, but everything was fuzzy. "What are you doing here?"

"Jesus Christ. I'm getting you out of here. Let's go."

I yanked my arm free of Sam's grasp. "Let go of me. I'm not leaving."

"The fuck you're not." Sam had a firm grip on my wrist and led me away from my friends.

Ari and Mila both called out, and I tried to pry my arm free again. Everything blurred as Gus grabbed Sam from behind. I tried to yell for him to stop, but Sam swung back and before I realized what was happening, Cruz was there. There was a scuffle, and I got knocked down on my ass. I tried to get up, but the room was spinning, and I crawled around on the ground. Ari pulled me to my feet. Gus had Sam in some sort of hold and he was leading him toward the back per Cruz's insistence. Cruz's hand found mine, and Ari held on to my other hand as we got pulled through the crowd and down the hallway into the back room. There was shouting and yelling. Sam was so angry.

Cruz turned to face me. "Fuck, Jade. Are you okay?"

Was I? My stomach was twisting, and I felt sick, but aside from too much tequila, I thought I was fine.

"Yes." The word didn't even sound like the English language, so I decided not to say anything more.

"What the fuck is your problem?" Sam shouted at Gus.

"You're my fucking problem. We don't let girls get dragged out by the arm against their will, asshole." Gus kept his voice even, and Cruz put his arm on the large man's shoulder.

"It's a misunderstanding. He's family." Cruz stared at Gus, who finally nodded and left the room.

"Jesus Christ, you're bleeding," Cruz said. I looked up to meet his concerned gaze.

Blood dripped down my leg. Cruz grabbed a roll of paper towels and bent down to clean me up.

"What are you even doing here, Jade?" Sam's voice was so loud it made my head pound.

"Leave her alone. She was having fun and just got a little carried away," Cruz said.

"This is because of you. Look at her. Do you even know why she drank herself into a fucking comatose state? No, you don't, do you? Because this is all fun and games to you. You don't give a fuck about her," Sam said, and I swore the walls were vibrating now.

"I'm going to be sick," I whispered, and Ari pulled a trash can in front of me.

"You don't know what the fuck you're talking about," Cruz argued. But their voices blended together.

"Make them stop, Ari. Please," I said before I dropped to my knees and heaved into the garbage can. Once I opened the floodgates, there was no holding back. I vomited repeatedly and Ari tried to clean me up each time I paused to catch my breath.

"Did she tell you she hates Halloween? Because her fucking mom died thirteen years ago today. But let me guess, you don't go that deep. You don't do the emotional stuff, right? Because you're too cool for that shit. Well let me tell you something—you're fucking with the wrong girl."

I tried to block out the shouting as I continued to puke. The darkness of this day had found me. Just like it always had. Ari rubbed my back. I pulled back and looked down at myself. I was wearing this stupid costume, and I had puke on my hands. And I was sick. I was so sick. There was a paper towel soaked in blood stuck to my shin. Cruz and Sam were arguing, and Ari's gaze was so sad.

The tears started to fall and there was no stopping them. I sobbed in front of all three of them. And I didn't care. I didn't care about anything. Grief threatened to swallow me whole, and I wanted it to. I wanted to drown in the heaviness of the day.

"Sam." I said his name loud enough to cause them to stop yelling. "I want to go home. I want to see Dad."

He helped me to my feet and pulled on the door, but it was stuck.

"The fucking door is stuck," Sam said, and he pulled hard on it a couple times before it finally opened.

I didn't look back or say anything to Cruz or Ari. Sam settled me in the front seat of his car and buckled me in. We didn't speak on the drive, but the tears continued to fall. I heard him on the phone with my father, and when we pulled up in front of my childhood home, Dad was there.

And it was exactly where I wanted to be.

Chapter Twelve

CRUZ

"WHAT ARE YOU GOING TO DO?" LENNON ASKED.

"WHAT ARE YOU GOING TO DO?" LENNON ASKED.

To say last night was a shit show would be a massive understatement. I don't even know what the fuck happened. I knew Jade was drinking too much. Maybe I should have interceded. I didn't realize she'd had as much to drink as she did. She's never out of control, and I wasn't fucking prepared for it. I tried to stop Gus from swinging at Sam because he didn't know who he was. Sam thought I was fighting him when I dove off the stage and he took a swing at me. It was a disaster. And Jade left with him. Not with me. He knew about her mom. I didn't. Sam had an eighteen-year advantage with Jade. I couldn't compete. But I sure as hell wanted to.

"She's not answering her phone or texts. Her friend Ariana just sent me her address in Bucktown, so I think I'm going to just drive out there and try to talk to her. Shit, I don't know what else to do."

"You really like her, huh?" my brother asked.

"Yeah. I do. She's just good, you know. In every way. I feel bad that I didn't know about her mom's passing."

"You can't blame yourself for something she didn't tell you. I think if she knew how much you actually like her, she'd be more likely to tell you what's going on."

"Yeah. What happened with the dude from the label?" I asked. After I jumped off the stage and the shit show began, all hell broke loose.

That's Halloween for you. There were several fights that had to be broken up after Sam and I were dragged to the back room. Some dude hit another guy over the head with a beer bottle and got arrested. Dex jumped into the mix because he loves a good bar fight, and he left with a black eye.

"Apparently he thought we had stage presence, and he liked how we engaged with the crowd," Lennon said, and we both laughed.

"Jesus. Are you serious? I was afraid I fucked things up."

"No. You've always got my back. And I've always got yours. Besides, Luke wants to hold out for AF Records, and I trust him. We don't need to rush this. You want me to drive with you out to Bucktown?"

"Nah. I've got this. Thanks." I clapped him on the shoulder and reached for my keys.

My palms were sweaty, because I didn't know what to say to her dad. I wasn't sure what Sam had told him, or what he'd heard, so I didn't know if he hated me. But I had to do it. I needed to know what the fuck happened last night.

I knocked on apartment 2D and shoved my hands in my pockets while I waited. The door opened and a tall man with dark hair stood on the other side of the door. He didn't have Jade's eyes, but I could tell they were related.

"Hello, Mr. Moore, I'm Cruz Winslow," I said. I extended my hand to him, and I hoped he missed the tremble in my hand.

He studied me for a minute before reaching out. "Cruz, I've heard quite a bit about you."

I didn't know what the hell that meant. If it was from Sam, it was bad. If it came from Jade, I assumed it would be better. I think? After last night, I didn't have a fucking clue.

"Oh yeah."

"Yes. Relax. Jade likes you, and that's what matters to me. Sam's just looking out for her. Don't let him rattle you."

I released a long breath I didn't even realize I'd been holding.

"Well, thank you for not passing judgment. I honestly don't know what happened last night. I only jumped in because I realized the bouncer was going to get rough with Sam. Gus was just looking out for Jade. I think Sam thought I jumped in to fight him."

"Nah, he figured it out. He actually stuck up for you. The first time he met you I got an ear full. But last night he said he overreacted, and you took control of the situation and got her out of there. I appreciate it. I don't think you or Sam could have stopped what went down last night. Jade was determined to prove she was okay, and I think she realized it's not the end of the world if she's not. Hell, if she needs to grieve every Halloween for the rest of her life, she can. There's no right or wrong way to lose the people you love, and it's a bumpy road trying to navigate it. Even all these years later."

"I can imagine. I know it's been a long time, but I'm very sorry for your loss," I said.

Jesus. I was sweating. Her dad was nice but intimidating. Just his appearance. He looked strong, like he could potentially bench press me without a problem. And I wasn't a small dude.

"Thank you. I'm guessing you came out here to see my girl?" Jack Moore was probably the only guy on the planet who could call Jade his girl without sending me into a jealous rage. I could see how much he adored his daughter.

"Yes, sir."

He led me down a narrow hallway and knocked on the door before cracking it open. "Jady bug, you have a visitor."

"I don't want to talk to Sam. Not right now, Dad. Please."

"It's not Sam." He nodded for me to go in and surprised me when he pulled the door closed to give us some privacy.

"Hey," I said, moving to sit on the edge of her bed.

She lifted her face from the covers. Her eyes were swollen, her nose red, and she was fucking beautiful.

"Oh my god. You must hate me." Her voice cracked.

"Why would I hate you?"

She pushed to sit up and used the sleeve of her Chicago fire sweatshirt to swipe at the tears streaming down her face. "I'm really sorry. I don't know what happened to me last night."

"You have nothing to be sorry about. I came here because I was worried about you."

She shook her head and tucked her hair behind her ears. "Did I mess things up for you? With that guy who came to watch you perform?"

She was sobbing now, and something in my chest tightened.

"No. And I wouldn't give a shit if you did. But a good fight only makes for a more appealing band," I said, and put my hand on her cheek. I used my thumb to clear away the moisture that continued to fall down her pretty face.

"I'm so sorry if I embarrassed you. I can't believe what a mess I was. I literally hate Halloween. Forever," she said, but it came out as more of a croak.

"That's fine. I don't give a shit about Halloween. But you should have told me about your mom. I would have been there for you."

"I didn't want you to feel sorry for me. And I don't really know where we stand or what we are. So I didn't think it was fair to dump my baggage on you. I just wanted a *normal* Halloween."

"Don't I always tell you I want *more Jade?* That includes the baggage. I love me some Jade baggage," I said with a laugh, and she finally smiled.

"Okay."

"And as far as where we stand, I don't know what kind of title you want to put on it, but I want to be with you. Only you. I like you so fucking much it scares the shit out of me. I can't stay away from you. I want to be with you. All the fucking time."

Her gaze met mine. "Really?"

I laughed. "Really."

She pushed back the blankets and climbed in my lap. Her hands tangled in my hair, and I pulled her even closer. Her face settled in the crook of my neck and I wrapped my arms around her. We sat like that for a few minutes in silence. It was the most intimate thing I'd ever done, and I'd had my fair share of sex. This was more personal. I liked it.

"So since we're making this official, that means telling me when something's bothering you." I stroked her hair.

"That goes both ways," she said.

"Fine with me. I told you about my fucked-up family and you didn't run."

She pushed up to look at me. "I just realized—you met my dad."

"I did. He's a nice guy."

She covered her mouth with her hand and moved to her feet. "I need to brush my teeth. I must smell like puke."

I laughed. "You smell good to me."

She opened her bedroom door and walked out in the hallway toward the bathroom. Her room was small, but quaint. Dark wood covered the floors. Her furniture was white, and there were white blinds hanging on the window. Her bedding was light gray and pink, and it smelled like Jade. Peaches and coconut. There was a model of the human body on her desk, and a light in the shape of Saturn hung on the wall. She was such a science nerd. I loved it. When she returned, her hair was piled on top of her head, and her face was scrubbed clean.

"You want to go to breakfast with me and Dad?"

"Sure," I said, pushing to my feet.

It was a short walk over to their favorite coffee shop. The wind bustled but the sun was out, making it tolerable. I liked seeing Jade and her father together. They laughed, and talked, and it was all very normal. Jack Moore adored his daughter. He was a good guy. Protective but fair. They bantered back and forth with such ease. I realized how non-traditional my family was. We'd never go have a casual breakfast and catch up. The Winslows didn't do coffee shops. Or unplanned family meals.

"So, did we learn anything about doing shots of tequila?" Her father gave her a firm look and waited for an answer once we were seated at a booth in the back.

"We learned that we don't like tequila. In fact, if I never see it again, it'll be too soon."

"And what did we learn about putting ourselves in vulnerable positions? If Cruz or Sam hadn't been there, things could have ended differently," Jack said. His tone was stern, and he didn't hide the concern in his gaze. It was all so foreign to me that I just sat back and took it in. She was his whole world. He loved her. Probably the way a parent should love their child, but it was unfamiliar to me. That kind of worry or care from a parent.

"Well, if Sam hadn't been there, we wouldn't have put on such a horrifying show," she said.

"Don't put this on him. He went there because I told Uncle Jimmy that I was worried about you. If I'd shown up, it would have been all the more embarrassing. Don't blame him, Jade. If you hadn't been three sheets to the wind, he wouldn't have had to drag you out of there."

Jesus. These two were so logical. No big blow-ups. Just straight shooters. My father had never talked to me like this. We only talked about the band. About money. About stuff. *Not life.*

"I know. I'm sure he's mad at me. I'll call him tonight and apologize." She gave her father a tender look, and he was putty in her hands.

"There you go, Jady bug. So Cruz, tell me about you. You grew up here in Chicago?"

"Yes, I grew up in Glencoe." I didn't like talking about my family, but I wanted to be respectful.

"And you're a junior? What are you studying?"

"Yep. I'm studying Art History."

The waitress set our plates down, and we dug in. The place was buzzing with people. Clearly we came at the right time to this local hot spot. The line extended out the door now.

"Nice. So is the band a hobby or something you want to take further?"

Isn't that the million-dollar question.

"I honestly don't know. If it were only me in the equation, it would be a hobby. But my brother is the one who started Exiled. He's a very talented guitarist, and he wants to take it the whole nine yards. So, I'm just kind of letting things play out. My dad is pushing for us to sign with a label and that would definitely mean I'd have to leave school and go on tour."

Jade leaned into me almost like she sensed my discomfort. I liked it.

"Your father is Steven Winslow?" he asked.

"Yes."

"I've seen a few of his movies. Talented guy," he said.

"He's very good at his job." I'd leave it at that.

"I was telling Cruz about how fun our Thanksgivings are. I think he and Lennon should join us if they stay in town this year," Jade said, changing the subject because she knew me well.

"You're both welcome to join us. We have a good crew that comes every year. This one makes a mean turkey, and her stuffing is out of this world." He flicked his thumb at his daughter.

The rest of breakfast was small talk and laughter. No tension. No animosity. And I liked it more than I ever would have guessed.

"Come on, tell me that's not the best ice cream you've ever had?" Jade said, licking the top of her double decker cone. Sprinkles were falling on her sweatshirt and on the ground and she just kept trying to catch them with her tongue.

"It's damn good."

"Yours is plain. You didn't do any candy or sprinkles on it. Mine is so much better," she said.

I leaned forward and licked the side of her cone, chomping on a mouthful of sprinkles. She waited patiently for my review.

"I don't know," I teased her.

"What do you mean?" She threw her hands in the air. "Mine is definitely better."

"Yours is busy. You've got two flavors going and it's crunchy and messy. My cone is no nonsense. Just good fucking ice cream."

She leaned forward and licked the top of my cone. Her nose scrunched and she shook her head. "You're crazy. Mine is so much better."

I just smiled. If I'd known dating Jade would be this great, I'd have tried to make this happen much sooner.

"Come here," I said.

She narrowed her gaze and leaned over the small table between us, while she held her cone off to the side. "You're not getting any more. I'm keeping it to myself."

I chuckled before covering her mouth and kissing her hard. When we pulled apart, she got up and walked over to sit on my lap.

"Thanks for coming here today. Are you going to let me show you around Bucktown a little more before we head back to school?"

"Yep. I'm in," I said, and I stole another taste of her ice cream. She was right. Hers was better.

We spent the next six hours cruising around Jade's hometown. Everywhere we went, people knew her. She'd grown up here. She showed me her dry cleaner, her drug store, her high school and her dad's firehouse. She didn't take me inside because she said we'd never leave if they saw her. But she promises to bring me back and introduce me to everyone. Her favorite park, the Six-O-Six was an abandoned elevated rail line that ran for three miles. We walked along the trail surrounded by green lush plants, and she told me all about her childhood.

"You see that house over there? The one with the black door?"

"Yeah," I said.

"Well, in middle school someone started a rumor that it was haunted. They said the lady that lived there was a witch named Mary Worth. You know, that urban legend where you say her name into a mirror? *'I believe in Mary Worth,'* over and over until you see her face? Rumor has it she lived in Bucktown," she said, looking completely serious.

"How can you believe in urban legends? You're a freaking science wiz."

Her head tipped back with a laugh. "A science wiz can't believe in witches? Have you never been to a slumber party with a Ouija board?"

I reached for her hand and intertwined my fingers with hers.

"I can't say I have. Our parties were more about making out and getting drunk." I chuckled.

"In eighth grade?"

"Yep. So tell me, what does Mary Worth, the urban legend of Bucktown, do in her big brick apartment building?"

She paused and turned to face me. Pops of gold dance in her green gaze where the sun hit her from above. "That's the thing. If you can ring the doorbell without her grabbing you and pulling you in to your slow, painful death—you'll officially break her spell. Send her packing. And guess who did just that?"

My laughter boomed around us and I tugged her close. "Let me guess. Was it you?"

"*Hells to the yes*," she said, thrusting one fist in the air. "I saved Bucktown, and most of these people don't even know it."

"I guess that makes you an urban legend, too."

She laughed before pushing up on her tiptoes and kissing me. It was short, and sweet, and she tastes like strawberry ice cream.

"Something like that. It made me quite famous at St. Anne's Middle School. Someone started the rumor about Mary Worth, and everyone believed it. And I finally ding dong ditched that house and ran for my life. A group of kids waited across the street. They called me lightning Jade for about three days until all the hoopla died down."

She pulled me back along the path and our hands were still connected.

"Tell me your favorite childhood memory," she said.

I thought about it for a minute. "If it involves stealing a car, does that make it bad?"

"You didn't."

"Well, it was one of my dad's many cars, and I was fifteen, so only a year away from getting my license. Adam and I took it to a gas station. We were going to try to get beer but seeing as we didn't have fake IDs at fifteen, we settled for candy and Red Bulls. Lennon was too scared, so he decided to guard the fortress, which is another way of saying he hid at home," I said with a laugh. "Anyway, I had the seat pulled so far forward and getting that car out of the driveway without my dad's driver noticing was no easy task. But we did it. And we both vomited for hours because we ate and drank so much sugar."

She laughed and shook her head in disbelief. "Wait, you had a driver? Why didn't you just ask him to take you?"

"Because where's the fun in that?" I said.

Jade and I ended our day at her favorite pizza place, and the owner came around the corner and lifted her off the ground when he hugged her.

"Jady bug, it's good to see you."

"Hi Al, this is my friend Cruz," she said.

Al was a big, tall Italian guy with a strong Chicago accent. Tattoos decorated his arms and he had warm eyes.

"Oh, is this a *special friend*?" he teased.

Jade slapped his arm. "Why do you always have to make things weird?"

"Because you like it that way. Nice to meet you, Cruz." The older man extended his hand to me.

"You too. I heard you have the best pizza in Bucktown," I said.

"You speak the truth, my friend." He squeezed my shoulder before moving back around the counter. "So, what'll it be? A large cheese, half pepperoni? Take some home to your old man?"

Jade turned to me to see if I was good with cheese and pepperoni, I gave her a nod and reached for my wallet. She fought me on paying for the ice cream and I wasn't fighting her on this. I handed Al my card.

"I already like you, kid," Al said before he called out our order to the kitchen.

"I already like you too, kid," Jade said, taking the seat across from me at a table.

"The feeling's mutual."

I liked this girl a lot.

More than I'd ever liked anyone.

And it was scary as hell.

Chapter Thirteen

JADE

CRUZ SHOWED UP AT MY DOOR AT SIX O'CLOCK SATURDAY MORNING TO pick me up. He was going on no sleep, because he had a show last night. Ari and I were at the library because we had another round of tests this week. He pulled me down the hallway and hurried me to his car. I brought my books and one change of clothes per his insistence. I had no idea what he was up to, and butterflies swirled in my belly.

"What's the rush?" I asked once he pulled away from the curb.

"It's a surprise," Cruz said with a wink.

"A surprise, huh?"

He took my hand and I gazed out the window as we breezed down the freeway. Cruz brought something out in me. Something unfamiliar. Maybe a sense of adventure. As much as a type A, OCD person was capable of at least. I was more relaxed when I was with him, more in the moment. Peaceful and happy. Those weren't two words I'd used to describe myself two months ago.

"What is this?" I pushed forward when we pulled into a parking lot of a large warehouse looking building.

"You'll see. Come on," he said, reaching in back to grab my backpack and his duffle bag.

He clasped my hand and led me inside the building. Airplanes flew overhead, but we weren't near the airport. It was a bit overcast and gloomy outside, and fall was in full motion. The cool weather forced me to wear both a sweater and a jacket.

"Cruz, good to see you my friend," an older gentleman said when we stepped inside.

"Hey, Ponch. Thanks for doing this on such short notice. This is Jade."

"Hi. Nice to meet you," I said. My voice was quiet because I didn't know what we were doing here.

"Happy to meet you. I understand you've never been on an airplane?" Ponch was in his mid-fifties, with warm blue eyes and a big round belly.

My teeth sunk into my bottom lip as I gazed out the window to see planes scattered around.

"I haven't, no," I said, and smiled because the look on Cruz's face was adorable. He looked like a kid on Christmas morning. Ready to burst at the seams. He wore distressed jeans, a grey sweater and a black peacoat. He wasn't nearly as bundled as me.

"Alright, Cruz will take you outside and show you around. I'll be out in a few minutes."

Cruz took my hand and led me outside to a gigantic parking lot filled with airplanes. He opened a door to another building, and we walked into a large warehouse. There was an airplane parked inside.

"What is this?" I asked as we walked up a staircase and into a lounge area.

"It's a hangar. This is where my dad keeps his planes," he said, pouring sparkling water into two small plastic cups.

"You have your own plane?" I sipped the water and stared out the floor to ceiling glass, looking down into the hangar.

"Yes."

"So, when you go see your parents, you fly on a private plane?"

"Usually, yes."

"Wow. Who flies the plane?" I had a million questions racing through my head.

"We have three pilots. Ponch is my favorite, so he'll be flying us today."

My stomach dipped. "What? Flying who today? I thought we were going to study?"

He chuckled and reached for my hand. "Relax, baby. We're going to study. We'll just be doing it at the New York Public Library."

Sending.

Sending.

Sending.

There was no signal. I couldn't process what he was saying.

"What are you talking about?"

He pushed the door open and we stepped back outside. The sun was blinding, and I used my hand to shield my eyes. Cruz kept tugging me toward an airplane, but I came to an abrupt stop.

"What's wrong?" he asked.

"What is happening? Who's going to New York?"

He smiled, and it did something to me. It happened every time. My heart melted. Every. Single. Time.

"*We* are. You've never been out of the state of Illinois, so we're going to fix that. They have a great library there, so we can kill two birds with one stone," Cruz said.

The breeze bustled around us and he looked gorgeous. His messy hair moved in the wind, as his honeyed eyes studied me. His cheeks were a little pink from the cold, and he leaned down and kissed me.

"You're taking me to New York? For how long?" I said against his mouth.

"That's up to you. It's an hour and a half flight. We can fly home late tonight, or we can stay the night if you're comfortable with that."

I started laughing and couldn't stop. Cruz smiled, and he looked at me like I had three heads.

"I'm going to New York?" I shouted at the top of my lungs.

"Yes. Come on, crazy. Ponch is ready."

"I can't believe we're doing this," I said as we boarded the plane.

I'd never been on an airplane, so I literally had nothing to compare this to. But I'd seen movies and I knew what the inside of planes looked like. This was smaller, but much swankier. There were twelve navy blue seats total. I dropped down into the spacious chair beside Cruz and buckled up. There were several televisions, and the seats reclined.

"Good morning, I'm Veronica and I'll be taking this short trip with you. What can I get you to drink?"

Yep. Apparently, we had our own flight attendant too. She was tall and blonde and probably late-twenties. Cruz looked at me, waiting for me to respond.

"Um. I would love a water. But I'm happy to get it myself," I said. I was so freaking awkward. This was overwhelming. Ridiculously overwhelming. And the most exciting thing to ever happen to me, aside from being accepted to Northwestern University.

"Two waters," Cruz said, and Veronica stared at him for an unusual amount of time. I pushed away the tinge of jealousy.

"Do you care if I text my dad? Or is that against the rules on an airplane?"

"You can text him," he said with a laugh.

Me ~ Take three guesses where I am right now.

I waited all of three seconds.

Me ~ Can't wait for your response because we are about to take off. On an airplane! Cruz is taking me to New York to study at the library there. I'm not making this up! I won't be in the same state as you for the first time in my life. That's weird, right?

Me ~ DAD! If you aren't fighting a fire right now, you need to text me back.

Dad ~ Sorry. I was in the shower. How are you flying to New York? For how long? You're at the airport?

Me ~ I'm coming home tonight or tomorrow. Cruz's dad has a plane. And some kind of airplane hangar? Not sure what that even is, but it has bubbly water and the swanky cookies you like!

Cruz laughed, and I glanced over to see him staring at my screen.

Dad ~ Who would have guessed your first flight would be on a private plane? I'm happy for you, Jady bug. Be safe and give Cruz my phone number in case of an emergency. Text me when you land and let me know when you will be returning. Don't spend the entire time at the library. Live a little, kid!

I couldn't contain my excitement as I powered off my phone. Cruz handed me his cell and told me to program my dad's number in it.

"Here you go." Veronica set down our waters, and I didn't miss the way she looked at Cruz again.

"Thanks," I said.

He didn't acknowledge her and shifted in his seat. He was uncomfortable. A sick feeling settled in my stomach.

"I think she likes you," I whispered close to his ear. We were getting ready for take-off, and my heart was racing.

"It's possible," he said, fidgeting with his phone. He didn't meet my gaze.

"Do you know her?"

"Yes," he said.

Warning bells sounded in my head like fireworks on the fourth of July.

"You know her? As in, *know her?*" I said, half joking, before taking a sip of water.

"Unfortunately, yes."

Water sputtered from my mouth all over my lap. "Oh my god. She's pushing thirty."

"I don't know how old she is. I don't really care. It was nothing. It was two years ago. Lennon bet me I couldn't make the mile-high club. She overheard the conversation and propositioned me. I've never spoken to her since. She hasn't been on a flight with me again, so I assumed she quit."

I didn't speak. I didn't want to let this ruin the moment. But it was a big, fat reminder to be careful where Cruz was concerned. I could be dropped tomorrow just as easily.

"You can't be mad at me about something that happened two years ago, baby. I was an asshole before I met you, that's not a secret." He took my hand and intertwined his fingers with mine.

"You still manage to be a pretty decent asshole now."

He chuckled. "I told you the truth. I could have just lied."

"And what would be the point? Why would you want to be in a relationship with someone you couldn't be truthful with?"

"I don't, which is why I told you. I only want you."

"I hate that you have such a—*colorful past.*"

"What matters is now. Moving forward with you."

"I guess. I hate her. Is that normal?"

"Yes. It's normal." He laughed. "But there's nothing there. I promise."

I nodded, and he leaned over and kissed me.

"Are we going to spend the entire day at the library? Or can we explore a little?" he asked.

I dropped the Veronica issue because he was right. I couldn't punish him for his past. But I could tread cautiously with Cruz Winslow. Though he made it difficult to do so. I wanted to jump all in. I was crazy about him, and it was terrifying to feel so strongly about someone. To care this much.

"I think we should do both. Where would we stay if we don't go home today?"

"My family has an apartment here. But I know you haven't spent the night with me yet because we're taking things slow. But it is possible to sleep with someone without having sex, in case you weren't aware. And there are multiple bedrooms in the apartment so we could technically have our own rooms. But I don't know if I could sleep knowing you were down the hall," he said. His warm honeyed gaze met mine.

I wanted to take the next step with him, but I was afraid. Afraid he'd tire of me when I did. That he'd lose interest and drop me like he did Veronica and the loads of other girls in his wake.

"It does seem silly to come all this way, just to turn around and leave. You know, NYU is my top choice for medical school. Although it's near impossible to get into. It would be a shame to be here and not walk by it," I said.

The plane started to move, and I lifted the armrest and scooched closer to Cruz. I laid my head on his chest and closed my eyes. It was loud and we were moving fast now.

"Jade," he whispered against my head. "Look out the window. This is my favorite part."

He wrapped his arm around me and pulled me as close as I could sit without climbing on his lap. I peeked one eye open and watched the ground disappear beneath us. I leaned forward and looked down, before quickly returning my cheek to his chest and squeezing my eyes closed. That was enough of a view for now. His chest vibrated when he chuckled.

"Do you know that Carrie Bradshaw married Big at the New York Public Library? Actually, she didn't. Scratch that. She was supposed to marry Big, but he had cold feet and he no-showed. It was a whole thing. But ever since, I've thought it would be cool to get married at a library. Can you imagine the setting?" I was clearly nervous, because I was rambling. It was my thing, I guess.

"That sounds awful. I don't even like going to the library to study. Who would choose to throw a party there?" He stroked my hair.

"Cool people."

"Cool, single people, maybe," he said, and his tone was all tease.

We laughed and I gazed out the window the rest of the flight. Veronica checked on us twice before we prepared for landing. I avoided eye contact. There was no logic behind my disdain for a woman I didn't even know. A woman who slept with my boyfriend two years ago, before I knew him. But she shared something with him that I hadn't. I'd never been a jealous person, but when it came to Cruz, I saw sides of myself I'd never seen before. And jealousy was one of them.

"Jade," Ponch called over the speaker.

I jolted upright. "Is he talking to me?"

"He is," Cruz said.

"Present," I called out. Unsure what the protocol was when responding to the man asking for you while he held your life in his hands.

"You want to ride copilot for the landing?" he asked.

"Do I want to ride copilot? I don't know." I whispered to Cruz.

"You do. It's cool."

He walked me up front to the cockpit. There were so many bells and whistles and I tried to take it all in.

Cruz buckled my seatbelt like I was a child, but it was so endearing it didn't offend me. He returned to his seat and I focused on the captain. He explained what some of the gadgets and buttons did, and handed me the walkie-talkie so I could announce that we were preparing to land.

"Prepare for landing," I said. And because I was in the moment, I continued in my deepest voice. "I'm the captain now."

Cruz laughed, and Ponch had a grin spread clear across his face. He was focused on landing the plane, so the last thing I wanted to do was distract him. He pointed to the controllers and talked me through what the process was.

When the wheels touched down, I cheered. This is quite possibly the coolest thing I'd ever done. When we exited the plane, Cruz told Ponch we were going to spend the night here and head back tomorrow. He took my hand and led me to a car waiting for us on the runway. My guess was, it wasn't the norm to depart a plane and walk to your awaiting vehicle. I was so excited to be here I could barely contain myself.

"Hey Donny, this is Jade," Cruz said. This was all normal for him. He was relaxed and comfortable.

"Nice to meet you, Jade."

I shook his hand. "Great to meet you. Thank you for picking us up."

"Where are we off to?" Donny said.

"Are you hungry? There's a great breakfast place near the apartment," Cruz asked.

"Sure. Sounds great to me."

Cruz gave Donny directions and we stopped to grab a bite to eat. The café was crowded, and the scent of warm bread and pastries filled the space. My stomach rumbled and we found a small table and ordered.

"Thanks for bringing me here. Seriously, this is unbelievable. I can't believe I'm here."

"I think we should study in different cities more often. It'll be a great way for you to see some new places."

"Your dad doesn't mind if you use the plane to fly around just for fun?"

He chuckled. "My dad wants me to use it. It makes him feel like he has something on me in a sick way. He loves when I ask for things."

"That's odd, right?" I said.

"You're not even scratching the surface. But I'm glad we're here. You know NYU is right around the corner if you want to stop there first. I didn't know you wanted to go to medical school in New York."

"Yeah, it's a pipe dream. But it's an incredible school, and they're the first med school to offer free tuition for all four years," I said as the server set our food down.

"It's not a pipe dream. You're fucking amazing. They'd be lucky to have you. Don't sell yourself short."

"They don't take many out-of-state kids and med school is super competitive. But you're right—you don't know until you try. I've got a couple years before I have to cross that bridge. I'm trying to graduate in three years."

"That's an impressive goal. Especially with your major. But if anyone can do it, it's you."

"Thanks. We'll see how it goes," I said.

"I'm glad we came."

"Me too. So, you have an apartment here?" My stomach dipped at the thought of sleeping in the same bed with Cruz. I'd been tempted to stay the night a few times but made a conscious effort not to move too fast. But it wasn't because I didn't want to.

"Yeah. We've had it for a few years. I'm glad we're staying the night." His tone was flirty, and he waggled his brows.

"Don't get cocky. I'm not Veronica. Nor am I like that naked girl that was at your house before we started dating."

"Are you worried that I think you are?" he said.

"Am I worried you'll have your way with me and never talk to me again? No, I don't think you'd do that. But sure, you could tire of me. You seem to have a pattern of doing that."

He pulled my chair close to him. "Jade. I didn't talk to those girls before I hooked up with them. I didn't know them or like them. It was a mutual thing. Something to do. It sounds bad, but it's the truth. And they were in it for the same thing. There were no broken promises. No one got hurt. You're so different. I could never tire of you. I've never felt this way about anyone."

"Neither have I." Admitting this was scary.

He leaned forward and kissed me. "I'd never pressure you. Hell, I don't want to push things either because I don't want to fuck it up."

I smiled. "Me either."

We ate a few more bites, but I was too excited about being in New York to eat.

"You want to get out of here?"

"Yes. But I'm paying for lunch. It's the least I can do," I said, and grabbed the check.

"You're ridiculous. I brought you here. You haven't let me pay you for tutoring for weeks. And now Lennon has you proofreading all his papers, so you're helping him, too. The whole family owes you."

"I don't tutor you. We study together. And I'm helping Lennon. It's not a job."

He rolled his eyes. "Let's go see your dream school."

I led the way out the door. Ready to explore. Ready for new adventures.

Ready for all the things with Cruz Winslow.

Chapter Fourteen

CRUZ

TODAY WAS DEFINITELY THE BEST DAY I'D EVER SPENT IN NEW YORK, AND several hours had been at a fucking library. We'd stopped by the medical school at NYU, went to see the Statue of Liberty and a few other quick touristy things before going to the NYC public library. I took her to Bryant Park for hot chocolate when we left the library.

Jade flipped out over the apartment and I ordered take-out so we could have a late dinner. We ate in the dining room which offers amazing views of the city.

I gave her one of my T-shirts to sleep in because she only has a change of clothes for tomorrow. She came bounding into bed. It was the first time she'd ever spent the night with me, and I was actually nervous, which was completely foreign to me. Nothing was going to happen, so it wasn't about taking that step with her. Not that I ever got nervous about sex, obviously. It was more about how much she meant to me and making sure I didn't fuck it up. The Veronica thing disappointed her, which was the last thing I wanted to do. I couldn't change my past, but I could control what I did moving forward.

"You smell very fruity," I said with a laugh.

Her head falls back. "There are so many lotions in there. I just put a little squirt of each one and made myself a little moisturizer salad."

Her legs were crossed as she sat in the middle of the bed, her dark hair falling around her shoulders, and her face was clean and shiny. Absolutely fucking perfect.

"I've never heard of a moisturizer salad," I said before tipping her back and tickling her.

She laughed and squirmed beneath me, which immediately got a reaction down south. I've grown used to having a constant boner. I kissed her hard, claiming her. When we came up for air, I pulled her up so we could get in bed. We both rolled on our sides to face one another. The moon shined through the floor to ceiling windows which illuminated her pretty face. She begged me to leave the blinds open, as she liked seeing the view of the city from the bed. I hadn't appreciated this view in years. But Jade saw the beauty in all things. We were on the top floor, and it really was magnificent.

"I can't believe I'm here," she whispered.

"In New York?"

"Well, yes. But here, in bed with you, too."

"Me either," I said. I stroked her hair, and she moved closer.

She rubbed the tip of her little nose against mine. "I've noticed you're not smoking as much."

"Yeah, I'm cutting back."

"I'm glad," she said, and her lips grazed mine.

"You probably hate the smell."

"Well, I don't like cigarettes, but that's not why I'm glad."

I ran my fingers up the back of her neck and into her hair and tilted her head to the side for better access. I teased her lips with mine.

"Tell me why then," I said against her mouth.

"Because they're bad for you, and I don't want anything to happen to you."

So. Fucking. Sweet.

"Nothing's going to happen to me, More Jade. You're stuck with me."

I covered her mouth with mine, needing this girl in a way that was completely unfamiliar. My tongue tangled with hers, and the little sounds she made drove me fucking crazy. I moved my hands to her waist, and she tugged her T-shirt up a bit, so I followed her lead and my fingers moved beneath the fabric. Her hands were on my shoulders, and I felt the tremble in her touch.

Take it slow, douchebag.

I was so out of my element. This had never been an issue. Most of the girls I took home were down to have sex. Hell, most of the time, they were the ones moving things forward. I rarely took the lead. But Jade was different. So fucking different.

She placed one hand over mine and urged me to move higher. I laughed against her mouth. "Are you eager, baby?"

She was panting. "I guess so."

"All you have to do is say the word. I just don't want to push you. But I'm dying here, in case you can't tell," I said, pressing myself against her so she could feel for herself.

"I'm not ready to have sex. But I'm sure there are other things we can do." Her voice wobbled. A heavy weight settled in my chest with the realization of what a big deal this was to her.

"I know you haven't had sex before, but I'm sure you've messed around with your old boyfriends from high school." I needed to know why she was so nervous. If it was just about trusting me, or if this was all new for her.

"Not really, no. We just kissed." She avoided my gaze, staring over my shoulder at the wall.

"Hey," I said, pulling her hands between us and kissing them. "Don't ever be embarrassed with me. I love that I get to be your first—everything."

Her gaze locked with mine. "Me too."

I wanted to tell her I loved her. Because I did. But I didn't want her to think I was just saying it to get in her pants. Nothing could be further from the truth.

My mouth moved over hers, and my hands slipped back beneath the cotton T-shirt. Her skin was soft and smooth. I took my time traveling up her stomach. Exploring every beautiful inch of her body. Her mouth was so sweet, I couldn't get enough. I kissed her deeper and cupped her breast. Her head fell back on a gasp, and I took my time exploring her perfect tits. I kissed my way down her neck, and she arched into me. I pulled the T-shirt up and over her head. There was too much fabric between us. I wanted to strip everything away so it was just me and her. More Jade. My mouth closed over her breast and I teased her nipple with my tongue. Jade gasped and moaned, and I swore in that moment I could die a happy man. Right here with her.

"Cruz," she pleaded.

My hand moved down her body until I reached the band of her panties. I was worshipping her breasts with my mouth and I wanted to pleasure her. She froze as my fingers slipped beneath the silk fabric.

"Nothing bad is going to happen, baby. Let me touch you. I want to make you feel good."

"Okay." Her voice was needy and gruff. I'd never seen this side of Jade. And I had yet to see a side that I didn't love. But turned-on, sexy Jade—well, she was hard to compete with.

I moved my hand slow and gentle along her most sensitive area, allowing her to set the pace. I loved feeling how turned on she was. My own erection was on the verge of an explosion, but I didn't even give a shit. I just wanted to please her. She moved her hips faster. Her breathing was frantic, and I pulled my mouth back up to meet hers. I kissed her as she cried out my name with her release. She was gasping and sweaty, and I'd never seen anything sexier.

"Oh my god," she finally said.

"That good, huh?" I propped myself above her as she laid on her back on the bed.

Her hand found my cheek. "Yeah. That good."

Her cheeks were flushed, and she tried to cover her face with her hands, but I didn't let her. "No hiding. Didn't you say you shouldn't be with someone if you can't tell them who you are? I love who you are."

"I love who you are, too." She met my gaze and smiled.

I lay down and rolled on my side to face her. She moved to her side and scooched close to me. I wrapped my arm around her, ready for sleep.

Her hands settled on my chest before making their descent to my *happy place*. She stopped at the waistband of my joggers.

"What are you up to?" I tilted her chin to look up at me.

"I want to make you feel good, too."

"You don't need to, baby. There's no rush," I said, but the boner in my pants was telling me to fuck off.

"I know. But I want to. Teach me," she said just above a whisper.

She pushed my sweatpants down, and I guided her hand to the base of my erection. This had to be the most erotic thing I'd ever done, and I'd done some crazy shit over the years. But something about teaching Jade how I liked to be touched, was the sexiest thing I ever saw. She moved her hand slowly at first, but she followed my lead as I moved my hips faster. I tilted her head up and covered her mouth with mine as a loud moan escaped me, and I released weeks of pent up desire. Jade pulled her hand back and kissed me.

"You're amazing," I said.

"I have a good teacher." Her cheeks pinked, and her warm breath tickled my skin.

I laughed. "As usual, you're the top student in the class."

I stood and pulled her up, and we made our way into the bathroom to clean ourselves up. She was watching me in the mirror, and I tossed the towel in the hamper.

"What?"

"Nothing. I just like looking at you sometimes," she said.

I wrapped my arms around her waist and settled my chin on her shoulder. My chest pressed against her back. "Oh, yeah. I like looking at you all the time."

"I've wondered what your tattoo says." She turned and traced the script on my arm with her finger. "*Wars begin in the minds of men?*"

"Just a saying I like."

"Me too."

She moved to my back and traced the words just below my neck. "*Inhale the future, exhale the past.* I like that one too," she said.

She came to stand beside me, and we stared at the two images in the mirror. Of course, she slipped my T-shirt back on when she got off the bed and covered up her gorgeous body. I studied the reflections looking back at me. All her soft edges to my hard ones. We just stood there in silence for a few minutes before Jade pushed up and kissed my cheek. She took my hand and led me back to bed, before settling her cheek on my chest as I wrapped my arms around her. I was tangled up in this girl in every way.

"How early did you get up?" I asked when I woke up to find Jade in the dining room studying.

"I got up a few hours ago and decided to get everything done so we could explore today."

Damn. What was it like being this good? This responsible. This driven.

I pulled up a chair beside her. "What are you working on?"

"I finished my chem homework and Lennon sent me an essay to proofread. I'm just reading it now," she said.

She had on my T-shirt and a pair of leggings. Her hair was in a messy knot on top of her head and she was fucking stunning.

"Thanks for helping him so much. School doesn't come easy for him. But he can't just rely on Exiled. He needs to have a back-up plan."

"Like you do?"

"Right. But music is everything to him. Always has been. Lennon's had a rough road. He struggles with a lot of shit," I said, picking up her water bottle and taking a sip.

"Drugs and alcohol?"

"Yeah, the shit I told you about. It all stems from depression. It's something he's dealt with for a long time, and his coping mechanism is to numb himself. He's been clean for eighteen months. Basically, since he came to college, away from my father's influence. When he was living at home, he'd get into trouble every time my parents were in town, or when we'd visit them. The year I left for school, he had a really hard time."

"Your parents know he struggles with drugs, and they still expose him to them?"

"Yes. As sick as it sounds, it's the truth. My mom wrestles with it, but she struggles with her own addictions, so she can't be of much support to him. And my dad flat out doesn't care. He doesn't think it's a problem. He thinks drug use is normal. My brother overdosed shortly before he came to school, and my father wasn't around to pick up the pieces."

Jade stood up and moved to sit on my lap. She wrapped her arms around my neck and rested her face on my chest. She always knew what I needed.

"I'm so sorry. What happened when he overdosed? Were you there?"

"Yes. I called 911, and he entered a thirty-day program. It's something he'll always need to work on and be aware of. The fact that he still drinks is risky, but I have to choose my battles. There's a fine line between support-ing him and enabling him. I'm not sure which I'm doing most of the time."

She pulled her face up to look at me. Her jade gaze locked with mine. "He's lucky he has you. You're so good to Lennon, and I can see how much he loves you when I watch the two of you together. Has your mom tried to overcome her struggles?"

"I don't think she wants to make a change at this point in her life. She's pretty checked out. But when it's just her and I, she's herself. For brief win-dows, at least. But when she's in crowds with my dad, all the social pressures get to her, I guess, and she checks out. I think it's gotten worse this last year. I've removed myself, and I don't see them as often. The last time I saw her, she slept half the weekend away. I found a bottle of painkillers in her bathroom. I shouldn't be pouring this on you. My family is fucked up. The worst part is, no one says anything. I swear I'm the only one that calls them out on their bullshit."

"Do you have any idea how brave you are?" She looked at me like I just brought her the sun and set it in her hands.

I laughed. "Far from brave, Jade."

"You're so hard on yourself. Maybe because you didn't grow up in a house like I did, with someone telling you how smart and talented you are every day. But let me tell you, if someone I love overdosed right in front of me, I wouldn't bounce back so easily. You just handle whatever life throws at you.

And life has thrown you more than most could handle. You're in a band because you know how much it means to your brother. And I know you enjoy it, but not the way the others do. Yet, you make it a priority because that's what you do, Cruz Winslow. You take care of everyone around you, and you don't ask for anything in return."

I stared at her. A lump formed in my throat, making it difficult to breathe. Overcome with everything I felt for this girl.

I held her face in my hands. "I love you."

She sucked in a breath and a single tear ran down her face. "I love you, too."

Her arms came around my neck and I hugged her tight. Damn. I'd never told a chick I loved her before, but I did. I loved her so much it was painful.

She pulled back and emotion welled in her gorgeous jade stare. "I've loved you for a while."

I tucked the loose hair that broke free from her elastic behind her ear. "Yeah? Me too. I've never said it to anyone before."

"Neither have I. I mean, not counting my dad," she said and smiled.

"Lots of firsts happening here, *More Jade*."

"Yep. I like it. Because they're all with you."

"Me too. What would you like to do today? And what time do you want to go home? I need to send Ponch a text," I said.

"I think we should go to the Met for sure."

"Ah, you're into art now?" I teased.

"I know it's your passion, so I'd love to go with you."

"Where the hell did you come from?" I said, grazing her lips with mine.

"Bucktown," she whispered.

I chuckled against her perfect mouth. She kissed me hard before pulling back. "Okay, lover boy. Let's go, or we'll never get out of here."

Museums were my thing. Thankfully, my mother was a lover of art, so it was something we shared. She would take me to museums on our travels, and I developed a love for art, the culture, the creativity. All of it.

"I've never seen anything like this," Jade said as we entered the Metropolitan Museum of Art.

"Yeah, the art and artifacts here span more than six thousand years of history. It's pretty amazing."

"It is."

"This is my favorite area," I said, leading her into a new section of the museum.

"Oh, wow. I like this."

"It's Egyptian mummies and ancient Egypt artifacts. Some of this stuff dates back to the Ptolemaic period. It's fascinating."

Jade and I spent a few hours at the Met before we grabbed lunch. She wanted to see Grand Central Station on our way to the hangar. To say that it had been an amazing weekend was an understatement. I didn't want it to end.

"Hey Ponch, thanks for being so flexible with us," I said.

"Not a problem. Did you enjoy New York, little lady?"

"I love it here. Thank you so much for extending things today. We went to the Met and to Grand Central. I helped land a plane yesterday. I get to check so many things off my bucket list," Jade said with a big grin.

Ponch laughed. "I'll save you a seat again today, if you want to help me land again."

I led her outside to the plane, and I was pleased to see that Veronica was not our flight attendant. Mary had worked for my dad since I was born.

"Cruzie, how are you?" She was full of personality, and always this happy.

"I'm good. Great to see you. This is my girlfriend, Jade."

"Aren't you cute as a button, Jade. I'm Mary, nice to meet you."

"It's nice to meet you as well," Jade said, shaking the older woman's hand.

We took our seats and Jade leaned in close to me. "Please tell me you didn't sleep with her, too. I really don't want to hate Mary."

I laughed. "No. No one else that works for my dad. I promise."

"Thank God. I wish we didn't have to leave. This was so fun. How am I going to go back to dealing with Meagan now?" she said.

"Does she know you're moving out in December? You can stay with me every night if you want." I wriggled my eyebrows.

"Yeah. She knows. She's moving into a single, which is a good idea because she's not easy to live with. I'm so happy I'll get to room with Ari. And I'm not staying at your place every night. I need to have a place of my own. You can stay with me sometimes too."

"Why would we stay in a twin bed with Satan's daughter sleeping beside us, when I have a king bed and my own room?"

She studied me. "You make a good argument. But I need to sleep in my room sometimes. I can stay with you on the weekends."

"Why? For what purpose? Did you like sleeping together last night?"

Her cheeks pinked and she glanced around to make sure Ponch and Mary weren't listening, like we were discussing something sinister.

"Of course, I did. But what happened to taking things slow?" Her gaze searched mine.

"Fuck going slow. We already did that. It's been almost three months since I met you. I'm ready to turn things up."

"I'll bet you are." She laughed and buckled her seatbelt for take-off.

"Get your mind out of the gutter. We don't have to decide anything today."

Once we were in the air, Jade pulled out her books and worked for the next hour until Ponch called her up front. She squeezed in every minute she could. She wasn't like anyone I'd ever met. She was genuine and real. Hardworking and determined. And I loved everything about her.

JADE

I HUGGED ARI GOODBYE AND MADE MY WAY TO THE BACK ROOM TO MEET Cruz after his show. It was the first time I'd been out in a while, but with Thanksgiving being a few days away, I didn't have any tests this week. I loved watching him perform and I promised I would come to The Dive tonight. He was difficult to say no to, which was why I'd slept at his house every single night since we'd returned from New York over a week ago. I couldn't argue with him, I slept better with him next to me. He hadn't tried to take anything further physically, it was me who'd grown impatient. He stopped things from going further when we got too heated. He said he wanted me to be sure I was ready.

I wasn't one of those girls who had this long list of rules regarding my virginity. I didn't. I just wanted to be in love. And I was now—so what was the problem? I'd never experienced an attraction like I had with Cruz. Nothing compared to this. So, there was no reason to hold back, except my boyfriend was afraid of taking my virtue too soon. He was an enigma. He could be crude and vulgar, but he had this old-fashioned gentleman side to him that no one else saw.

"Hey." Cruz met me in the hallway, and I sensed his discomfort. His shoulders were stiff, and his honeyed gaze distant.

"Great show," I said, studying his movements.

"Yeah, thanks. Uh, apparently my father is here. I haven't seen him yet, but Luke said he's in the back. Do you want to meet him?"

"Of course. Yes. I would like that."

He grasped my hand with a firmer grip than usual and led me to the back room where Lennon was huddled in the corner intently listening to who I assumed was their father. He looked to be about my dad's age, mid-forties, and tall like Cruz. The similarities ended there, as he favored Lennon's coloring with dark hair and blue eyes. He was an attractive man and dressed to the nines in a black suit. Their conversation came to an abrupt end when they both looked up.

"Hey, Jade. Thanks for coming tonight," Lennon said.

I liked Cruz's younger brother, but I worried for him. He'd been very down the last few days because they hadn't heard anything from AF Records and things were moving slow. He had all his eggs in one basket. I guessed it to be the reason their father was here. I was torn on how I felt about Exiled getting signed. I didn't want Cruz to leave. I knew that he wanted to finish school, and selfishly, I wanted him to stay with me. But I knew how important Lennon's happiness was to him, so I struggled with how selfish I was when it came to Cruz.

"Of course. You guys were amazing."

"So, this is the infamous Jade?" Cruz's father walked toward me with a bright smile and an extended hand.

"Mr. Winslow, it's nice to meet you."

"Don't age me, sweetheart. Call me Steven, please. You're sure easy on the eyes. Cruz has always had an affinity for beautiful things." His voice was husky and worn.

"She's a human being, not a thing." Cruz was on the defense. His shoulders were stiff, chin up, and there was an edge in his tone. He didn't like his father, and he didn't hide his disdain.

Steven's laughter vibrated off the walls. "Eh, big college boy is getting technical. Sorry about that. I meant no offense."

Nothing about Steven Winslow felt genuine.

"None taken," I said, glancing up at Cruz.

"So Jade, tell me, when Exiled signs with a label, will you be going on tour with them?" Steven looked down at his phone while he dropped a bomb on the room. Cruz and I hadn't talked about what we'd do. We preferred to pretend it wasn't happening.

Everyone stared at me and the room grew silent. Cruz squeezed my hand before jumping in. "We haven't even signed with anyone. Don't get so ahead of yourself. Jade's studying to be a doctor, she's not going on tour with the band."

Steven slipped his phone in his suit pocket. "She's young. People change paths all the time. Why don't you let her decide for herself?"

"Is there a reason you've graced us with your presence?" Cruz's tone was harsh and cold.

"Yes, I got a call from AF Records. After the holidays, they'd like to come see you perform. We need some new material. Labels are looking for bands that think outside the box. Expand a bit, boys. Write some new shit these next few months and dig deep."

Luke watched Cruz before jumping in. "What he means is that we don't have to stick to only alternative rock. I know you guys like to bring in some R & B, and some slower ballads—don't be afraid to have some fun. Mix it up."

"I like it," Dex said.

Cruz lets a sarcastic laugh escape. "Sure, you do."

"What the hell does that mean?" Dex asked.

"It means you're an ass kisser. You'd sell your soul to the Devil if you thought my dad wanted you to," Cruz said.

Dex lunged at Cruz and my hand slipped from his. I grabbed Cruz's shirt and pushed between them. No way was Dex touching Cruz in front of me. I was aware I wasn't much of a match for him. But he'd still have to go through me either way.

"Don't touch him," I said, pointing my finger in Dex's face, surprising everyone in the room including myself.

Lennon, Luke, and Cruz laughed first. Adam and Dex followed. But Steven just watched me with an amused smile on his face.

"Thanks, baby." Cruz kissed my forehead.

"Let's all relax. Take the edge off." Steven pulled a joint from his pocket and lit it. He offered it to me.

"No thanks," I said, wondering why the hell a forty-something-year-old man was pushing everyone to party.

"We're out. Lennon, are you coming?" Cruz said, and my gaze pleaded with his younger brother to come with us.

"Yeah. I've got a test tomorrow, Dad. Cruz and I will meet you after for breakfast though, okay?"

"Those tests won't mean much in a few months, but suit yourself," Steven said with a cocky smirk.

Dex stepped up and took the joint to his lips, exhaling all the smoke in my face as we walked past. Cruz shoved him back before we made our way outside.

"He's such an asshole," Cruz said as Lennon and I both slipped into the car.

"Who? Dad or Dex?"

"Both."

I glanced over at my boyfriend. He was visibly angry. He hit the steering wheel with the butt of his palms. I reached over and put a hand on his back.

"Don't let him get to you," I said.

"He's offering you a joint and who the hell knows what else he'll offer you, Lennon. You need to be on guard where Dad is concerned. I know you want to sign with the label. But that doesn't mean you have to sell your soul to the Devil. You've worked hard to get where you are. Don't let him derail you."

"You worry too much. I'm fine. I'm sorry if he made you uncomfortable, Jade," Lennon said.

"Not at all."

"That was badass, you jumping in to fight Dex, though," Cruz said and we all burst out in laughter.

"I don't know where that even came from," I said.

Cruz turned and his gaze locked with mine. "You're a little scrapper, baby."

"When I need to be."

"You do know I can take Dex easily, right? The dude can't fight for shit," Cruz said.

"You guys shouldn't be fighting anyway. Don't play into your dad's hands."

"She's right," Lennon said from the back seat.

"Well, I'll feel better when his ass is on a plane tomorrow afternoon."

"I still can't believe Mom wants to go to Japan for Thanksgiving. I don't know what she's thinking," Lennon said.

"I talked to her today. It's too far to travel for a long weekend. I told her we'll meet them in Park City for Christmas." Cruz pulled in the driveway.

"Yeah, Christmas will be better. We'll have more time off. And I'm glad we're coming to your house, Jade," Lennon said.

"Me too. Prepare yourself for a lot of fun."

We walked into the house. Lennon stopped and hugged me. "Thanks for coming tonight, Jade."

"No problem. See you tomorrow," I said.

Cruz took my hand and led me to his room. He shut the door and pulled me into the bathroom, before dropping to sit on the closed toilet seat and reaching for me. His arms wrapped around my waist and his cheek rested against my stomach. I stroked his hair, and we just held each other in silence for a few minutes.

"Take a shower with me?" He looked up to meet my stare.

"What?"

"You heard me. Come on. It'll be fun," he said.

"I've never done that." My voice was just above a whisper.

"Neither have I. I've never wanted to. Usually the shower is an escape to get away from people. But I want to shower with you. Come on. I'll wash your hair. And your body," he said with a quirked brow.

"Okay." I was nervous, but I wanted to do it. I wanted to be close to him. In every possible way.

He lifted my shirt over my head and unclasped my bra. I crossed my arms over my chest because I felt so exposed. He tugged my arms back down to my sides. Yes, he'd seen me undressed before. But I hadn't been standing in the light.

"Don't hide yourself from me," he said.

I tugged his shirt over his head and took in his chiseled chest and defined abdomen. He was beautiful. It still shocked me that I was dating him sometimes. He pulled me close and unbuttoned my jeans, pushing them down my legs. I closed my eyes because that's the only thing I could think to do. He chuckled.

"Look at me, baby," he said.

I opened one eye to see him pull his jeans off before leaning over to turn on the shower. The bathroom fogged up within a few seconds, and he took my hand and led me in. Hot water ran down my back and it felt so good. Cruz poured shampoo into the palms of his hands and massaged it into my hair. Heaven. I lathered up the soap and washed his chest, taking my time on his chiseled abs. Feeling each hard ridge beneath my touch. I traced the script on his chest with my finger. Damn. Showering alone would never do after this.

He kissed me and moved his lips down my neck. My back was against the wall and he dropped to his knees and kissed me in places I'd never been kissed. My head fell back, and I tried to keep from screaming. My hands tangled in his hair and he looked up to meet my gaze, I swear I've never loved anyone the way I loved him. And I never would. I closed my eyes and enjoyed his touch as he buried his face between my legs. He made me feel things I never knew existed. I cried out my release, and he stood up and kissed me.

"See, showering together is so much better than showering alone," he said.

My legs were jelly and my head dizzy. He laughed before turning off the water and stepping out of the shower. He wrapped me in a towel, and I was still dazed when I slipped on his T-shirt and climbed into bed.

He pulled me close and pushed my damp hair away from my face. His chin rested against my forehead.

"How do you feel about your dad being here?" I said, my voice just above a whisper.

"I can't stand him, yet I'm completely dependent on him. It sucks that I don't respect the man who gave me life, you know? He's just—he's not a good guy."

My hands rest on his bare chest and I run them back and forth, an effort to soothe his worry away. "I can't imagine how hard that is. Do you think he's right about Exiled getting signed in the next couple of months?"

"I don't know. We have good momentum and they seem genuinely interested. But this business is competitive, and I won't believe it till we sign on the dotted line."

"And what will you do if it does happen?" My voice trembled. I couldn't imagine Cruz not being here. The thought made me sick.

"I don't know. I'm just hoping it drags out until after I graduate." His fingers drew little circles on my arm, and I fought to keep my eyes open.

"Do you want to go on tour?"

"I want Exiled to get signed because I know how much it means to Lennon. But at the same time, I don't want to do this for the rest of my life. I don't want to leave school, and I don't want to leave you. But I'm part of a band, so it's not really up to me," he said.

"I don't want you to leave."

"It probably won't happen for a while, so let's not even worry about it." He kissed my forehead and I moved even closer to him. Every part of my body was touching his, and the sound of his heartbeat lulled me as I drifted away.

Loud voices startled me from sleep. I was disoriented. "Cruz?"

He wasn't beside me. My phone said it was three thirty-eight in the morning. I focused on the voices and one of them was Cruz. I slid off the bed and made my way to the door, cracking it open just enough so I could hear them.

"Stay the fuck away from my brother," Cruz said.

"You're not his keeper. He's a grown man." It was Dex he was arguing with.

"You think you're going to do that shit in my house? You can get the fuck out. Find a new place to live. I don't want it around my brother, or my girlfriend who's sleeping in the next fucking room. You need to find a new place to live. I'm not doing this anymore."

"Yes, oh mighty one. Heaven forbid your little puppet Lennon, or the virgin princess Jade, were to be exposed to a few lines of coke. Their castle might implode, right?" Dex's evil laugh sent a chill down my spine.

"Shut your fucking mouth about her. You don't know what you're talking about."

"Come join us, baby," a female voice said. Are there girls here? She said *us*.

"You can leave. The party's over. Take your shit with you. You can take him as well," Cruz shouted.

"What the fuck, dude. That's expensive shit. You don't just throw it out the door," Dex said. His tone was loud and slurred.

"You don't have to be an asshole. We were leaving," another female voice said.

The door slammed. I hear more voices. Adam and Lennon.

"He's out of control," Adam says.

"He is, but you need to stop treating me like a child. I can take care of myself." Lennon spoke now.

"Can you? Do you think I like being a goddamn babysitter? Stop putting yourself in bad situations. Why the fuck did you come out here with them? I find you sitting on the couch with all that shit spread across the table. So, if I hadn't walked in, what then, Lennon?"

"I wasn't going to do anything. I was just talking to them. You know, Dad gave him that shit, right?" Lennon said.

"Listen, everyone's tired. Let's get some sleep and we can figure this out in the morning. Dex needs to find a new place to live. He's not going to school and his partying is out of control. Cruz is right, Lennon, this isn't good for you to be around. We can be in the same band without living with the dude," Adam said.

"Let's talk about it tomorrow. I have a test in the morning," Lennon said.

I tiptoed back over to the bed, processing what just happened. I was just in a house where clearly there were drugs out in the open. Could I get in trouble for being here if the police were to come? And did Dex call me a virgin princess? He doesn't even know me. I hope they do kick him out. I don't like him.

"Are you fake sleeping, More Jade?" Cruz chuckled when he slid back into bed with me.

I laughed. "How'd you know I was awake?"

"I saw the door close when I came down the hall."

I pushed to sit up. "He had drugs and girls out there?"

"Yeah. With Lennon sitting a foot away from a mound of coke. I've told him I don't want that shit in this house," he said.

"He's insane. But he left?" I asked, wanting to make sure he'd left for the night.

"Yeah. He's gone. He needs to get his own place. He can afford it. His dad is loaded, and I don't want him here."

"Why did he call me a virgin princess? He's such a jerk. Did you tell him?"

"Hell no. I would never tell anyone. It's nobody's business. He's just an asshole."

"You don't think Lennon did anything, do you?" I asked.

"No. But I don't know that he wouldn't have."

"Is that what he had the problem with? Cocaine?"

"Amongst other things, yes," he said, pulling me down to lie beside him.

"How is he going to handle it on tour? Isn't that lifestyle way worse?"

"It's up to him. I mean, I don't do any of that shit and neither does Adam," he said. Frustration radiates from him.

"I love you," I said, and I heard his breathing settle into a rhythmic pattern.

"Love you."

CRUZ

THREE HOURS IN THE STUDIO AND MY VOICE WAS FRIED. THANKFULLY I'D cut back on smoking because we'd been putting in a hell of a lot more time in the studio than we were used to. My vocals were strained. We were cutting a new demo and we had a ton of new shit on it.

We'd put music to something I wrote. Something inspired by my girl. The guys loved it, and Luke thought it was going to set us apart. It was a slow ballad, and Lennon wrote the music to go with it. I hadn't shared it with Jade yet, because I wanted to surprise her and sing it to her when we worked out all the kinks in the music.

"You guys miss me living there. Just admit it," Dex said as we made our way out to the parking lot.

Moving him out may have actually salvaged the band. We weren't fighting twenty-four-seven anymore. I didn't have to worry about what he brought around my brother or my girlfriend, and we had some separation.

"Sure, dude. We miss your crazy ass," Lennon said.

"I'm sorry about all the shit that went down." Dex looked at me and I nodded.

"It's all good. I'm leaving today with my parents. We're going back east for Thanksgiving," Adam said. Always the peacekeeper.

"You two are staying in town, right?" Dex asked Lennon and me.

"Yeah. We're going to Jade's house for dinner. Should be fun," Lennon said.

I'm happy my brother agreed to go with me. He loved Jade, and I thought we could both use a normal holiday this year.

"What are you doing for Thanksgiving?" I asked Dex. He'd offered an olive branch, and I'd take it.

"It's the first year since my parents split, so it sucks. I'm going to spend it with my mom in New York. Dad's off the rails in Mexico somewhere with his twenty-two-year-old girlfriend."

I couldn't tell if he was horrified or impressed. I cringed all the same. The only thing that kept my dad from looking like an old dude who wanted to relive his youth is that he loved my mom. She may be the only thing he loved in this world. It was his one saving grace, even if he'd managed to slowly bring her over to his way. It was the only normalcy I grew up with. I had parents that actually loved each other, even if they were the most self-ish assholes on the planet.

I dropped Lennon off and headed over to pick up Jade before she left for Bucktown in the morning. I hadn't spent a night away from her in weeks, and I wasn't looking forward to her not being here. She was standing outside when I pulled up to the dorms.

"Hey," she said, getting in the car.

"What's wrong? You look all flushed."

"Meagan is the Devil," she said, and I laughed.

"What'd she do?" I asked, pulling onto the road.

"She just grilled me about us. *You and me.* She can't seem to wrap her head around what you're doing with me, and she has no problem telling me so." She was all huffy and angry, and I fucking loved it. Jade was as real as you got. She didn't hide her feelings and she didn't have a dishonest bone in her body.

"Fuck her. She doesn't have a clue what she's talking about. I can't wait till you're out of there. You know, you could just move in with me now," I said.

"Move in with you? Are you insane? I can't live with you. I'm moving in with Ariana for the rest of the year." She looked at me like I had three heads.

"Well, what about next year?"

She laughed. "Next year Ariana and I will need to find a place. You don't even know if you'll be here. And I'm eighteen years old. It's a little young to be shacking up, don't you think?"

"You're nineteen next month," I reminded her.

Yes, Jade's birthday happened to be on December twenty-fifth. She shared a birthday with Jesus himself. That was how fucking special this girl was. I wasn't the least bit surprised when she told me.

"That's still too young." She laughed.

"We're old enough to do whatever we want. And I don't know what will happen with the label. They liked the demo and they want to meet after the holidays. This could drag on for years."

138

"Patience is a virtue you know," she said.

"*Your* virtue is the only one I care about."

We still hadn't had sex and it wasn't because Jade didn't want to. I didn't want to rush her. She shared a birthday with the Messiah, for fuck's sake. I didn't want to taint or tarnish her goodness. But I was dying without sex. Sleeping next to Jade every night was like Chinese water torture, but in the best way. There was nowhere else I wanted to be, but it was painful at the same time.

Blue balls are real.

"I can't believe you brought your grade up to a B in bio. It's so impressive," Jade said when I slipped back behind the wheel. Professor Lockhart posted grades today and I had an eighty-four average going into the final. I just wanted to pass the class, but it was all due to her.

"Says the girl with the highest grade in the class."

"Stop." She shook her head. "I'm so glad you and Lennon are coming for Thanksgiving. It's going to be weird not sleeping next to you for four nights though," she said.

We parked and made our way down the sand toward the water. Today was the last day of classes, as no one would be at school tomorrow, the day before Thanksgiving. We spent a few hours on the beach before we went back to my place.

"You count the nights, not the days?" I asked.

"Yep. My favorite time of day is sleeping next to you."

I leaned forward and kissed her. "Same."

⁓ℛ⁓

"Are you sure they don't care if I come?" Lennon asked as we got on the freeway to head to Bucktown.

"I'm positive. Jade really wants you there."

"Well, she knows you won't come without me, so I'm guessing she really wants you there," he said with a laugh.

"Stop stressing. She wants you there. Her dad invited you too. Last time I was out there, he said we were both welcome."

"All right. It'll be nice to see what normal people do on Thanksgiving," Lennon said.

"Are you bummed about not seeing Mom?"

"Nah. I'm not in the mood for the crowd and the craziness, to be honest. This semester is kicking my ass, and with all the practice we've been putting in at the studio, I could use a chill weekend."

"Yeah, this will be nice," I said.

"I've never seen you get a chick flowers before. Well, aside from Mom. You really like her, huh?"

I glanced at the bouquet and the two bottles of wine in the back seat. My parents may not have been around much when we were kids, but Clara taught us manners early on. I knew better than to show up at a house for dinner empty handed. And the flowers, well, they looked like something Jade would like.

"Yeah. I like her," I said.

"I do too. And, she's good for you."

"Meaning?"

"Meaning you don't drink or smoke nearly as much as you used to. You study all the time now. It's fucking amazing. You're not nearly as big an asshole as you used to be." Lennon laughed and I rolled my eyes.

"Shut the fuck up. I'm still an asshole, trust me."

"I'm just giving you shit. I'm happy for you. Jade's a good girl. What are you going to do if we sign with AF?"

I knew they'd all been talking about it. I sensed it every time I walked in on a conversation and everyone shut up.

"I mean, of course I want to finish school, so I don't know what the fuck I'll do if it actually happens sooner."

I was avoiding the question. I could take classes online and finish my degree if I needed to. But leaving Jade would suck. And long-distance relationships were a shit show.

"I think it's going to happen, bro. Do you think Jade would take a break from school and come with us on tour?"

"No. And don't suggest it," I said. My tone was harsher than I meant it to be, but I didn't want my brother or my father pressuring her.

"You don't want her to come?"

"Of course, I do. But I don't want her dropping out of school for me. We've only been together a few months, and most of that time we weren't even dating. I'm not going there. Look how well it turned out for Mom dropping out of school to go follow Dad around. No fucking way."

"You're nothing like Dad," Lennon said. "Those are totally different circumstances."

"How do you figure?"

"Mom liked school, but she admits that she was there to find a husband. She wasn't into her studies the way Jade is." Lennon shifted in his seat. He was nervous. Afraid I'd jump ship. He had every reason to be, because I thought about it. More than I should. But I wouldn't do that to him.

"I'm not going to abandon you, little brother. But I'm also not going to fuck up Jade's life. Not that she'd even consider leaving school. She wouldn't. And she shouldn't."

"That's not what I'm worried about. Well, it's not *all* I'm worried about. Believe it or not, I want you to be happy too. And for the first time in our lives, you seem happy. Really happy," Lennon said.

"I am. It'll be fine. Stop worrying."

"You know I appreciate all you do for me, right?"

"I know you do. We're good," I said, pulling in front of Jade and her father's apartment.

I got out of the car and leaned in the back seat to grab everything, when someone landed on my back. I didn't even have to turn around to know it was my crazy ass girlfriend, who was part spider monkey. I reached for the wine and pretended I didn't notice her attaching herself to my body.

"Hello? I know you feel me back here," she said, and her lips grazed my ear.

"I always feel you, More Jade."

I pulled out of the car and stood up, and Lennon chuckled, taking the wine and flowers from me. Jade wrapped her legs around my waist, and her hands around my neck as she laughed hysterically. I tilted my head back and she kissed me. Hard. Damn, this girl owned me.

I'd spent my entire life not being owned by my father. By his power, and his money, and his bullying demeanor. But this gorgeous little dark-haired girl with jade eyes, strolled into my life—and I was done for.

She slid down my body, dropped to the ground and faced me. "Hey, there."

"Oh, hey. I didn't see you," I said, tugging her closer.

She pushed up on her tiptoes and kissed me before turning to my brother. "Hey, Lennon. Thanks for coming. I hope you're hungry."

"Starving," he said.

She looked at the flowers and her whole face lit up.

"These are from Cruz, he picked them out," my brother said, handing her the bouquet of white and pink flowers.

She studied the blooms and then stared at me. "How did you know my favorite flowers were peonies and hydrangeas?"

I gave myself a silent pat on the back. "I didn't. They just looked like you."

She closed her eyes and smelled them, and Lennon laughed. He and I weren't used to the little things being acknowledged. My mother always had fresh flowers at our homes. If you walked in with a bouquet, she'd have the housekeeper put them in water. She certainly wouldn't take the time to smell them or appreciate the type of flower you gave her.

"Come on up. Everyone's excited to meet you. Oh, big scoop," Jade said, stopping to huddle between my brother and I. "Sam and Cara are back together. *She's here.* Inquiring minds want to know, am I right?"

Not really. I didn't give a fuck about Sam's relationship, but I'd fake it because Jade did.

"I've barely slept since they broke up. I'm so relieved," I said, my tone flat. Jade and Lennon broke out in a fit of laughter.

The Moore's apartment wasn't large, yet they managed to fit a good group of people in their place. It smelled like turkey and pumpkin pie, not something I was used to. Everyone was kicked back on the couch watching football or working on a puzzle at the coffee table. Jade introduced us to the whole group as the only ones I knew were Jack and Sam. I met Uncle Jimmy and his wife Maria, Sam's parents. Everyone called the dude Uncle Jimmy. Even his friends. He was tall like Jade's father, but stockier. I met John and Teresa, and their two kids, Sienna and Piper. And Vinny and his new girlfriend, Emma. John and Vinny were also firefighters. Each one of them pulled me and Lennon in for a half bro hug, like we were part of the family. The whole scene was totally foreign to me—the warmth of this group. The doorbell rang, and in walked a female firefighter. Her name was Sara, and I didn't miss the way she looked at Jade's father. I glanced at my girl, who was completely clueless. She hugged Sara and dragged her over to meet me.

"Heard lots about you, Cruz. And this must be your brother, Lennon?" she said. Sara had blonde hair, blue eyes, and wasn't much taller than Jade. But she had a more athletic build and looked like she could hold her own out there.

"Nice to meet you, Sara."

"Jade's pretty particular about who she includes in Thanksgiving, she's terrified there won't be any leftover turkey if we open this up to too many people," she said, and Jade's head fell back in laughter. "So you both must be special to her."

"Hey, the leftovers are the best part," Jade said.

Sara looked at Jade the way a mother looked at her child. They'd clearly known one another for a long time.

My girlfriend tugged me by the hand and told Lennon to follow as she led us into the kitchen.

"This is Sam, and Cara," she said. She was awkward as shit because the last time I saw Sam it wasn't on the best terms.

They both rose from the small kitchen table. Lennon shook their hands, and I reached for Cara's and we both said hello.

"Hey, I told Cara Exiled is playing next weekend at The Dive, so we thought we'd drive over to see you play. I may or may not have lied about knowing who your band was the day we met," Sam said with a sheepish grin.

I laughed. "Not a problem, *chief*."

Sam's head fell back in laughter. "Dude, I'm sorry. I was a total douche-bag to you."

"Nah, you were looking out for her. I get it."

"Well, thank you for not letting me get my ass kicked by that bouncer. I didn't stand a chance." Sam shook his head.

"That was a crazy night," Lennon said as Jade pulled up another chair and we all sat around the table.

Jade taught us how to play Sequence, her favorite board game, and she was up and down every five minutes checking on the turkey or stirring the potatoes. She was in her element. Sam told me about his years playing soccer, and it surprised me that we had so much in common. I actually didn't mind the dude.

When we settled around the dining room table, there were name tags for each of us. They used a card table at the end of the dining table to make it long enough for all of us to fit. There were white table linens and small pumpkins running down the center of the table. Two small bouquets sat on each end, and the flowers I brought were placed in a large vase in the center of the table. The linen napkins were orange and green with a random purple one on Jade's place setting. It all worked. It was so different from the Thanksgiving set up Lennon and I were used to where everything matched. It was perfect, and sterile, and cold. I'd take this any day of the week. Jade had crayons and coloring sheets for Sienna and Piper, and she took her seat beside me.

Jack Moore said a prayer and thanked each of us for coming. My brother sat across from me and beside Cara, and he couldn't stop smiling. He liked it as much as I did. We dug in and it was by far the best Thanksgiving meal

I'd ever had. The food was home-cooked and delicious. Everyone went back for seconds, and I watched my girl as she moved around the table smiling and laughing. These were her people, and she didn't need much more. She poured more wine in her father's glass and met my gaze.

"Jady bug, are you going to make us do those weird questions again?" her father asked, and everyone laughed.

She pulled her gaze from mine and came around to sit beside me. "He is so full of it. He looks forward to this every year," she said. "Okay, lift your plates. You'll find a piece of paper beneath and we're going to go around and read our questions and just answer the best you can. Keep in mind your papers are folded, so I don't know who got what question."

"Oh man. Last year she got all philosophical, and she didn't like my answer," Sam said, rolling his eyes.

"That's because your question was, *what are you most thankful for this year*, and you said pizza. That was a lame answer."

"Hey, Cara and I weren't together then. Pizza was the best thing I had going at the time," Sam said. "Hashtag no judgment, J-bird."

I sipped my wine and laughed as they went around the table and answered the ridiculous questions. They were so comfortable with one another. It was charming and funny, and I was enjoying myself. Which wasn't the norm for me on the holidays. I preferred brooding in my room. Alone.

"My turn," Jade said. She unfolded her paper and smiled when she read her question. "Serves me right. Okay, here goes. 'If you could do something different this year, what would it be?'"

Jack clasped his hands together and winked at Sara, who sat at his right, and watched his daughter. "I can't wait to hear this one."

"Well, I definitely wouldn't have had those four shots of tequila, that's for sure," she said, and the entire table erupted in laughter.

"And how about wearing a little more clothing next Halloween too. No more going out in your underpants," her father said.

Even I had to laugh at that one. Although she looked hot as hell, she didn't have much on that night.

"And maybe we don't fight Sam when he's trying to help us?" Sam added.

"I think we get it, people. Bad night. Let's move on," Jade said.

We're going back and forth across the table, so Lennon lifted his plate and pulled out his question.

"What? Who made these questions up?" he bellowed out, looking right at Jade and there was more laughter.

"They're good questions. Let's hear it," Jade said before sipping her wine.

"If you could have any superpower, what would it be?" Lennon said, and he paused to think about it. "Hmmm… I think it would be cool to fly, but there's nowhere I'm dying to go, so I'll skip that one. I think I'd choose time travel."

"Why?" Jade asked, and she looked mesmerized as she listened to my brother, like there was some deeper meaning in these answers.

"Because you can go back and change the mistakes you've made. Right your wrongs. And if you don't want to be somewhere, you can just pop over to another decade. Those 70s babes were hot," Lennon said, wriggling his brows.

I studied my brother's gaze, and I'll be damned if Jade wasn't right about these ridiculous questions. Lennon met my gaze, and I knew in that moment he was talking about his overdose. *Right his wrongs.* I nodded, and Jade tilted my plate so I could get my question.

I looked down at the paper and smiled, shaking my head. Because it was so her. "What are you most thankful for this year?" I said. There was no hesitation. "That's easy. *You.*"

Vinny hit the table with his palms and chuckled. His voice was all tease. "You gave your boyfriend the easy one, Jady bug. That's cheating."

"I did not. You're just mad that you had to tell us about getting called Vinny poopy pants in second grade," she said, tipping back in her seat as the table roared with laughter.

I'd never spent a holiday this relaxed.

And I liked it.

JADE

"I CAN'T WAIT TO SEE THIS BRACELET," ARI SAID.

"Yeah, I hope it looks good. I wanted to get Cruz something sentimental because he has everything. I love that you can put a message on these. What did you end up getting for Jace?"

"Well, he gets *me* every day, and I'm the gift that keeps on giving," she said. "But I got him a bunch of little things, a T-shirt, a flannel, and a cool beanie. It should get delivered today, so we can wrap gifts this weekend."

"Yes, perfect. He will love that," I said, and the man returned from the back room with my purchase.

"Here you go. Let me know if everything looks okay, and I'll ring you up," he said. He looked to be about sixty years old and had a hunched back and a kind smile. I found out about this shop online, and I loved the idea.

"*Love you more, xoxo Jade.* Oh. My. Gosh. This is adorable. He's going to love it," Ari said after reading the inscription on the brown leather band while she stood beside me.

"Yeah, I hope so. I'm going to give it to him before he leaves for Christmas break."

"He can't handle being away from you for one day. How is he going to deal with being away from you for two weeks?"

I laughed. "He'll be fine. Are you excited to meet Jace's parents?"

"I'm a little nervous. He said they're really quiet, so hopefully I don't overwhelm them."

I tucked my debit card back in my wallet and thanked the man for the bracelet before leaving the store.

"They'll love you. It's impossible not to."

"I can't wait for you and me to finally live together when we get back from break. Is Meagan speaking to you this week?" Ari said with a dramatic eye roll.

"Yep. Now she's all over me. She wants me to set her up with Lennon. The girl is seriously insane."

"Wow. She really wants to date someone from Exiled. Isn't she back together with her boyfriend?"

"Yep. And she thinks I'd set her up with Cruz's brother when she's dating someone. Lennon is so sweet. I would never do that to him," I said.

Lennon and I had grown close since spending Thanksgiving together. He hung out with Cruz and I more now, and I helped him with his papers when I could.

"Exactly. Oh, Jace told me we need to start looking for a place for next fall soon. He said rentals are hard to find. I'd love to find a small two-bedroom house instead of an apartment. It would be nice to have a small yard, and not have neighbors living above and below us, but I don't know budget wise if that's even reasonable. Rentals in Evanston are not cheap."

"Yeah, I agree. Cruz said he might know someone moving out of their place. I'll ask him to check with his friend. The most I can afford is eight hundred a month, so if you can do that as well, we could go as high as sixteen hundred. I don't know if a house is possible in that price range. We'll be lucky to get a two-bedroom dump for that," I said as we walked back to campus.

"At least we'll be together." Ari bumped her shoulder into mine and chuckled.

"True. You want to head to the library? I may as well set up permanent residence there. I have all five finals next week. It's going to be a stressful couple of days."

"Yeah, no going out for me until after finals either," she said.

I don't know how Cruz handled the stress with band practice, his shows, and balancing his classes. He did it all, and always found time for me. I couldn't wait to give him his Christmas gift.

I really did love him more.

~*~

I flipped the page of my chem book, the only audible sound in the library. It was almost two A.M. and it would be closing soon. I just wanted to finish this last chapter.

"I knew I'd find you here," Cruz whispered against my ear.

His two arms came around my waist and his chin rested on my shoulder. He smelled like beer and cigarettes, a scent I normally despised, but somehow he made it appealing. He rubbed his scruff against my cheek.

"Hey, what are you doing here?" I turned to face him.

His honey-brown gaze looked tired, and I pushed up to kiss his plump lips.

"I tried your phone and you didn't pick up, so I figured you'd be here. Come on, let's get out of here, they're about to close."

I slipped my books in my backpack and he reached for it and slipped it over his shoulder, before intertwining his fingers with mine and leading me out of the library.

"How was the show?" I asked as I zipped my coat up and we stepped outside.

It hurt to take a breath at first because the temperature had dropped below freezing. I pulled my hat from my pocket and slipped it on my head. Cruz wore a black beanie and his peacoat. He pulled me close and wrapped an arm around me as we stepped to the curb and slipped in the Uber he called for us.

"The show was good. Long. Couldn't wait to get out of there and come find you," he said.

"Sorry I had to miss your show again tonight. I can't wait for finals to be over."

"I'm fucking proud of you. You're the hardest worker I know. Don't give that shit a thought," he said, and reached for my mitten-clad hand as we stepped out of the car.

"Is everyone home yet?" I asked as we walked inside.

The house was quiet and much cleaner now that Dex wasn't living there. They'd put a couch and a TV in the spare room, which was where Lennon and Adam played endless hours of video games.

"They're hanging with a couple girls, so I don't think they'll be back for a while."

"I thought Lennon liked the girl from Australia?" I said, dropping to sit on his bed.

"Lennon likes everyone he meets from moment to moment."

"What time do you guys leave tomorrow?" I had one more final exam tomorrow morning, but Cruz finished today.

"Probably around noon," he said, dropping down beside me and brushing my hair out of my face with his fingers.

"I want to give you your gifts." I pushed to stand and reached for my backpack.

"Ah, you got me something, did you?"

"Of course, I did."

I handed him three packages, all wrapped in coordinating red and white gift wrap with gold bows. He opened the first one and laughed so loud I couldn't help but do the same.

"*My girlfriend is cooler than yours,*" he said, reading the writing on the white T-shirt. "Are you cool now, More Jade?"

I chuckled. "I'm the president of the Barry Manilow fan club. How much cooler does it get?"

"I love this. Thank you." He folded it up, and I handed him the next package.

"Oh, wow. I love this." He pulled out the black leather journal with his initials monogrammed in gold.

CWC. Cruz Christian Winslow.

"I thought you could write your songs in it. That way you won't lose them," I said.

Cruz wrote songs and poems on notebook paper, and he shoved them in his pockets, or they were loose in his room on sticky notes.

"I love it. I'll put the song I wrote for you in here first," he said, leaning forward and kissing me.

"When do I get to hear this song?"

"Soon, baby. We're just working on the music. I want it to be perfect when I sing it to you."

Butterflies swarm my belly. I don't know how he does it, but he always manages to fluster me. I bite down on my lip and hand him the last package.

"What do we have here?" He opened the package and studied the brace-let before turning it over and reading the inscription. "Thank you. I love it. And I love you more."

He leaned forward and kissed me before gazing back down to study the bracelet he'd secured around his wrist. He jumped up and walked over to his closet, pulling out a bunch of shopping bags and bringing them over to me.

"I may have gotten you something too," he said, his voice was all tease.

He handed me the first bag and I pulled out a shoe box. Black and white checkered Converse. I'd wanted these for a while. How did he know that? "I love them. Thank you. You know my shoe size?"

He laughed. "I do."

I slipped on my new shoes, clicked my heels together, and smiled. "They're perfect."

He lifted the next bag from Office Max, which happened to be my *happy place*. He dumped it out on the bed, and there were endless packs of colored markers, pens, Sharpies, and highlighters. There were sticky notes and index cards. Binder clips and washi tape. I couldn't form words, because this was the best gift I'd ever received.

"I can't believe you did this. I love it," I said, but it came out like a squeal. I was actually squealing because no one appreciated office supplies quite like I did.

He laughed as he watched me. "My girl likes office supplies, what can I say?"

"Best gifts ever." I pulled all the pens and markers together and placed them back in the bag. I couldn't wait to organize everything in my desk. I was already envisioning my entire top drawer filled to the hilt with an array of colorful supplies.

"There's one more. The rest I'm saving for your birthday. But I wanted you to have these now," he said.

He handed me a small box with Ethan Lord Jewelers written on the top. My heart raced because I'd never received jewelry as a gift before. I wasn't big on wearing it, but I didn't know if that was because I didn't like it or because I just didn't have any. I lifted the top off and took in the beautiful stud earrings.

"Oh, my gosh. Are these jade?"

"Yep. They were made just for you. I noticed you wear studs and thought you might like these," he said, watching as I slipped them in my ears.

"I love them."

"I love you." He cleared off his bed, and I slipped into one of his T-shirts.

"Love you more," I said, rolling on my side to face him.

"So, let's talk about your birthday."

"Okay." He pulled me closer, my head nestled in the crook of his neck. My legs tangled with his, and his nearness warmed me.

"I know you want to be with your dad on Christmas, but do you think you could come out and stay with me the next day? I've already checked with Ponch, and he can fly you out any time that day, and we could stay at a hotel in Park City for a few days."

I pushed back so I could look at him. "You don't want me to stay at your parents' house?"

"I'll be ready for a break from them, I can only handle small doses. We can celebrate your birthday and hang out in downtown Park City and then go stay at my house for New Year's. Trust me, two nights with the Winslows will be plenty."

"Okay. That sounds amazing. Yes. I would love to. My dad goes back to work the day after Christmas, so this will be great."

"Okay, I'll set it up."

Cruz's body tensed when he spoke of his parents. I met his dad the one time, and his disdain for his father was impossible to miss. I wanted to meet his mother and see them together. I wanted to know them. They were a part of him whether he liked them or not. He kissed the top of my head, and that was the last thing I remembered before sleep took me.

"Pull in right up here," I said to Dad as he pulled into the parking lot in front of the hangar. Something had changed between Dad and Sara, and I was happy about it. He wouldn't admit they were dating, but they were spending a lot of time together, and I knew she was crazy about him. She'd spent Christmas with us, and it made leaving him easier because I knew Sara would look after him. And I was excited to spend a few days with my boyfriend.

"You're pretty serious about this boy, huh?"

Where did that come from? "Um, sure. Yeah."

Sara laughed. "Smooth, Jack."

"What? I like Cruz. He's a good kid. But it seems to be getting really serious. Just want to make sure you're being safe," he said.

"Oh, God, are you seriously giving me the birds and the bees talk now?"

Sara and I laughed, but Dad remained dead serious. This couldn't get any more awkward.

"Jady bug, you need to be safe, okay? I'll leave it at that."

I put my hand on his shoulder from the back seat. "Dad, I've got this. You're jumping the gun. I'm not even there yet."

Not that I didn't want to be, but it was actually my boyfriend who didn't think we were ready to take the next step. I'd spare my father the gory details. Relief spread across his face at my words.

"Ah, good to know. Well, I'm here if you need any, er, any advice on safety."

"This is painful to watch," Sara said, and we broke out in a fit of giggles again.

"It really is, Dad."

"Listen, I know you don't have your mom to go to, and I just want to make sure you know how all of this works."

Sara and I gasped at the same time. "I'm begging you to stop. I'll talk to Sara if I need any advice on how *it all works*, okay? Do you guys want to come in and meet Ponch?"

"Sure," Dad said, and we all stepped out of the car.

I introduced Dad and Sara to Ponch, and they checked out the plane before I hugged them goodbye. Dad had a wrinkle between his brows where they pinched together.

"Stop worrying. That's my job, remember?" I said, and my tone was all tease.

"Call me when you land. Love you."

I waved and accepted Ponch's invitation to ride copilot the whole way. Seeing as I was the only passenger and I had no homework for the first time since school started—I was all about riding shotgun.

The hotel was massive and beautiful. I'd never stayed at anything remotely close to this. The dark wood on the floors matched the wood on the ceiling, and there were beams forming triangles every few feet. Large chandeliers hung above, and the oversized space was warmed with cozy couches, chairs, and fireplaces that decorated the lobby. It looked like something straight out of a magazine. We made our way to our room, and the views were breathtaking. Snow covered mountains sat like a photograph outside our window. The gray sky hovered above the towering evergreens with white tips covering the high peaks. The fresh snow lay like powder white carpeting as far as I could see. Icicles hung outside our window and reflections of pink and blue danced around where the sun peeked through the clouds. Cruz turned on the fireplace in our room, and I sat back and took it all in. It was almost overwhelming to be staying here.

"You okay?" he asked, studying my face.

"Yeah. Of course. This is just—*wow*. It's amazing. I'm a little awe-struck."

He kissed me and I melted into him. "I missed you."

"Me too. So how was Christmas with your parents?" I asked.

"A shit show. So, typical holiday with the Winslows," he said with a laugh. But I saw the disappointment in his gaze.

I fell onto the bed and he stretched out next to me. He closed his eyes when I ran my fingers through his disheveled hair. I traced the line along his chiseled cheekbones with my finger and made my way down his nose, stopping at his lips. I brought my mouth to his and kissed him. I felt so complete when I was with him. It wasn't logical. But he made me feel— complete. Like this was where I belonged. With him.

He took control of the kiss and rolled me on my back, propping himself above me. We were both panting, and he pulled away. Like he always did when things got too heated. I wrapped my arms around his neck and held his body close to me. His desire was impossible to miss, and it stirred something in me I'd never felt before.

"I should give you your birthday gift," he said.

"I have everything I want right here." I lifted up and kissed him again.

"Baby, I'm not going to be able to stop if we don't cool things off now."

"I don't want you to stop," I said, and the desperation in my voice surprised me.

He studied me, searching my face for something, I don't know what. He didn't speak.

"Please." It's all I said before his mouth covered mine again.

His hands slipped beneath my T-shirt and he reached around and unclasped my bra. I couldn't get my shirt off quick enough, and he yanked his sweater over his head with one hand. He kissed my neck and made his way down my body. I was on fire. The overwhelming sensation left me breathless. The desire so strong I'd die if he stopped now. He reached the waistband of my jeans and pulled them down my legs, and my pink panties followed. Yes, he'd seen me naked before. But this felt more intimate somehow. I wanted to take the next step. The last step. The only step left between us. I reached for his waistband and pushed his joggers and briefs down his legs. He stood and kicked everything off, baring himself to me again. This time I wasn't nervous. Wasn't afraid to look. I wanted to memorize every beautiful inch of his body. I sat forward and watched him as he climbed back on the bed.

"Are you sure about this?" he asked. His voice was gruff.

Sexy and needy.

"I'm positive. I want to be with you, Cruz. No more waiting."

His mouth moved over mine again, and he kissed me for what felt like forever. I writhed beneath him because I needed more. He pulled away, and I reached for his shoulders and pulled him back.

The sexiest smile spread across his face. "I need to get a condom, baby. I'll be right back."

I laughed because how desperate was I?

Sheesh, Jade. Get a handle on yourself.

He climbed back over me and sat up on his knees. He rolled the condom on, and I couldn't look away until he settled between my thighs.

"I love you more," he whispered.

My whole body started to shake. I couldn't speak. I was nervous, excited, turned on, and desperate. Not a good combo when trying to appear cool and confident.

"Relax, baby. There's no pressure," he said, whispering the words against my ear.

"I know. I'm just—I'm ready. I'm so ready," I said.

He chuckled. "Me too."

He kissed me again. Slower. Softer. My fingers ran through his hair, and he teased my entrance. I stopped breathing as he pressed forward.

"Breathe, Jade," he said as he moved slowly.

He pulled back and watched my face as he continued to move inch by inch. I gripped his shoulders and bit down on my bottom lip. It was both painful and amazing at the same time.

"Okay," I whispered.

"Am I hurting you?" He was so focused, I could see the restraint in his gaze, as he took his time.

"No. Maybe a little. I don't know." I arched into him because I wanted more. I wanted everything. Even the painful part.

"Oh my god, baby. You feel so good," he whispered against my ear.

All the discomfort dissipated, and he started to move in a rhythmic motion. I followed his lead, and his hand moved between us, touching me just where I needed to be touched, and my eyes squeezed shut with the sensation.

"Cruz," I said as my hips moved of their own volition.

His mouth moved over mine, and I exploded into a million little pieces. He followed me and called out my name. It was the only thing I heard.

We were the only two people that existed in this moment.

And I never wanted it to end.

CRUZ

"HOW DO YOU FEEL?" I ASKED AS SHE STRETCHED HER ARMS ABOVE HER head.

I'd been awake for a while wondering if she'd wake up pissed that she lost her virginity to an unworthy asshole.

"I feel amazing." She pushed the hair back from her pretty face and looked up at me.

I relaxed at her words. "No regrets?"

"No. Why would I have regrets? You exceeded my expectations, Cruz Winslow," she said, wriggling her eyebrows.

I laughed. "I'm not concerned about my performance, because, well, that's self-explanatory." I winked before continuing, "I'm just making sure you're okay with everything."

"I'm the one that pushed for it. Of course, I'm okay. I've been ready for a while, but my boyfriend is secretly chivalrous and protective of my virtue." Her cheeks pinked and a grin spread across her gorgeous face.

"Only chivalrous when it comes to you. I don't really give a fuck about anyone else," I said. And it was the truth.

She laughed. "Yes, you do. You love your brother and Adam. And your mom."

"Sure, but I don't worry about their virtue."

"Well, I hope not. That would be weird," she said with a chuckle.

I pulled her against my body as I lie on my side. God, I couldn't get enough of her. She lost her fucking virginity twelve hours ago, and I wanted more, like the selfish prick I was. I still couldn't wrap my head around the fact that she'd saved herself for nineteen years, and she'd chosen me. I didn't deserve her. But I sure as shit wanted to be that guy. The guy she needed me to be. I wanted to give her—everything.

"What do you want to do today? Do you like to ski?"

"I love skiing," she said.

"Okay, I brought you some ski clothes from the house because I thought you might want to hit the slopes."

She ran her fingers through my hair, and chill bumps covered my arms. Like a fucking eager middle school boy who watched porn, I was completely turned on just by her touch.

"So, do I look different?"

I pulled back and took in her face. She wasn't kidding. She was dead fucking serious.

"Different how?"

"I don't know? More womanly maybe?" she said.

"You know, when you first woke up, I was thinking, '*wow, she looks so womanly this morning.*'"

She slaps my chest. "Shut up. I'm serious. They say people get an after-sex glow."

"You had an after-sex glow before you even had sex," I said.

"Thanks, I think?"

"Let's get dressed, grab some breakfast, and hit the slopes." I sat up, but Jade reached for me and pulled me back down.

"Maybe we could work on my glow before we get ready."

I rolled her on her back. "You don't need to ask me twice. I just thought you might be sore. You know I always want more, Jade."

She laughed and wrapped her hands around my neck, and my mouth covered hers. If Jade wanted some extra after-sex glow, who was I to deprive her.

I HANDED HER A PACKAGE BEFORE WE STEPPED OUT THE DOOR.

"Every time we're in this room, you distract me, and I forget to give you your birthday gift."

"I thought you gave me my gift last night." She quirked her brow.

I laughed. "That's the gift that keeps on giving."

She pulled the box from the bag. "Tiffany's? So swanky, Winslow."

"Nothing but the best for my girl," I said, wrapping my arms around her from behind and resting my chin on her shoulder.

She opened the box. "Oh my gosh. It's gorgeous. I love the two little hearts. One is yours and one is mine."

I chuckled. "You already have mine."

She spent five minutes studying the two hearts before she held her hair up for me to help her clasp it behind her neck, and she admired it in the mirror. "I love this so much."

I kissed her quickly and hustled her out the door, or I'd have her undressed and beneath me if we didn't leave now. We walked downstairs, as the resort sat directly on the slopes.

Jade couldn't ski for shit. She was a self-proclaimed *excellent skier*. My girl was a lot of things, the best at most—but skiing was not one of them.

"Shoot. Why do I keep falling? This hill is too steep." She wore white bibs, a white ski jacket and a black hat and gloves. Her hair fell around her shoulders, and her cheeks and nose were pink. Her jade eyes stood out in contrast to the white snow that her ass was currently sitting in.

"We're on the bunny hill. They don't get any flatter."

"Well, it didn't feel all that flat when we hiked up to the top, did it?" She was flustered, and I fucking loved flustered Jade.

Yes, we hiked up the bunny hill because she informed me that she would never dream of getting on a chairlift because they aren't trustworthy. It made no fucking sense, but I followed her ass up the hill. I definitely needed to quit smoking because between the altitude and the exercise, I was ready to call it a day. I'd rather go back to how I started my day—in bed with my girl.

"It sure as shit didn't. I thought you said you've skied before? You walk up the big hills too?"

"No. Dad and I don't ski on hills," she said, like I should just know this.

"No hills? You cross country ski?"

"Call it whatever you want. It's much better than this. There're no miserable chairlifts, and you don't fall down much at all." She reached for my hand and I pulled her to her feet.

"Yeah, that's a completely different sport."

"A better sport," she whispered, and her words were barely audible. But I heard them.

I laughed. "You want to go back to our room and practice the new sport I taught you last night? Go for a little more glow?"

Her head fell back, and she chuckled. "Not a bad idea. But I'm no quitter. Come on, let's hike up one big hill and give it a shot," she said.

I reach for her arm. "We can't hike up that hill. What if you just try the chairlift, I promise I'll hold on to you."

She studied me. "Fine. But no goofing around on it. Don't swing it or mess around."

We made our way to the chairlift and she stayed quiet. But she did it. I was impressed. We made our way up, and she gripped the side rail with one gloved hand. I had my arm around her, and I scooched closer when we approached the top.

"Be careful. We're tipping to the side," she said, panic in her voice.

"We're fine. I promise."

"Okay." She relaxed beside me.

She sat forward as we approached the top of the hill. We pushed off the chairlift, and she squealed as she glided down the small slope.

"Not too bad, right?" I said and kissed her.

But now how in the hell was I going to get her down this big ass hill? The chairlift was hardly the most challenging part of this endeavor.

"It wasn't awful. Let's do this."

"Slow down. This is a lot steeper than the bunny hill, baby. Remember how I showed you to slant the top of your skis together to slow down?"

"Yep. The snow plow thing. Got it."

I told her to go first and I'd follow close behind her. She surprised the shit out of me when she took off and bent her knees and swooshed from side to side. Like she'd been doing this for years. She came to a stop about halfway down the hill.

"Holy shit. How the hell did you do that?"

"I don't know, but I still kind of hate it," she said with a laugh.

"I couldn't tell. You were hauling ass."

"That's because I'm freezing and I want some hot cocoa, and maybe we can head back to the room for a little bit." She wriggled her brows and it was cute as hell.

"You don't have to ask me twice. Let's go," I said.

I followed her hot little ass down the hill, and we decided to head to the room before getting hot chocolate. I had other ways to warm her up that were much more effective.

We loaded the SUV and got on the highway to head to my parents' house. I was dreading it. I didn't know what Jade would think of them. We had a fun couple days at the resort and I wasn't looking forward to leaving our bubble. And it was New Year's fucking Eve at the Winslow's. That was the equivalent of porn night at the playboy mansion. My parents took ringing in the New Year to a whole new level.

"So how many people do you think will be there tonight?" she asked.

"Who knows. A hundred or more."

Jade laughed. "A hundred people at their home? I don't even know a hundred people."

She changed three times before we left. She was nervous to meet my mom. I didn't know why. She would be lucky if they spent ten minutes with her because they'd be in party mode. She wore black leggings, a white turtleneck sweater, and tan lace-up boots with fur coming out of them. Her hair was down, and she looked stunning.

"Don't be nervous. But keep your expectations low. They'll be consumed with the party, and probably drunk by the time we get there," I said, glancing at the clock on the dash. It was noon—also known as cocktail hour at the Winslow's.

"I don't care. I'm just looking forward to meeting your mom and actually speaking to your dad since we were so rushed the last time we met."

I shook my head. She thought they were normal. Her dad stopped what he was doing when she arrived. He wanted to hear about her day, her classes, her life. My dad didn't give a shit. He never had. Mom was iffy. If she wasn't numbing herself on the latest prescription cocktail, she might show Jade a little attention, but it would depend on her current mental state.

We pulled in the long driveway and Jade looked at the house before turning to face me. "This is your house?"

"Yes."

"Wow. It's so big. Did your parents ever leave you and Lennon home alone here?" she asked.

"Sure."

"I'd be scared to be in a house this big alone, you know? Think of how many beds you'd have to look under before you could go to sleep."

It was so Jade to think of that. Most people just cared about the size. The money. Not her. She didn't care that the necklace was from Tiffany's, she just liked the hearts. The meaning behind it.

I laughed before getting out of the car and reaching for our bags. "I never thought about it. There's always staff here, so you aren't really ever alone. You ready?"

"Yes," she said, and I led her inside.

"Come here, my sweet boy," Clara said when I stepped inside. "Did you two have a fun week in Park City?"

She'd worked for my family since I was a baby, and I'd spent more time with her than either of my parents.

"Yes. Clara, I want to introduce you to someone." We shared a quick hug. "This is my girlfriend, Jade."

"Hi, Jade. Cruz has talked quite a bit about you and Lennon has been singing your praises the last few days as well. The girl who finally captured this boy's heart. I'm pleased to meet you," Clara said, taking my girlfriend's hands between hers.

"I've heard so much about you as well. It's so nice to finally meet you."

"Please, come in. Your parents are floating around here somewhere, and Lennon is in the game room. He's been bored, so he'll be happy you both are here," she said.

Jade fidgeted with the two hearts resting between her collarbones. I took her hand and led her through the house. We stopped along the way and I introduced her to Sabine, who was Lennon's nanny most of his life, and still worked for the family, organizing events and gatherings for my parents. That was one thing I'd give my dad. He never let go of any of his employees. We had several people who had been employed by my father longer than I'd been alive. I introduced Jade to Diego, my father's driver, and Brad, who provided security for the large events at our home.

"So many names to remember. I like them all so far, but I really like Clara and Sabine a lot," she whispered as we made our way toward the game room to find Lennon.

"Cruz," my mother called from behind me.

"Hey. I thought you'd be in your room," I said. She'd always been a striking woman. She modeled for the first few years after she met Dad.

"Well, I wanted to come meet this special girl of yours," Mom said.

"Hi, I'm Jade. It's so nice to meet you, Mrs. Winslow."

"Please, call me Juliette. Aren't you gorgeous? Lennon told Steven and I so much about you last night, and I couldn't wait to meet you. It's difficult to get much out of this one," she said, flicking her thumb in my direction.

"I told you about Jade," I said, rolling my eyes.

"Yes, but you leave out all the fun details. Lennon told us how brilliant she is, and I understand you want to be a doctor, is that right?"

"Yes. I have a long way to go, but that's the goal," Jade said.

"My father was a doctor. He studied at Northwestern as well."

"Yes, Cruz shared that with me. He sounds like an incredible physician, too."

"He really was. He's retired now, but he's still as brilliant as ever. Come with me. Let's go sit in the living room and visit. Cruz, you can tell Lennon to meet us in there. I'd like to spend some time with Jade before the party tonight," my mom said.

The theme song for *The Twilight Zone* played in my head. Since when did she spend any time with anyone? She took Jade by the hand and led her back toward the living room. I stopped in the game room to let my brother know we were here.

"What's up, asshole?" I said, leaning in the door frame.

Lennon looked up from wracking pool balls. "Finally, douchebag. I've been stuck here for days with no one sane to talk to. Where's Jade? Did she realize you're an asshole and leave you?"

"You wish. She's in the living room with Mom. Come on, let's go check on her," I said.

"Look at you all flustered being away from her for a few minutes." Lennon laughed as we made our way down the hall.

"Shut the fuck up. So how has it been?" I asked.

"Mom's actually been good. A little more present than usual. Dad's fine. The same. Busy. But Clara and Sabine stayed up and played three hours of chess with me last night."

I laughed. "So, nothing's changed then?"

We entered the living room and I was shocked to see my mother so engaged with my girlfriend. They were sitting beside one another on the couch, and my mother was holding Jade's hand. What the fuck is that about?

"Hey," I said, dropping to sit beside my girl.

Lennon gave Jade a hug and dropped in the chair across from us.

"Clara, can you bring us a few glasses and a nice bottle of white, please?" Mom said, her voice louder than usual so it reached the kitchen.

"Of course, Juliette. I'll be right there."

"Thank you, and why don't you see if Steven is available to join us," she asked.

Well this was a first. We didn't do family pow wows. Never had. But somehow Jade's presence was drawing everyone in. Hell, she did it to me, I shouldn't be too surprised.

"So, tell me about your family," Mom said.

I felt Jade stiffen beside me a little and I wanted to jump in, but she squeezed my hand to stop me.

"I grew up in Bucktown, about thirty minutes away from Northwestern. My father is the captain of his firehouse, and my mother passed away when I was five."

Mom gasped. She showed real emotion, and I was struck by her interest. I sat back while they got to know one another.

"I'm so sorry to hear that. Was she ill?"

"Not really. We had no warning. She had a rare congenital heart defect," Jade said. Her voice wobbled a bit, but otherwise she appeared comfortable talking to my mother.

"I'm sorry, sweetheart. I don't know if Cruz shared with you that my mother was taken far too early as well. I was only seventeen when she was killed by a drunk driver in a car accident."

Jesus, Mom. Why so heavy? It's New Year's fucking Eve.

"I didn't know that. I'm so sorry for your loss." Jade squeezed Mom's hand.

"Starting the party without me?" my father asked, and his laugh was loud and rattled around the room.

Clara poured the wine and handed us each a glass.

"Come sit, darling. I'm just enjoying some time with Cruz's lovely girl-friend. I know you two met briefly, but we're looking forward to spending some time with you, Jade."

"Thank you for having me. Your home is gorgeous," Jade said, taking a sip of wine.

"Are you ready to have some fun tonight? We've got a lot of big names that'll be here, so get ready to gawk," my father said, ruining the moment.

Of course, he had to start name dropping and reminding everyone how fucking big time he was.

"Sounds like it's going to be fun," she said.

"Did you enjoy your flight in? It sure beats flying commercial, am I right?" Dad said, and his laughter led to a coughing fit.

Karma's a bitch, jackass.

"Um, I've actually never flown before our flight to New York, so I have nothing to compare it to. But it was very comfortable. Thank you so much for flying me here. Ponch let me land the plane again," Jade said, and I sensed her discomfort. Dad had a gift for reminding people what he'd done for them. All the fucking time.

"Don't give it a thought. We're thrilled to have you here. Tell me, what did you bring to wear tonight?" My mother changed the subject, and I swore I saw her shoot my father some sort of look that shut him up.

"I brought some dark jeans and a blouse," Jade said.

"Come with me. You're too beautiful not to sparkle. I'm a bit taller than you, but I have something that I believe will work perfectly," Mom said, and reached for my girlfriend's hand and led her out of the room.

"Looks like Mom is awfully fond of Jade," Dad said once the three of us were left alone in the living room.

"There's nothing not to like." There was zero humor in my voice.

"Listen to me, son. I like her. It's nice to see you settling down a bit. But don't get sidetracked. Big things are about to happen and there's no room for flexibility. So, unless she's on board to join you on tour, I'd cut the cord. Things are happening," Dad said.

"Jesus, Dad. Have you ever heard the saying *timing is everything*? Can't you just enjoy the moment. Having both your sons here, and meeting Cruz's girlfriend," Lennon said, surprising the shit out of me. I was going to rip into my father, but I sat back and let my brother take the reins.

"I like her. And I'm happy you're both here. But business is business. How do you think we pay for all these homes, the planes, and all the shit you both love so much? It's about pushing all the time, boys. And you're lucky to have an example to look up to." Dad tilted his head back and slammed the entire glass of wine. Like I said, everything was extreme. "Clara, I need a scotch."

"Good talk. I'm going to go find Jade and show her around. Meet you in the game room in a while," I said to my brother, because I was done talking to my father. He was well on his way to getting drunk, and I didn't need to be around for it.

꩜

"You cheated. You knocked that ball in with your elbow," Jade said with her hands on her hips, and I couldn't help but laugh. Lennon was a full-on cheater when it came to playing pool. In his defense, the kid had practiced endless hours, but he'd just never taken to it.

"It was an accident. I was taking a shot," Lennon said, and he didn't hide the dumb ass grin spreading across his face. He liked that she called him on his shit, and so did I.

Music came from the front room, which meant the party would be starting soon. The DJ was setting up and guests would start arriving within the next thirty minutes.

"Oooh, I need to go get ready. Your mom is letting me wear the most gorgeous dress I've ever seen."

"Meet you out there in an hour," I said to my brother.

I led Jade to my bedroom, where Diego left our luggage.

"Are you sure your parents don't mind us staying in the same bedroom?" she asked.

I laughed as I shut the door. "I'm positive."

"I really like your mom."

"Yeah. She can be great when she's *present*. Hopefully she can stay there for the next few days. Sorry my dad is such an asshole," I said, opening my closet to find something to wear.

"He's fine."

He was anything but fine, but I dropped the conversation because I wanted her to have fun. Jade and I got dressed, and she was putting her makeup on when someone knocked on the door.

"Come on, you two. Don't leave me alone out here," Lennon whined through the door.

Jade laughed and let him in. "We're ready."

"Wow. You look beautiful," my brother said, ogling my girl.

"Stop looking at her, asshole." I shot him daggers.

Jade wore a fitted black sequined mini dress that I was pretty sure my mother had worn as a top with pants before. But Jade was small, and my mom was a tall woman, so I guess it was a brilliant idea. She paired the dress with the black and white checkered Converse I got her for Christmas. It was very Jade to wear a formal dress with tennis shoes and still manage to be the hottest girl in the room. It took zero effort for her.

"You two are ridiculous. Your parents aren't bad. I actually really like your mom, and your dad is harmless."

"Well, sit back and enjoy the show tonight, because you're in for a real treat," Lennon said.

We made our way out to the great room. There were already fifty to sixty people there. Most of them were decked out in designer duds and each one trying to outdo the next. Jade took in the scene with wide eyes and a huge smile.

"This feels like one of those famed Hollywood parties you read about," she whispered.

Lennon and I laughed because that's exactly the kind of party this was.

"Let's go mingle," I said, leading her through the room.

"Jade," my mother shrieked, and everyone turned to see what the unusual outburst from my soft-spoken mother was about. Mom held both Jade's hands in hers. "Look at you in this dress. You look gorgeous."

"Thank you for letting me borrow it. I hope I didn't ruin the look with my tennis shoes," my girlfriend said.

"Well, if I had a pair of size six shoes lying around, they'd be on your feet. But you actually pulled this look off quite well. Very hip, sweetheart." My mom took Jade in, and her face beamed. I'd never seen her gawk over anyone like this, aside from my dad.

"Thank you. Coming from you, that's a huge compliment," Jade said.

"Come with me. I want to show you off." Mom winked at me and I rolled my eyes.

So much for staying under the radar.

Chapter Nineteen

JADE

"NO THANK YOU," I SAID TO STEVEN WHEN HE OFFERED ME YET ANOTHER SHOT.

I know people liked to go big on New Year's, but I was sticking to wine and beer after my one and only experience with shots. Cruz's father wasn't giving up though, and he continued to push. I didn't want to get sloppy, not that anyone would notice. This place was crazier than The Dive. People in their fifties and sixties were putting down shots like this was a fraternity party. I leaned against the back of the couch as Steven's friend, Walker, told me what Cruz was like as a little kid. I noticed people were going in groups down the hallway toward the master bedroom. They'd come out a few minutes later, and no one was the wiser. Cruz had gone to check on his mother, as she'd disappeared a while ago. He seemed hesitant to leave me alone with his father, but I assured him I'd be fine. He returned to my side and was notably agitated. I squeezed his hand and focused on the man speaking to me.

"He was a no-nonsense little shit, even when he was eight years old. Not Lennon though, he was easier to mess with," Walker said.

"Are you fucking kidding me?" Cruz kept his voice low, but his father scanned the area to make sure no one was listening.

"Relax, Son."

"Relax? What the fuck is this guy doing here? After what he did to your son? And talking about my childhood like you and I were ever friends. We weren't. And neither were you and Lennon. Stay the fuck away from my brother." Cruz tugged on my hand and led me out back.

My heart raced at the awkward exchange, and my arms came around my shoulders when we stepped outside. It was chilly and a cold breeze blew through the patio. The scattered heaters weren't providing enough warmth at the moment for guests to be outside. Cruz paced along the patio. There were cocktail tables scattered around the outdoor area with white linens, candles, and flowers. Music boomed inside and out, and I placed a hand on my boyfriend's back to calm him down.

"What happened in there?" I asked.

He ran his palm along the back of his head. It was a habit he did when he was angry.

"Walker is my dad's—agent, manager, who the fuck knows. He's been around since I was a kid, and he's a fucking drug dealer. He's the asshole who gave Lennon enough prescription pills and coke to kill himself."

I gasped and wrapped my arms around his middle. "Why is he here? He still works for your dad?"

"Yep. Dad called it *bad judgment*. His son nearly died. And this asshole is invited to a New Year's party at our house? Lennon left the party and is in his room. And have you noticed my mother is MIA?"

"Yes. Where did she go? Is she sick? I keep seeing people go back to their bedroom."

"Jesus, Jade. It's so fucked up. I shouldn't have brought you here. I wanted you to see where I come from, because I don't want to hide anything from you. But it's not pretty. Yeah, it all looks shiny and fancy, but it's all bullshit. My mom is upset that Walker's here, so she is locked in her room. She's already downed a couple Ambiens and she's gone. That's her current numbing pill of choice. She shuts down. And those people heading down the hallway are going to the laundry room, where my dad has a stash of whatever his drug of choice is stocked in there for them."

I searched his gaze and a piece of my heart broke for him. I was so connected to this boy, and his pain had somehow become my pain.

"I'm sorry. And I'm glad I'm here with you. I'm not here to judge, I'm here because I want to be with you. Your mom won't come back out?"

"Nope. And Lennon is in his room playing video games. He won't come back out either. It's Steven Winslow's show tonight, and he doesn't care what his wife and kids think of it."

"Well, I've had enough partying for the night. It's almost midnight, why don't we grab a few cupcakes, a couple waters, and go watch a movie in your room. We can see if Lennon wants to join us. Everything will be better in the morning when the party is over," I said.

He kissed my forehead and wrapped his arms around me. "Where did you come from, Jade Moore."

"Bucktown," I said, and he laughed.

"Let's stop at the kitchen and then go find Lennon."

We had a plate full of snacks and three bottles of water. We stopped by Lennon's room, and he didn't answer when we knocked. Cruz peeked inside and his brother was already asleep.

"Good for him," he said, pulling Lennon's door closed.

We set up a full picnic on Cruz's bed and I convinced him to watch *The Proposal* because he'd never seen it. His room looked more like a hotel room than a twenty-one-year-old guy's room. It had been professionally decorated, the bedding was chestnut colored and top of the line, and the cherry wood furniture was grand and traditional.

After we finished all the snacks, we tucked in under the heavy comforter and finished watching the movie. Laughter and loud voices trickled in for hours, but exhaustion finally kicked in and allowed me to drift off.

A loud shatter startled me from sleep. The room was dark, but little bits of light peeked through the plantation shutters. I felt around the space beside me, but no one was there.

"Cruz," I whisper-shouted, hoping he was in the bathroom.

A loud voice came from the main house, but I couldn't make out the words or the voices. I hurried to my feet and found Cruz's hoodie on the chair beside the dresser and pulled it over my head and slipped on my black leggings. The sound of something being smashed came from the living area, and I rushed out the door. Once at the end of the long hallway I stopped and remained beside the wall, just out of sight. Cruz and his father were arguing.

There was another voice that I couldn't place. I peeked around the corner and there was broken glass all over the floor. I didn't know where it had come from. A chair was flipped on its side and Cruz had his hands in the air as he shouted at his father.

"Why? Why do you ruin everything good in your life?" my boyfriend said, and I wrapped an arm around my stomach because the sadness in his eyes sent a sharp pain to my middle.

"You're being dramatic. It's not a big deal," Steven said to his son. He was still wearing last night's suit jacket and button up, but he looked disheveled.

There was white powder piled on the coffee table, and three little lines were beside it. I didn't know much about drugs, but I was fairly certain it was cocaine. There were two people sitting on the couch as I scanned the room. Walker, the man from last night, and Lennon. My heart sank, because I knew what happened before even being told. Lennon was leaning back against the cushion. He stared off in space, dazed, like he had no clue what was going on around him.

"He's high on a hell of a lot more than that shit, and you know it. What did you do? Go in and wake him up and drag him back into your piece of shit existence?" Cruz said, and veins bulged on his neck.

He shoved his dad out of the way and reached for Walker. He lifted the man to his feet and shook him by his shirttails.

"Why the fuck can't you leave him alone?"

Walker pushed my boyfriend back. "Your brother came looking for it, just like he did the first time. Quit blaming me. Once an addict, always an addict."

Cruz grabbed him and threw him over the couch, and Walker landed on his ass on the wood floor. He laughed. He didn't care what he'd done to their family. I wanted to rush over and stand beside Cruz, but my instincts kept me in place.

"Shut the fuck up," Cruz said, backing away and pointing his finger at his father. "This is your problem now. I'm done."

He turned and his gaze locked with mine. We didn't speak a word, he stormed past me and grabbed my hand, leading me back to his room. He started throwing clothes in our bags and picked up his phone.

"When can you have the plane ready, Ponch?" He paused and his stare was distant as he listened. "Thank you. We're on our way," Cruz said, tossing his cell on the chair and pacing around the room.

"I'm sorry, baby. We need to leave." He told me before dropping to sit beside me on the bed. He buried his face in his hands.

I ran my hand along his back, before wrapping my arms around his middle. "I don't care. I'm so sorry this happened. What about Lennon?" I whispered.

"I don't care. I can't do it anymore. He's a grown man. I'm done being his babysitter. He doesn't give a shit about his life, so why should I?" His gaze was tired and glossy, and my heart chipped away a little more.

"I understand your frustration. Do you want me to go get your mom, and maybe she can get involved and ask Walker to leave?"

He pushed to his feet and threw a few more things in his bag. "I tried. She's out of it. Mumbled something and fell back asleep. She's a fucking pill popper too. They're all fucked up. I don't want to be around it anymore, and I don't want you to be exposed to this shit either."

"Okay, let's go." I hurried to the bathroom and threw my hair in a ponytail. I slipped a bra on beneath Cruz's hoodie and followed him out the door.

We walked through the house and Steven was arguing with Walker, but Cruz didn't stop or engage. He opened the door and I walked outside with him right behind me. There was a car waiting there, and I had no idea if it was his family's driver or a service, but the man nodded when we stepped outside.

Before Cruz pulled the car door closed, his father called out to him, "Cruz, let's just take a minute and talk about this."

"I'm done talking about it. You made your bed, now you can lie in it," he said and pulled the door shut.

The car ride and the flight back home were quiet. We both fell asleep on the flight, as we hadn't got much sleep last night. It felt like weeks had passed since I left for winter break. I'd visited another state, lost my virginity, downhill skied, attended a Hollywood party, met Cruz's parents, and witnessed a drug-induced fight.

Life with Cruz Winslow was never boring.

The weeks blurred together after I started my spring semester classes. I moved into Ari's dorm room, and I was much happier. I still slept at Cruz's house every night, because Jace stayed in our room, so it worked out well for everyone. But I still came home every morning to get ready, and Ari and I ate breakfast and lunch together most days. I was trying my best to keep my life balanced, but Cruz and I spent a lot of time together. I was growing dependent on him, and it terrified me.

"So is Cruz finally speaking to Lennon?" Ari asked as she scooped scrambled eggs onto her plate.

"Not really. It's very tense between them. Lennon just tries to stay out of his way. He's apologized so many times and is just waiting for Cruz to come around."

"It was noticeable at their show this weekend. You could feel the disconnect, you know?" she said.

"I'm sure. Cruz is resentful. He's given up a lot for his brother, and he wants him to take control of his own life. I'm not surprised you could tell. The tension is palpable at their house."

"When are you going to come out with me again?" she whined.

I laughed. "I'm sorry. This semester's class load has been a lot. I promised Cruz I'll come next month when the AF Record label guy comes to watch them."

"Isn't he going to play the song he wrote for you?" she said as we walked to our usual table.

"Yeah, I'm dying to hear it. He won't sing it to me until they have it ready with the music. He said he had a drink with you and Jace after the show last night."

"He did. I think he and Jace have a little bromance going. Cruz said his friend's house will for sure be available for us. He didn't know what the rent was but said it's super cheap. I don't know how, being so close to campus," Ari said.

"I know. I told him what we could afford, and he said it's less than that. We can go see it in a few weeks."

"I can't wait to have our own little house. What are you doing for Valentine's Day?"

"Pizza at the beach," I said, smiling because it was kind of our thing now.

"Fun."

"What are you and Jace doing?"

We left the dining commons and headed for campus. I didn't have any classes with Cruz this semester, but Ari and I had taken an elective together. It was a screenwriters course, and studying Harry Potter hardly felt like a real class, as it was my favorite series of all time.

"He's making me dinner at his apartment," she said, wriggling her brows.

"Awww... he's so sweet."

"He really is. See you at lunch." Ari waved as she walked to her English class.

"Hey Jade," Brayden said, jogging up beside me.

"Oh, hi." He had three classes with me this semester. He was also a human biology major, though he was a year ahead of me.

We took our seats in Anatomy. I liked to sit up front, as it helped me focus. Brayden sat beside me the first day of class, and they'd become our permanent seats.

"He posted the scores for the first test last night. How'd you do?" he asked.

"I did well. How about you?"

"Ninety-one. I can't complain," Brayden said.

I'd received a ninety-eight on the test. I was still kicking myself for changing the answer on the question I missed.

"Awesome. Congrats."

"Are you still dating Cruz?" His question caught me off guard. I'd been with Cruz for months now, and I thought Brayden was more than clear about it.

"Yes. We've been together for a while now."

"Oh, I just wondered. I never see you at The Dive when Exiled is playing," he said, opening his spiral notebook as Professor Kross wrote something on the whiteboard.

"I don't go out much. I just don't have time. How do you do it and maintain your grades?" I whispered. I really was curious because I was drowning in work.

"Well, I go out more than I should. You must be on an accelerated program because you're in so many sophomore classes."

"Yeah, I'm trying to graduate in three years."

"That's impressive. You must have tested out of a bunch of first year courses."

"Yeah, and I'll take summer classes as well." I took the cap off my pink pen and faced the front of the room as the lecture began.

"Damn. You're taking on a lot. This program is hard enough doing it in four years. You're going to be a great doctor someday," he whispered.

I smiled and turned my attention back to Professor Kross. Class ended and we walked outside. Two arms came around my middle and I knew it was Cruz before I even turned around. I always felt him before I saw him. His chin settled on my shoulder and his scruff tickled my cheek.

"Hey," I said, turning to face him.

"Hey, yourself, More Jade."

"Well, I'll see you later," Brayden said, and my boyfriend glared at him. Cruz was ridiculously jealous, and he had no reason to be.

"I'll see you in class this afternoon." I waved at him before he walked off.

"I hate that dude," my boyfriend grumbled.

"You do not. You don't even know him."

"I know enough. He wants you. That's all I need to know."

"He does not. We're friends," I said as he strode beside me through campus.

"He practically took all the same classes as you."

"Because we're the same major." I laughed.

I stopped in front of Herbert Hall and faced him. His dark blond, disheveled hair was longer than usual. His long sleeve white fitted Henley showed off his defined shoulders and stomach. He was wearing black joggers and Converse. My fingers itched to pull him closer, but I didn't want to be late for class.

"Trust me. He wants you." His hand wrapped around my waist and he tugged me against his body. I was instantly warm. His lips found mine and he kissed me hard. "Love you."

"Love you, more," I said, resting my forehead against his. My voice was breathless.

He chuckled. "I'll pick you up at four o'clock."

I pushed up on my tiptoes and planted another kiss on his perfect mouth.

Cruz Winslow was my favorite distraction.

Chapter Twenty

CRUZ

"I'M GLAD YOU GUYS ARE IN SYNC AGAIN," LUKE SAID WHEN WE FINISHED rehearsals.

"It must mean Cruz finally stopped menstruating," Dex said.

I flipped him the bird. We'd all been in a funk. Well, I'd been in a funk. I'd had a beef with everyone but Adam. Dex not living at the house had improved our relationship, and he'd straightened up these last few weeks. It was good timing as AF Records was coming to see us in mid-April. That gave us less than a month to get our shit together. My anger toward Lennon had simmered some, but this was the longest I'd ever gone staying angry at the little fucker. I'd moved forward with my brother, but I didn't fully trust him anymore. Unfortunately, I didn't love him any less. But I had more to think about now than just Lennon.

Jade was mine, and she meant everything to me. I looked at the future differently. I used to not give a shit about tomorrow, and now I cared too much. Being with her gave my existence an actual purpose, and I'd never felt this way before. I understood what her dad meant when he said everyone had one perfect match. Jade was mine. I'd never experienced a connection like I had with her. Her happiness was my happiness and her sadness—my sadness. Loving Jade was like finding the missing piece to a puzzle you'd searched for your entire life. She was the only person I'd ever loved that didn't let me down.

Lennon and I hashed it out. He'd fucked up. He reminded me that humans occasionally did so. But his fuck-ups were life altering, so I had a hard time forgiving him each time he played Russian roulette with his life. Jade and my brother had grown close, and he got her to broker the deal for us to finally talk it out. Walker was a piece of shit. He'd woken Lennon up that night claiming our father wanted to see him. It was a shitty thing to do—but, at the same time, Lennon needed to grow the fuck up and stand his ground. He couldn't blame everyone else every time he slipped. And neither could I. Didn't mean I didn't think Walker was a piece of shit, but I couldn't control everyone who came into contact with my brother. I'd agreed to forgive him, and he was trying to get back on track and he'd even stopped drinking since New Year's. I didn't know how long it would last, but I was letting Lennon take the reins of his own life.

"Fuck off. If you two weren't complete douchebags, I wouldn't have to be an asshole," I said.

"As much as I hate to admit it, he's right." Adam tipped his head back and guzzled his water.

My best friend always had my back, especially where the band was concerned. Adam knew more than anyone that going on tour was not something I dreamed of doing. He was as concerned as I was about my brother and Dex spiraling if we were to take Exiled the whole way.

"Yeah, yeah, yeah, we've cleaned our asses up, stop bitching," Dex said, leading us out the door.

"See you in thirty minutes?" Adam asked as he got in his car. He'd started seeing Tory a few weeks ago, and Jade and I were meeting them for dinner.

"Yep. I'll go pick her up and head over."

"Cruz." My brother jogged over to my car.

"What's up?"

"I know you're surprising Jade for spring break. When are you leaving?"

"Sunday morning. Why?"

"I was going to see if I could fly with you guys. Ben and Seth are going to be in France for spring break, and they asked me to meet them there," he said.

There were times that I looked at my brother and my chest squeezed because he looked like a broken little kid. Hell, maybe he still was. I hated him for making me soft. For making me care about his untrustworthy ass.

"Do you think that's a good idea?" Fuck. I spoke to him like I was his father and I knew it annoyed him because it bugged the shit out of me.

But I didn't know how to stop doing it. Ben and Seth weren't bad kids. They'd been friends of Lennon's since we were kids. But they partied like normal college kids, and that was dangerous for my brother. He didn't know when to stop.

"Jesus, dude. I'm not five years old. Yeah, I've had some issues, I'm more than aware. Hell, I'm reminded every time I look at you and I see the disappointment. But I need to find balance in my life. I can't be all in or all out. The most I'm going to do is have a couple beers with them. Nothing hard. And no drugs. Hell, they don't mess around with that shit anyway."

But you do.

I bit my tongue. Lennon knew who he was, he didn't need his asshole brother reminding him of his mistakes every day. The thing about Lennon that sucked the most—he was one of my favorite people in the world. His heart was huge. He was talented as shit, and funny as hell when he wasn't being a fuck up.

"All right. Yeah, of course you can fly with us. But I'm not babysitting your ass when we're there. Jade's never been, and I don't want this trip to turn into another shit show."

He smiled, and fuck if I didn't want to hug him. But I didn't. I'd taken a much-needed step back from my brother for the first time in my life after his slip in Park City, and it had forced him to make decisions for himself.

"Thanks, Cruz. You know I love you, right?"

Jesus. He was making this a challenge. "I do. Love you too, brother."

He squeezed my shoulder and jogged to his car. I watched him drive away, and for the first time in two years, I started to think Lennon might actually be growing up.

❧

"I'm so ready for spring break," Tory said as we took our seats at La Trattoria.

Jade and Tory had met twice, and they'd hit it off.

"Same. I need a break. I had my last midterm today," Jade said.

"Where are you guys going for break?" Tory asked, and Adam laughed as he tore off a piece of bread. His girl was chatty as hell and she asked a shit ton of questions, but Jade didn't seem to mind.

"He won't tell me," my girlfriend whined, and it was cute as hell.

"It's a surprise," I said.

"What about you two? Do you have any plans?" Jade asked.

"I'm going with a group of girls to Daytona Beach and I'm trying to get this one to go with me," Tory said, batting her lashes at Adam.

"I'm thinking about it," my best friend said. Adam was a relationship guy, always had been. But something seemed different with this girl. He liked her a lot. Even so, Adam was way too haughty for spring break in Daytona, but love could make you do crazy shit. I, for one, could vouch for that.

"I don't even know if you're allowed in the state of Florida." I laughed hard. "Don't you have a warrant out for your arrest?"

"That's your fucking fault, Winslow."

"Oh yeah? I made you go a hundred and ten on the freeway?" I said, using my hand to cover my smirk.

"Uh, let's see. You pushed me to rent that goddamn Lambo and insisted no one was out on the road at that hour," Adam said, his head falling back with a dumbass grin.

"And I was almost right. We were the only ones out there, aside from the one cop hiding on the side of the road."

The table erupted in laughter, and I caught my girl staring at me. She claimed my laughter was her kryptonite. I needed to remember to laugh more.

"Jesus. I almost shit my pants I was so scared," Adam said.

"I suggest checking with the state before visiting. Pay that shit off."

"Yeah, if you get signed, you're going to be traveling a ton. You might want to clear your record for the future," Tory said, and Jade's shoulders stiffened.

"Yeah, that's not the only state I need to check with either," Adam said under his breath so only I could hear.

I nudged Jade with my shoulder, and she smiled, but it was forced. The idea of leaving her sucked, but I didn't want to stress about it until I had to. So much needed to happen before we got to that point. Our waiter set our plates down and I sneaked a ravioli from Jade's plate.

"So, Jade, are you going to go to the show when AF Records comes to watch them? Maybe we could go together?"

"Yes, I'm definitely going, and I'd love to go together. I want you to meet my roommate Ariana. You're going to love her."

"I can't wait. What are we going to do if these guys leave?" Tory said, and I wanted her to quit talking about it, so I shot Adam a look.

He was sitting across from me, and Jade right beside me. I rested my hand on top of hers in her lap.

"Let's not worry about that, yet," Adam said.

"I know. I'm so torn because I know how bad you want it to happen, but I can't imagine not having you here."

Adam and Tory had been seeing each other for just a couple of weeks, but they were inseparable.

"Don't worry about it. You aren't getting rid of me that easy," my best friend told her.

Tory dropped the topic and I appreciated it. We spent the rest of the night laughing our asses off, and no one mentioned the fact that everything might change in a few months.

⠀⠀⠀⠀⠀⠀⠀⠀⠀⠀⠀⠀✦

"Is your friend going to be here?" Jade asked as she, Ariana, and I made our way to the front door of the rental house.

The small white house with gray shutters was only a few blocks from campus and even closer to my house.

"No. He owns it and uses it as a rental. Turns out it's empty now," I said. I kept it brief for a multitude of reasons.

"It's so cute," Jade and Ari said at the same time, and laughed.

Kay swung the door open. She was the property manager, and she and I had already discussed how this would go down.

"You must be Jade and Ariana. I'm Kay."

"Yes, hi. This place is adorable," Ari said, and Jade squeezed my hand and looked over with a big grin on her pretty face.

"Did you find out how much the rent is? This looks pretty fancy," my girlfriend whispered.

"You worry too much. We'll get all the details from Kay."

Natural light flooded the front room, and Jade gasped when we stepped inside. She turned slowly, taking in the space. It was light and airy, according to my realtor. Yeah, I bought the place. She needed a house and I didn't want her in a shitty apartment. I'd prefer she lived with me, but she wouldn't even consider that yet, so this was the next best thing. Jade needed a place and I had a shit ton of money. I called it my reward for having a piece of shit father. We had large trust funds, and the dude who managed our money had urged me to invest in something. It was a win, win. But if I told Jade I owned the property, she'd over analyze it. Kay was aware of the situation, and she'd manage the property for me. This was a lie that didn't hurt anyone. I wanted to help her and she wouldn't let me. So, I found a creative way to make it happen. The rent money from Ariana and Jade would go into an account that would be Jade's when she went to medical school. So, she was stocking away for her future. And why not invest in someone that had her heart set on saving the world? It didn't get any better than that.

"Are these the original floors? This wood is gorgeous," my girlfriend asked. Jade was renting the house, not buying it. But in typical Jade fashion, she'd researched everything out there—she'd done her homework.

"They are the original knotty pine. This little cottage got a complete overhaul before the new owner purchased it, but they kept all the history intact. They didn't change the moldings or the flooring, but everything else is new," Kay said, smiling at the two girls.

She was playing her role. I had the place cleaned up for them after I'd purchased it a few months ago when Jade's dad mentioned she needed a place. A contractor came in and made it pretty. I liked renovating homes. It was something I could see myself doing in the future. My parents bought and sold homes often, and I'd learned a thing or two watching them. It was easy to make money when you had money. That's why I wanted the funds from this place to go in an account for Jade. Why the hell do the rich bastards get to profit off everything. What about the girl who was killing herself to attain her goal? Her father worked his ass off to keep our city safe. They deserved it more than anyone I knew.

"That's amazing. It looks like he put new furniture in here. Is someone living here now? When will it be available?" Ari asked.

"He's not going to move in. He just wanted a rental. He figured college students wouldn't have furniture, so this all comes with it," Kay said, glancing over at me as she adjusted the collar on her navy suit jacket.

"Are you kidding me? It's gorgeous." Jade placed her hands on each side of her face and smiled.

She was so fucking perfect. She appreciated everything, and I loved it. I wasn't used to it. I was surrounded by spoiled fucking brats, including myself. I liked seeing the world through my girl's eyes.

"Yep. He brought in a professional designer to set it up." My realtor led them to the two bedrooms and they only grew more excited as they saw more of the space.

The kitchen was the final stop, and the girls did not hide their excitement. It was all white and clean, as that was the new trend.

"There's literally no way we can afford this. And there's three bedrooms. I don't know if we could find another roommate," Jade said, looking at Ari.

"You don't need a third roommate. You can use it as an office or a study room," Kay said, proving she followed instructions well.

"Well, I don't think we could afford it with just the two of us. What is he asking?" Ari asked, and I could see how nervous they both were.

"It's a thousand dollars a month. Five hundred bucks each. That includes utilities and landscaping." Kay read the details from her notebook and avoided looking at them. We all knew that was ridiculously low for this area. Hell, I'd have preferred they paid nothing, but I knew that would be too obvious.

"What? How is that possible? Rents are much higher in this neighborhood. Are you sure you have the numbers right?" Jade bit down on her lip, and I pulled her against my body. Her back to my front, resting my chin on her shoulder.

"Yes. He was very particular about who he would rent it to. He liked the idea of two young ladies who wouldn't be throwing wild parties." Kay was going rogue now, throwing in her own bullshit. I wasn't renting this place to anyone but Jade, but if it made it more believable, I was fine with that.

"We won't throw any parties, we barely even go to them," Ari said, and we all laughed.

"That sounds perfect, ladies. Would you like to sign the paperwork? The place is yours on May first if you want it. They just have a few things to finish up on the renovation, and you can move in," Kay said, pulling some papers from her leather portfolio.

"Oh my gosh. I can't believe we get to live here." Jade turned in my arms and kissed my lips. "Please thank your friend for us. Is it anyone I know? I hope it's not Dex's place."

"Nope. A friend of my dad's."

They filled out all the paperwork, and we dropped Ariana off at the dorms and Jade grabbed her suitcase and clothes for our trip tomorrow.

"Everything is just coming together," she said when she slipped in the car beside me.

"I told you it would all work out."

"I think you're my good luck charm, Cruz Winslow."

I hoped she was right about that. Because I sure as fuck wanted to be.

"I can't believe we're in Paris," Jade said when we stepped off the plane. She'd spent the first few hours of the flight guessing where we were going until she and Lennon begged me to just tell her.

"I told you I'd take you to new places whenever I could," I said, tugging her close to me as we walked toward the waiting car.

"Jesus, you two are made for Paris. Never thought I'd see my brother so sappy," Lennon said.

"Shut up, asshole. I'm not fucking sappy."

Lennon and Jade both chuckled.

"You're a little sappy, baby. But I like it," she said.

I rolled my eyes and slipped into the car. Jade and my brother played board games most of the flight, and I wrote. Writing was an odd thing. There were times I couldn't sleep because the words wouldn't turn off. The ideas poured from me like water from a fountain. Other times there was just nothing there. Right now, the ideas were flowing, and I'd been writing non-stop.

We dropped my brother off at the rental house he was meeting his friends at and Jade and I headed to our hotel. We were staying in the city, so we could walk to all the touristy bullshit. When we entered the grand hotel, her eyes grew wide as she took in the high ceilings and magnificent architecture.

"Oh my gosh, this isn't real," she whispered.

"We have a whole week to do whatever you want," I said.

"I want to see everything." She wrapped her arms around me and nestled her face into my neck.

"Then that's exactly what we'll do."

After checking in we made our way to the top floor and stood in front of the floor to ceiling windows, taking in the views. It was magnificent.

Jade and I spent the week eating croissants, pastries, and every French treat we could get our hands on. We spent two days at the Louvre Museum, and Jade appeared to enjoy it as much as I did. I agreed to take a baking class with her on our last day, which basically meant Jade learned how to make macarons and I ate most of them. I'd never spent spring break sober, and I'd never had a better time.

I was used to booze and sex, and yes, we were having a shit ton of sex in France, because—why not? But it was different. I wasn't wasted. And I was crazy about this girl. We had wine a few times with dinner, but most of the time we were dead ass sober. Unless you count the fact that I was fucking drunk on Jade Moore. She numbed my pain and made me want more out of life.

And I was all in.

JADE

THE LAST FEW WEEKS WERE SOME OF THE MOST MEMORABLE IN MY LIFE. I'd been to Paris with Cruz, and we'd had the most amazing time. He'd become the center of my universe, and I knew I should be cautious. I was going to drown in this boy, and my inner voice told me to reach for a life vest, but I didn't want to come up for air.

Today was the day. It was an exciting day. But it didn't feel like it. AF Records was going to be at The Dive tonight. They were ready to sign Exiled pending they liked their live performance. Which of course they would. There was no question there. I wanted to be encouraging, wanted to share in this achievement, but I couldn't. I'd never been a selfish person, but when it came to Cruz, I was a greedy bitch. I didn't want to share him. AF Records was a huge label. If they signed Exiled it would mean tours, and travel, and paparazzi. Fame, and fans, and partying. That wasn't me. I was school, and studying, and Oak Street Beach. I preferred the quiet most of the time and there was nothing quiet about what Cruz might be venturing into.

I lie in bed and rubbed my upset belly, bending forward in the fetal position when a sharp cramp struck below my belly button. I was letting everything get to me. I didn't want to be a walking stress ball. I needed to rally for my boyfriend and that's exactly what I was going to do.

"You slept in today," Cruz said as he strode into his bedroom with two Starbucks coffees.

"Oh wow, you've already been out?"

I slid up to sit with my back against the headboard and pulled my knees up to stop the cramping. It wasn't working, but I pushed the discomfort away. My last test was yesterday so I could actually enjoy the next few days before I was buried again.

"Yep. I didn't sleep much," he said. He avoided my gaze, and I knew he was as nervous as me.

Maybe for different reasons. Maybe for the same reasons. I honestly didn't know. He only talked about how much it all meant to Lennon, and Adam, and even Dex. He also said that he didn't want to leave me. I didn't know what Cruz wanted, because he was so wrapped up in what everyone around him wanted. We avoided the conversation. I didn't push it because I didn't want him to know how scared I was. How terrified I was about him leaving me. About losing him. Because really, how would it work? It wouldn't. And I didn't know if I could survive without Cruz. At least I didn't want to.

"Are you nervous?" I asked, taking a sip of coffee.

"Nah. I'm excited for you to hear the song I wrote for you."

Nausea hit my stomach, as the topic of tonight was impossible to avoid.

"I can't wait," I said, resting my head on my knees.

"Are you worried about tonight?" he asked, dropping to sit beside me on the bed and pushing the hair back from my face. "You feeling okay? You're a little flushed."

"It's nothing, just a little stomachache."

He kissed down my neck and took the coffee from my hand. He set it on the nightstand and tugged me to lie down on my back. I laughed when he tickled my neck with the graze of his lips. He knew how to make everything better.

"A stomachache, huh? Should I kiss it better?" he said.

Butterflies swarmed my belly, and I arched into his touch. He pulled my shirt over my head and kissed his way down my body. I tried to breathe as I writhed beneath him with a fire that only ever burned for him.

"You should definitely kiss it better," I said, my voice raspy and full of need.

"Oh, I intend to. I'm going to kiss all your worries away, More Jade."

And that's exactly what he did.

The Dive was packed. It was even crazier than Halloween. Exiled continued to grow in popularity, there was no denying it. Everything was falling into place for the band—and imploding for me at the same time. Tory put on some lipstick in the mirror in the back room, and Ari and I passed a beer between us. I didn't feel like drinking tonight. My stomach was still queasy and the last thing I wanted to do was get drunk and emotional on my boyfriend's big night. Cruz and the rest of the guys were with Luke getting ready to go out on stage.

"All right, ready girls? Let's go wedge ourselves up front," Tory said.

"You don't have to ask me twice." Ari laughed.

My two friends met thirty minutes ago, and they'd hit it off. It was a relief because it took the attention off my shitty mood.

"I need to use the restroom before we go out there," I said, trying to push back the fact that my stomach was in knots and I wanted to curl up in a ball and cry. I couldn't tell anyone how I was feeling because I was embarrassed about being so selfish. This was their big break. I needed to rally.

"No worries. You're probably about to get your period. I always get the worst stomachaches right before," Tory said as she pulled hard on the door handle.

"Oh my gosh, not again. Can you imagine if we miss the entire show because we're locked in here." Ari grunted as she tugged harder.

I reached forward and pulled hard several times. The damn door was stuck. Again. We all three took turns shaking, pulling, and screaming at the door. I wasn't sure what the yelling would accomplish, but it got out our frustration.

Tory hit her fist against the white wood. "Hey, someone open the damn door."

The door swung open and Luke smiled and said, "We can't have the three biggest fans of Exiled locked in the back room now, can we?"

I gave him a quick hug and hurried to the bathroom. I was doubled over on the toilet and thankful to have access to a private stall. My forehead was sweaty, and I leaned forward to rest my head in my hands. There was no reason to be on the toilet. I didn't have to go to the bathroom. I just needed to sit down and let these cramps run their course. I thought about Tory's words and tried to remember if I was due for my period. The last time I'd had it was the week before Valentine's Day. It was April tenth. I'd missed two cycles.

Oh, god.

Oh, god.

Oh, god.

It wasn't possible. Cruz and I were always safe. I was only nineteen years old. I'd only had sex with one person. Safe sex. No. I couldn't be pregnant, could I? I poked the sides of my breasts because I remembered seeing someone do that on TV. Maybe they were a little tender, I couldn't tell. I stood up and flushed the empty toilet and hurried to the sink. I put a paper towel under the running water and wrung it out before putting the damp towel on my forehead and trying to calm my breathing. I was freaking out.

You're overthinking this.

I'd been so stressed. People missed their periods all the time due to stress, right? I googled the question when Ari knocked on the door.

"You okay, girl?"

I glanced at my phone and saw tons of websites pull up for missed periods due to stress. *Phew.* I slipped my phone in my back pocket and opened the door with a smile.

"All better."

"Good, they just started. Let's get out there," Tory said.

With one hand tucked in Tory's and one clinging to Ariana's, we made our way through the crowd. The bouncer helped us get to the front, and the energy was palpable. The crowd was amped, and the band responded to it. Lights were flashing, and the music blared. I search behind me to try to see if I could find the guy from AF Records. I knew he was in his thirties, so in this crowd, he should stand out. I couldn't see much over the bouncing heads dancing in the mosh pit. The place was going off. Beyond anything I'd ever experienced here before. The song stopped and the crowd settled.

My gaze locked with Cruz's, and I relaxed. He smiled and his honey-brown gaze never left mine when he spoke. "So we have something new that we want to share with you tonight. I wrote this for the girl I love. It's called 'More of Me.'"

People screamed and cheered. Some girl yelled out, "Love me, Winslow."

Tory, Ari, and I all laughed, and I turned my attention to the stage. It was a slower ballad, I could tell by the music. Cruz pulled up a stool and dropped down to sit. I'd never seen him sit when he performed. His beautiful voice started singing and the words would forever be etched into my soul.

"The dark of the storm is all I see.
And like a dream she comes to me.
Now my world is upside down.

Makes no sense keeps spinning round.
When it stops she surrounds me.
In her light I finally see.
And she asks me…
Why would you want more of me?
She doesn't know just what I see.
Beautiful girl with eyes of jade.
Shines so bright can't find the shade.
Heart so pure even in her pain.
In the drought she is the rain.
Wasn't looking but I found her.
I'm the sickness she's the cure.
I'll drown us both in the waves.
She's the only one I want to save.
Makes no sense why she's with me.
Beautiful girl with lots of dreams.
And she asks me…
Why would you want more of me?
She doesn't know just what I see.
Beautiful girl with eyes of jade.
Shines so bright can't find the shade.
Heart so pure even in her pain.
In the drought she is the rain."

He sang it slow, and sultry, and sexy. Tears streamed down my face as I stared at the beautiful boy in front of me. He winked and I wanted to pounce on the stage and kiss him senseless. He wrote me the most beautiful song I'd ever heard.

Ari's fingers grasped my hand so tight I laughed when I met her glossy gaze. She was crying too.

"That was beautiful. I want Jace to be in a band and write me love songs," she said with a laugh.

"Girl. Adam better start writing songs right now. That boy loves you something silly," Tory said.

I mouthed the words *I love you* to Cruz before we headed to the bar for more drinks. My stomach started to twist and turn again, and I ordered a water. We stood off in the corner and tried to cool off.

"Jade, you look pale. Are you okay?" Ari asked.

I dabbed my face with a napkin. I was freaking hot. The sharpest cramp nailed me right in the center of my stomach, and I leaned forward.

"I really don't feel well. I think I might have eaten something bad. My stomach hurts so bad," I said, grasping the back of a barstool for balance. The guy sitting on it turned around and smiled. I nodded in apology.

"Let's find you a chair," Tory said as the band broke out in another song.

She pushed on her tiptoes to see, just as Jace joined us in the back corner.

"What's going on, beautiful?" He kissed Ari's cheek and a pink hue covered her pretty face.

"Just taking a break. Jade may have food poisoning. She's not feeling well," Ari said, searching for an empty chair.

"You know what, guys—I'm going to just go in the back room and wait there for a little bit. There's a couch and I can lie down and see if it passes. I'll come find you if I'm feeling better. Go have fun."

"Do you want me to come with you?" Ari asked.

"No. I'm fine. Promise," I said, and leaned forward to hug her.

"Okay, text us if you need anything."

I agreed, even though I glanced down at my phone and noticed I was at one percent and it was about to die. I didn't want them to worry. I just needed a few minutes to sit down away from this crowd. I'd drink some water and be good to go.

I stopped in the bathroom and splashed some water on my face. I bent over the sink when another cramp hit me hard. Jesus. Maybe this is what happened when you skipped a period. You got the mother load the next month. I made my way to the back room, shut the door and grabbed a bottle of water from the mini fridge. Dropping down on the couch, I pulled my knees up and tried to breathe. I'd never experienced stomach pain like this. I grabbed my phone and googled the symptoms of appendicitis. Everything pointed to the right side, and this pain was definitely not favoring any side of my stomach. I googled the symptoms of food poisoning, but my phone died, so I set it on the floor and hugged my knees to my chest and waited for the pain to pass. In the brief reprieve, I calmed my breathing and closed my eyes. Cruz would be done in a half an hour, and I could go to his place and soak in a hot tub with him. Thoughts of warm water and my boyfriend's arms around me allowed me to drift away.

A piercing noise startled me, and I sprung to my feet. The lights were off and I swore I fell asleep with the lights on. I heard distant shouting outside the door, and there was some sort of high-pitched alarm torturing my ears. I was so disoriented, and the room was all fuzzy. Was I dreaming? I blinked a couple times and focused my eyes around the small space. It was hazy. Smoky.

Smoky.

Filling with smoke.

Smoke alarms were going off.

I learned the rules of fire safety before most people learned their ABCs. But I'd never been in an actual fire. My father had described them to me hundreds of times. I'd had nightmares about fires. Watched movies about fires. Read articles about fires. But nothing really prepared you for an actual fire. Nothing. And I was in the midst of one.

I reached for my phone and remembered it was dead. I rushed to the door, holding my hand just a few inches away from it, something I'd learned at a young age. Heat vibrated from the wood, and smoke bellowed from the crack between the floor and the door. I knew better than to open it. I found two jackets and shoved them in the opening where the smoke continued to flow from beneath the door. There was a towel lying on the end table and I wrapped it around my nose and mouth and made a makeshift mask, tying it at the back of my head.

I searched the room. How had I never noticed that there were no windows in this room? It was an oversized closet and there was no way out. I knew the only way I was getting out of here was through that door. The fire was close, but it wasn't here yet, or the door would be in flames.

Think, Jade.

I ran to the mini refrigerator and grabbed a few bottles of water. Cruz's army jacket hung on a hook and I dumped two bottles of water all over it as fast as I could. Time was not on my side. I needed to move.

Move.

Fire spreads fast.

Act.

I tightened the towel around my face and found a T-shirt lying on the floor in the corner of the room and soaked it with water. I wrapped the wet shirt around the doorknob to cool it off and twisted. And pulled. And pulled harder.

The door was stuck.

It was fucking stuck.

Panic set in. I was trapped in this little room and I couldn't get out. Ari and Tory knew where I was, but I had no idea if they realized I was still in here. I didn't know what time it was or when the fire started. I didn't know where Cruz was, but I knew he'd look for me. I heard shouting in the distance and I pulled harder, but the door wouldn't move.

"Help," I screamed as loud as I could.

My voice was not recognizable. It was raspy and hoarse. How much smoke had I taken in.

I pounded my fists against the door and shouted. The hot wood burned against my skin. A sharp pain hit my middle but I continued to bang my fists against the door. I was going to die in here if I didn't get out now. I had no choice. I couldn't see as the room had filled with smoke, and my eyes burned despite the fact that tears were pouring from them.

I didn't hear the shouting anymore. I was alone. I was going to die alone.

Dad.

Cruz.

I dropped the T-shirt and tightened my grip on the handle. My skin sizzled, but I had a tighter grip on the handle. I pulled as hard as I could, but the door didn't budge.

"Someone help me." My screams were useless. No one was here. It was just me.

I backed away from the door and ran, throwing my body into it, as I cried and screamed for help. The door wouldn't budge. I remembered Dad telling me about left-and-right-hand-search patterns, and I searched every direction, including the ceiling, but I didn't see another way out. There was nothing.

No way out.

I lie down on the ground when I started coughing and couldn't stop. I pulled the coats from the bottom of the door, allowing a heap of smoke in and screamed through the crack. I shouted multiple times, "Help me."

What felt like a punch in the gut hit me in my middle and I moved away to escape the smoke and curled into a ball, wrapping myself in the soaked jacket. Sobs sounded between my coughs and I squeezed my eyes closed for a reprieve from the smoke.

The door opened and the wood splintered and shattered all around me. I squinted and moved to my feet. My boyfriend was covered in soot, his gaze wild and manic, and he hurried across the room. We didn't speak. My sobs were the only audible sound as he pulled me beside him and rushed me toward the door.

"We have to go now. There's a door at the end of the hall. Get down on all fours and keep your head down. Stay in front of me."

His hand was on my back, the most excruciating pain radiated across my middle, and tears filled my eyes. I glanced over my shoulder. The other end of the hallway was illuminated by a blazing fire that we were running from. It was getting closer.

"Baby, come on. You can do this," Cruz shouted, pressing his hand into my lower back and urging me to go faster.

There was a voice coming from a few feet ahead and two arms pulled me to my feet just as cool, crisp air enveloped me. My lungs begged for air. I gasped and bent forward, placing my hands on my knees, and coughed until I vomited. I couldn't stop. Cruz was coughing beside me when a blanket came around my shoulders.

"Jade. Cruz. Are you okay? I need help over here," someone shouted beside me and I recognized her voice, but it was more frantic than I'd ever heard it before. Sara. Dad must have called her. She lived closer.

I was crying and vomiting when Sara directed someone to assess Cruz. I wiped my mouth and my gaze scanned his body through my tear-filled vision. He was coughing, and talking, and calling out for me—but Sara walked me in the opposite direction.

She turned me to face her and shook my shoulders a little. "Are you okay?"

"I think so," I said through my cough.

"Jade. Look at me. Your dad is going to be here in a few minutes. Cruz is over there and he's going to be fine. The back of your jeans are soaked in blood sweetie. Are you hurt or is it something else?"

I couldn't speak. I thought about the cramping. The late period.

Oh my god.

"I'm late and I've had terrible stomach pain today. I don't know how this happened. Please don't tell Dad or Cruz. Please, Sara," I begged before leaning forward and vomiting.

Chapter Twenty-Two

CRUZ

"WHERE THE FUCK IS JADE?" I ASKED, DROPPING THE BLANKET SOMEONE had wrapped around me on the ground and scanning the shit show before me. Firetrucks, ambulances, paramedics and police cars were scattered everywhere I looked. Half the building was up in flames, and multiple hoses were aimed at it in an attempt to extinguish the fire. Dark smoke billowed from the broken windows.

"She's getting checked out," Lennon said, and I looked up to see his tear-streaked face.

"Are you hurt?" I asked.

"No, asshole. We all got out. You're the one who ran back into a fucking burning building and scared the shit out of us," he said. His voice was loud, and it cracked on a sob.

"He's okay, Lennon," Luke said as he and Adam flanked each side of me.

Yeah, I ran into a burning building when I found Ari and Tory and they told me Jade was still inside. Fire trucks hadn't arrived yet, and I wasn't about to leave her in there. Motherfuckers didn't have sprinklers at The Dive and the place went up in flames like something you'd see in a movie.

"Dude, I can't believe you ran back inside," my best friend said.

I sure as shit did. When the words left Ari's mouth, I didn't have a choice. None. The thought of dying trying to save Jade was better than the thought of living without her.

I wouldn't.

"Cruz." Jack Moore's voice sent chills down my spine. Maybe it was the sound of a man fearful that he'd lost the person he loved most in this world. I could relate.

"She's okay, Jack. She's with Sara." I leaned over and coughed hard again.

He put his hand on my back. "You okay? Were you with her?"

I couldn't speak as my throat constricted with spasms and I heard Luke fill him in. He told Jack I'd gone back in to find his daughter. He made me out to be some sort of fucking hero. But I knew better. Jade was here for me. She never would have been here if not for me. She didn't go out much, but she'd come to support me, and she could have died. At nineteen years old. I brought her to this piece of shit bar, where it wasn't safe, and she'd nearly died.

"Jack." Sara walked toward us.

The dark sky was illuminated by flashing lights, resembling a cross between a rave and a crime scene. But I saw the concern in Sara's gaze as the reds and blues spotlighted her face. I pushed to stand.

"Where is she?" I said through my cough.

"She's okay. I promise. Listen, she inhaled a lot of smoke. She's going to be fine. But I'm going to ride over to the hospital with her. She wanted me to make sure you two were together," Sara said.

"Take me to her." Jack Moore's tone was frantic and angry.

"How long have we worked together? I'm asking you to trust me. She's going to be fine. She's upset and scared. You two getting all worked up is not going to help the situation. Get Cruz checked out. Help out here, and I'll call you in an hour. I'm just going to take her over to County and have my dad check her out."

"Jesus, Sara. You want to take my kid to the hospital, and you don't want me to see her?" Jack said.

I leaned over and vomited again. What in the actual fuck? I couldn't stop puking.

"Yes. And your daughter won't forgive you if you don't help Cruz right now. You're needed here. I've got her. I promise." Sara handed him a bottle of water. "Get him to drink this, and I'll call you in an hour."

The next hour and a half was a blur. I learned that Sara's father was an ER doctor, and Jack stayed with me until a paramedic checked me out and cleared me. Most of the building was charred, but there were no fatalities, thank God. I thought of my girl and a sick feeling settled in my stomach. I could still see her huddled in the corner, wrapped in my jacket in a room filled with smoke. She'd covered her mouth and nose. She'd done everything right. But she'd been locked in a room with no way out, and it was a struggle to tamper down my anger.

I sat on the bumper of my car watching the chaos play out. Jack moved around the scene like a fine-tuned machine, jumping in to help where he could. The bleak surroundings were hard to take in. College students covered in soot, coughing and crying. People running to one another when they found their loved ones. Parents racing to the scene in hysterics searching for their children. It was heavy. And all I fucking wanted was to see Jade. I doubted she had a phone as I'd called it a couple hundred times and it went straight to voicemail. My phone was blowing up with texts from friends and family. My mom wanted to know if we were okay, my dad wanted to make sure the dude from AF Records had seen the show, and then asked if we all made it out okay.

Asshole.

Finally, the text I'd been waiting for. It was sent as a group text to Jack and I.

> Unknown Caller ~ Hey, it's Sara. Jade is totally fine and cleared to leave. She doesn't have a phone. It was lost in the fire. She's shaken up and wants to go home to Bucktown. Cruz, she asked that you text me to let me know how you are. She said to tell you thank you for coming for her and she loves you. She will call you tomorrow.

What the fuck? I wanted to see her tonight, and she wanted to go home? To her dad's? Did she blame me for being here?

> Me ~ I'm all checked out and good. Tell her I want to see her. Make sure she's okay.

> Sara ~ It's Jade. I'm fine. I promise. I love you so much. You saved my life. I just need to go home tonight, okay? I'll call you tomorrow.

> Jack ~ I'll take Cruz home. He can come back tomorrow for his car. I don't want him to drive. I'll meet you at the house in an hour.

I didn't respond because she didn't want to see me, and looking like a desperate pussy on a group text with her father wasn't high on my list. Adam and Lennon wouldn't leave my side, and they hopped in the car with Jack and I, leaving their cars at The Dive as well. Or—what was left of The Dive.

When we pulled up to the house, they both got out of the car, giving me a minute with Jade's father.

"I know you're worried, Cruz. But she's stubborn. When she gets scared, she retreats. Just give her a day. She's probably in shock. But I need you to know that I appreciate what you did for my girl." His voice cracked, and he put his hand above his brow, shielding his emotion. "You saved her life."

"She wouldn't have been there if it weren't for me," I said.

"Don't do that to yourself. There were a couple hundred kids there. It's a college hangout. Jade doesn't blame you and neither do I. I'm thankful she was with you, and that's the truth. Not many people would run back into a blazing fire, I know that first-hand. It was very brave of you to do so."

My throat closed, and a lump formed in the back. I was fucking exhausted. Fucking drained. I gazed down at the blisters covering my palms.

"Thanks, Jack," I said. It sounded like a fucking croak. I was struggling to keep it together.

He leaned in and pulled me into a hug. A fatherly hug. One I'd never shared with my own father. Steven Winslow didn't do hugs. He preferred fist pumps.

I stepped out of the car and waved. Adam, Lennon, and I sat up most of the night trying to wrap our heads around what happened. Nothing made any sense.

I slept half the day away and woke up coughing with a pounding headache. I grabbed my phone and saw a text from Jade.

Jack Moore ~ It's me, Jade. I hope you're okay this morning. I want to stay in Bucktown this weekend. I just need to spend some time with my dad. I can't thank you enough for what you did. You came back for me.

Me ~ Of course I did. Do you want me to come there? I need to see you and know you're okay.

Jack Moore ~ Please don't. I just need some time with Dad. I promise I'm fine. I love you.

A selfie came through. She looked worn and tired, with bags under her pretty jade gaze. This was what she was offering. A picture to prove she was okay. She didn't want to see me. She blamed me for the fire. There was no other explanation. And I couldn't really blame her for it. But I'd been there too. Shouldn't we be comforting each other? Isn't that what you did when you loved someone? I was done texting. I dialed Jack's number.

"Hey." Her voice sounded hoarse and tired.

"How are you?"

"Fine. Thanks to you," she said.

"You and I both know you wouldn't have been there if it weren't for me."

"That's not true. I wanted to be there. I would never blame you. You saved my life, Cruz," she said, and I heard the tremble in her voice.

I ran my hand through my hair. Fuck. I didn't want to upset her. She'd been through a lot. I'd never relied on my parents for support, but Jade and her father were very close.

"Okay. I get it. You need some time at home. I just miss you."

When did I become such a fucking pussy? Oh yeah, the day karma made me its bitch for all the people I'd fucked over, over the years. This had to be payback.

"I'll call you tomorrow, okay? I love you," she said, and she broke on a sob.

Instinct told me there was more going on. But I wouldn't push because Jade was a chick and even though I was acting like one, I didn't truly understand all the emotional shit that girls experience. I'd never cared to before, but I sure as shit cared now.

"Love you too, More Jade."

She hung up as soon as the words left my mouth. What the fuck was going on? Maybe her near death experience forced her to realize her boyfriend was a piece of shit.

"How are you feeling?" Lennon asked, dropping my car keys on the coffee table.

"Fine, how about you? Thanks for picking up my car."

My brother was showing actual signs of maturity. He never did things for me. It had always been the other way around.

"No problem. I got you a tea. Might help your throat," he said, handing me the white and green infamous coffee house cup.

"Thanks, son. You make me proud." Sarcasm oozed, and we both laughed.

"Did you talk to Dad?"

"Nope, not today. Is he worried my cough is going to interfere with his plans?" I asked, leaning back on the black leather sofa and taking a sip of the warm tea.

Adam came in the house and dropped down on the couch. "Did you tell him?"

"Not yet," Lennon said. His gaze bounced around the room. Anywhere but at me.

I moved to my feet. "What? Did you have a lapse? Did something happen?"

My brother rolled his eyes and shook his head. "Jesus, dude. No. Relax. AF Records wants to sign us. Apparently, he watched the first half of the show and he left after we performed the song you wrote for Jade. It's exactly what he wanted to see. He said that's the kind of music he wants us to write. Or you to write, I guess. He said it had heart."

"I thought he said it had soul," Adam said.

"Who the fuck cares. He liked it. Great fucking timing. The place nearly burned down, and we cheated death, but hey, we got a record deal. Let's celebrate," I said. My tone so flat no one could miss the disdain.

The irony was not lost on me. The song I wrote for Jade was the reason they were signing us. My love for the girl I didn't want to leave was ultimately what would take me away from her. And right now, she was barely communicating with me. I couldn't talk to her or come up with a plan.

"Listen, Luke talked to Dad. They're going to let us finish the semester, okay? You'll only have a year of courses to take online to graduate. We can make this work."

My brother didn't hide his desperation. And hell, I couldn't fault the dude. Lennon was getting everything he ever wanted. Unfortunately, *I* was a piece of the puzzle. A necessary piece. And it would suck to mess this up for him. And now that it was actually happening, I knew I didn't want to go. But I didn't know how *not to go*.

I scrubbed a hand down my face. "Fuck. I'm not ready to do this."

There. I said it. They'd both known it, but hearing me say it aloud was new.

"Maybe she'll come with us," Adam said because he knew Jade was the reason I didn't want to leave. "You don't know until you ask."

"I can't."

Asking Jade to leave her scholarship and go on tour with me was a dick move. It would be asking her to give up her dream. Just like me refusing to go was like asking Lennon to give up his. They were the only two fucking people I really cared about, and either way I'd be hurting one of them.

"What if you just commit for one year, and we work on finding a replacement over the next twelve months," Lennon said.

"Yeah, we'll figure it out. My head's pounding and I feel like shit. I need a nap," I said before moving to my feet and heading down the hall.

Campus buzzed with talk of the fire. People stopped me on campus to ask if I was okay. Word had spread that I'd been one of the last ones out. Rumors were flying and I'd heard some crazy shit over the last few days. Adam heard someone say that I'd run back inside The Dive for my stash of drugs. Another rumor was that I'd gone back in for my girlfriend, and she and I had jumped from a third-story window. Yeah, The Dive was a one-story building. Shows you how fucked up the gossip mill was. People had doctor's notes excusing them from class.

The Dive was facing all sorts of lawsuits and legal shit due to all the underage students that had been there and they hadn't followed fire code laws. Half the building was burned to the ground, and people were asking where we'd perform next. We'd signed our deal with AF Records yesterday. I hadn't even told Jade yet, because we were barely speaking. She'd replaced her phone and she sent me one text a day.

One.

She never responded to me after I'd reply. I was on my way to meet her now and I wanted to find out what the fuck was going on. I hadn't seen her since the fire, and I needed to know she was okay.

"Hey," she said from a table inside a Starbucks near campus.

Why we were meeting here, I had no idea. Why not at my house? This kind of shit was for people who met on a dating app, not two people who'd been dating for months and were in fucking love with each other.

"Hi." I sat across from her and she slid a cup toward me.

"I got you a caramel frap." She smiled.

She didn't lean over to kiss me. She was stiff and distant. Her jade gaze finally met mine.

"So, what's going on? You're barely speaking to me." I was done playing games. Time to hash this out.

She shook her head. Dark circles covered the space beneath her eyes and her cheeks were sunken. What the fuck was going on?

"I just need some time, that's all."

"Some time for what? I was there too, Jade. I'm not cutting you off. Aren't we supposed to lean on each other? Isn't that what you do when you love someone? Or do you need to think about that too? Maybe you blame me for the fire?"

She sat up in her seat and frowned. "Is that honestly what you think? I promise you I don't blame you. You saved my life. I'm so grateful for what you did for me. You ran back inside a burning building," she said, and tears streamed down her grief-stricken face.

"And we're both fine, baby." I wrapped my hand over hers on the table. "I don't understand what the fuck is going on."

She pulled her hand away and used the cuff of her sleeve to wipe away her tears.

"I can't explain it. Not right now."

Explain what? We were both there. I know what happened was scary, but we both made it out. I want to shout at her, but I don't. Something's going on with her and that won't help.

"Exiled signed with AF Records. We're going on tour as soon as the semester ends," I said, sitting back in my chair and waiting for any kind of reaction.

She nodded, and more tears streamed down her face.

"So, you're leaving."

"I don't know what the fuck to do, because my girlfriend won't talk to me."

"You always have me. I just need some time to process everything, you know? It's how I deal with things."

"How much time, Jade?"

"I don't know. Does it really matter? You're leaving anyway," she said, pushing to her feet and swiping at the liquid streaming down her cheeks.

"Really? That's it?" I sounded like a whiny little bitch, but I couldn't help myself.

"Well, you haven't asked me to go with you. Did you know Adam asked Tory to go with him?" she said, and now she's angry.

Jesus Christ. She's all over the fucking map here. She wasn't even talking to me and now she's pissed I didn't ask her to go with me?

"Are you serious? You aren't even fucking speaking to me, but you're mad I didn't ask you to give up everything you've worked for to go with me? Sorry I'm not a fucking selfish prick."

She turned on her heels and walked out the door. I don't go after her. I'm always fucking going after her. Halloween night and the night of the fire and since—I'm always chasing this girl. It's her turn to tell me what the fuck is wrong. A sick feeling settles in my stomach. The fear that if I don't chase after her this time, she might never come back.

Chapter Twenty-Three

JADE

I SPENT THE MORNING WITH MOM'S JOURNAL. SHE'D STARTED THESE journals when she was sixteen and wrote in them daily up until the day before she died. I'm grateful because they show me a side of her that I wasn't able to know in the short time I had with her. She was wise, and honest, and strong. Some of her journal entries have helped guide me through challenges in my life. She somehow managed to be there for me, even when she wasn't physically here. I guess that's the gift of a mom, right? They always find a way to protect their babies. It was instinctual. Well, I needed her more than ever right now. I couldn't remember a time that I'd ever felt so lost and alone. I knew it wasn't logical, because I had people who loved me, yet I felt painfully alone.

"I wish you were here, Mom," I whispered before pressing my back against the headboard in my room. I'd been staying in Bucktown since the fire happened, and today I was going back to the dorm. It was time. If I didn't get back to my regular life, it was going to raise questions that I didn't want to answer. I spent the next hour getting caught up in Mom's journal. Which somehow comforted me.

April 17th

I never thought college exams could be this stressful. Mom and Dad don't understand how much work this is. They expect a lot from me. I swear someday when I have a kid, I'll be more understanding. Professor Hagglen is not curving the final, and I need to get an A in this class. There just aren't enough hours in the day.

On a better note, Jack is amazing. He brings me sweet little treats to the library when I'm studying. I never knew I could love someone this much. He's sweet, and funny, and smart. He totally gets me. Not sure how I got so lucky, but I'm not complaining.

Okay, signing off for now. I have so much homework to do.
Ciao for now, J.E.

I traced my finger over her initials. Jaqueline Edington. Hence my name—Jade Edington Moore. My mom chose it because she and Dad both had names that started with a J. She liked Jade because it's considered the luckiest gemstone and symbolizes compassion and wisdom and a whole lot of other hoopla I always forget. She wanted her maiden name to be my middle name so that I would always have a piece of both of them with me. It didn't hurt that my initials spell out *JEM*, because Mom thought it was a sign that I was a gem. Yes, the spelling is wrong, I've never understood it. But I appreciated the thought that went into naming me.

I didn't feel lucky right now though. I closed her journal and zipped up my duffle bag before heading downstairs.

"Good morning, Jady bug," Dad said from the kitchen sink.

"Hey Dad. You heading to work?"

"Yep. Can I talk to you for a minute before I go?" he asked.

"Sure."

Our kitchen is old and dated, but it felt like home. Spanish tiles and an old wooden farmhouse table filled the space. It always smelled like coffee and garlic to me, but it had become a scent I found comforting.

"It's been two weeks since the fire. You doing okay with everything?"

I'd been commuting from school to home every day. I didn't want to be at school. I didn't like the person I saw when I looked in the mirror right now, and she was easier to look at in my safe cocoon at home where I wasn't reminded of what I'd done. Maybe I just didn't want to face Cruz. Didn't want to tell him the truth. Sure, the fire was scary, terrifying even. But the other thing—I couldn't say it aloud. I didn't want to think about it. I was drowning in shame. *I wasn't that girl.*

The girl who got knocked up at nineteen.

I knew better. I had a lifetime of dreams to chase. My irresponsibility almost changed the lives of three people. Me. Cruz. And the child we'd never know. I fought the tears that threatened and bit down hard on my bottom lip. The metallic taste caused my stomach to turn.

"I'm good."

"You're not good. If you don't want to talk to me, you have to talk to someone. I know that you were trapped in that room and it was terrifying. Hell, I've been there. But you can't just lock yourself away from everyone you love. It's not healthy."

He thought this was about the fire. Everyone did.

"I'm going to talk to Sara today. She's coming over in an hour," I said. It was kind of true, but not in the way he thought.

"Okay." Relief flooded his features. "Good. The firehouse has therapists you could talk to as well."

"No, I think talking to Sara will help."

"Okay. I'm sure Ari and Cruz are missing you being at school," he said.

They thought I was going through some sort of trauma after the fire. Which, in a way, I was. But not the way they believed. I knew I needed to get back to my regular life. But nothing was the same now. I was different. And Cruz was leaving to go on tour. We'd barely spoken since the day we'd met on campus. He was respecting my wishes, I guess. But what if I hadn't lost the baby? I'd be a college dropout with a guy who left to go on tour with his band. How was this even my life? I didn't recognize myself.

"Yeah. After I meet with Sara, I'm going back to the dorms today. There are only a few weeks of school left, and then I'll move into the rental house for the summer." I forced a smile.

I should be excited. I was moving into the cutest house with my best friend. I had an amazing boyfriend. But all I felt was sadness.

Disappointment.

Shame.

He pushed to his feet. "I guess my job here is done then."

He laughed and I made myself do the same. I didn't want him to worry. If he knew I'd gotten pregnant and lost the baby, he'd never look at me the same. Hell, I didn't look at myself the same.

"I'll call you when I get back to the dorms later today," I said and hugged him goodbye.

"YOUR HCG LEVELS SHOULD GO BACK TO NORMAL IN THE NEXT TWO TO four weeks. The truth is, Jade, there's no way to know if the fire caused the miscarriage. With all the cramping you'd had earlier in the day, the process had most likely already started," Dr. Peck said, sitting on her rolling chair, facing me.

Why was I crying? What was wrong with me? I didn't even know this woman. I'd never been such a blubbering mess. My arms wrapped around my knees and I rested my cheek there. I was so exhausted. Dr. Peck was Sara's gynecologist and she convinced me to come talk to her. Sara waited out in the lobby, and she was going to drive me back to school after. She was the only other person aside from me and Dr. Peck who knew what happened the night of the fire. I was thankful I could trust her.

"Yeah. I know. I just didn't know how it happened. We were very careful," I said, but it came out more of a croak.

Dr. Peck slid her chair closer to me and put her hands on my knees. "It happens all the time. You need to forgive yourself. You're human. Now you learn from this and you take more precautions. Let's write you a script for birth control. I do want to see you again in a month, just to check your blood work and follow up, but everything looks good."

"Okay," I said, nodding.

"Is your boyfriend supportive of what you're going through?" she asked as she washed her hands in the sink.

"I haven't told him."

She turned around and studied me. "You need to talk about it. Keeping all this bottled up isn't healthy. You both need to be aware that it can happen, even when you're being safe. This didn't only happen to you, although I'm sure it feels like it did. It happened to him too. Let him be there for you, he deserves to know too," Dr. Peck said before leaving the room.

Sara took me back to the dorms where I found a cupcake and a poster that read *Welcome Home* on my desk from Ari. She wasn't here, so I put all my clean clothes away and tucked my three month sample of birth control in my desk drawer. I thought about what Dr. Peck said. I knew I should tell Cruz. But I knew it would upset him. He'd blame himself, and what was the point of that? He was leaving in a few weeks. Long distance romance didn't work. Everyone knew that. Especially when your boyfriend was the lead singer of a rock band. Tory continued texting me, asking what I was going to do when they left. She hadn't decided if she was going to go with Adam. She obviously didn't know Cruz and I were going through something right now. We hadn't been speaking much, but that didn't change anything for me. I loved him so much—I ached for him. I needed to talk to him. See him. I didn't know how to tell him what happened, but I needed to figure it out.

~~~

I WOKE UP THIS MORNING AND KNEW TODAY I NEEDED TO MAKE A CHANGE. It was time to face this head-on. No more running. Plus, time was not on my side. Cruz would be leaving soon, and I didn't want things to end this way. Hell, I didn't want things to end at all. Being apart from him these last few weeks made it apparent that living without him wasn't an option. If that meant putting my dream on hold for a year to support him, I would do it. I'd never believed in the whole *support your man* philosophy, but I'd also never been in love before now. I wanted to do whatever I needed to make it work.

I pedaled up the walkway to Cruz's front porch. As I leaned my bike against the railing, the front door opened. Dex came bounding outside and my stomach dropped.

"Well, if it isn't Yoko fucking Ono herself," he said, crossing his arms in front of him. His face was pinched and angry.

I rolled my eyes. He was insane and I wasn't going to get into it with him.

"Excuse me." I tried to walk past him, but he blocked me.

"Listen, *you're* actually the one I should be talking to. I can't get through to your boyfriend, and from where I'm standing, you're the fucking reason we're all on edge. You've got this guy so messed up in the head, and he holds all the cards right now. We've worked our asses off and now he doesn't want to leave."

"This has nothing to do with me. I haven't even spoken to him," I said, trying to push my way past him, but he continued to block me.

"It has everything to do with you. How about you stop being a little bitch and make things right. Do you really think I'm going to allow *you* to get in the way of Exiled? Do you have any idea who you're fucking messing with?" He was so close to me, his spit hit me in the face.

All the tension that had been building for weeks rose to the top. I grabbed him by the shirt and pushed him out of my way.

"You know nothing about me. You don't scare me."

I stormed past him and he grabbed my forearm. I slapped his hand away, but he just gripped it harder and yanked me back. Out of my peripheral, there was a blur of movement. Cruz was on top of Dex before I realized what was happening. He had Dex pinned to the grass in the front yard.

"Don't you ever put your fucking hands on her, you piece of shit," Cruz said. Veins bulged on the side of his neck. I'd never seen him so angry or out of control.

"Then pull your head out of your ass. She's not worth it. All this over a little virgin pussy? Do you know how many chicks are out there, you dumb fuck." Dex squirmed beneath my boyfriend as he shouted hateful words, and I fought the urge to kick him. Hard. What the hell was his obsession with my virginity anyway?

"Shut the fuck up, Dex or I swear to God I'll hurt you," Cruz said.

Lennon and Adam pulled up in front of the house and jumped out of the car.

"What's going on?" Adam said, racing toward his bandmates wrestling on the ground.

"He put his hands on Jade." Cruz let Dex go and stood.

"I'm just trying to figure out why we aren't celebrating right now. Why we're not excited that everything we've worked for is finally happening." Dex moved to his feet and brushed off his dark jeans. His hair was disheveled, and he had leaves stuck to the back of his head.

"It's not what *I've* always worked for, you asshole. Maybe it's not what I want to do with my life. It has nothing to do with her, but you're too stupid to see that. You're high ninety percent of your life, and you can't see beyond yourself." Cruz was shouting now, and I moved beside him and put my hand on his arm.

"Maybe you should try it. You might be happier," Dex said. "She might like it too. Maybe it'll loosen her up a bit."

Cruz lunged at Dex, and Lennon and Adam jumped between them.

"Jesus, dude. Shut up and get out of here. You're making things worse. All he said was that he wasn't committing to more than a year. Calm the fuck down," Adam said, pulling Dex away and pushing him toward his car.

"I'm going, I'm going. It's all good. Just want our lead singer to be on board. Catch you later, Yoko," he said to me.

I gave him the finger and glared. Dex didn't scare me. He was the one who was scared.

"Are you okay?" Cruz asked and squeezed my hand. The little bit of contact sent chill bumps down my arms.

"Yes. I'm fine."

"I'm sorry, Jade. All this tour stuff has gone to his head. He's not sleeping and partying way too much. He shouldn't have touched you," Lennon said.

"Jesus. The guy is out of control. I'm calling Luke." Adam pats me on the shoulder with an apologetic smile when he reached for his phone and walked away.

Lennon followed him inside.

"So," Cruz said, his honey-brown gaze locked with mine.

"So." I smiled.

"I didn't know you were coming over. Are you done needing space? Or did you come here to dump me?" he asked, shoving his hands in his pockets.

"I came to talk to you," I said. "Can we go inside?"

CRUZ

I'D NEVER BEEN DUMPED, NOR HAD I EVER HAD MY HEART BROKEN. BUT I had a hunch I was about to experience both. I'd already felt it building. I hadn't seen her in two weeks. Two fucking weeks. We'd left the coffee shop angry, and we'd never talked about it. We texted once a day just to check-in. She needed her space. I'd followed all the rules. She blamed me for the fire, whether she wanted to admit it or not, and she'd never been the same since it happened.

She followed me into my bedroom, and I shut the door. I sat on the bed while she paced from the bathroom to my dresser. All I could think about was the last time we showered together in there. I forced myself to block that thought from my mind.

"What happened with Dex?" I asked, because his arm had been wrapped around hers when I walked outside, and I'd seen red.

"He called me Yoko Ono and said I was ruining Exiled," she said and shook her head.

I couldn't help but laugh. It was the first time I'd laughed in two weeks, and it was with her. More Jade. She lightened me. I was different when I was with her.

"He's such an asshole."

"Yeah. He said you don't want to go on tour because of me."

"That's not completely false. I mean, I don't know what's going on with us, right? So, it's hard to make plans. You asked for space, and I gave it to you. But I don't know where the fuck we stand. And I can't see a future that doesn't have you in it." I couldn't believe the words left my mouth. Sure, I'd thought them, but I'd never said them out loud.

213

She stared at me and her mouth hung open. If she came here to break up with me, I just made things very awkward.

"I can't see a future without you in it, either," she whispered.

I wanted to go to her, pull her onto my lap. But I didn't. My hands fisted at my sides.

"Are you going to tell me what's going on?"

"I am. I don't think you're going to look at me the same though, Cruz." Her voice trembled, and I forced myself to stay exactly where I was.

"There's nothing you can say that will change the way I feel about you. You know that."

"I thought I did." She fidgets with the sleeve of her sweatshirt. "The night of the fire, something else happened."

"Okay."

"Remember I didn't feel well that day? I thought it was nerves about AF Records coming to watch you perform," she said, and tears streamed down her beautiful face.

"Yes. You had a stomachache. I remember. That's why you went to lie down in the back room during the show."

She moved closer to me and searched my gaze, like she was looking for answers to a question she hadn't asked.

"I realized I was late," she said. Her voice was barely audible. But I heard it.

"Late?"

"My period," she said and swiped at the falling tears.

Holy shit.

Holy fucking shit.

I jumped to my feet. "You're pregnant? Jesus Christ, Jade. Why didn't you tell me?" I wrapped my arms around her. I couldn't stop myself. She'd been dealing with this alone. "I'm here. We're in this together. Fuck Exiled. I won't go. I would never let you do this alone. Is that what you thought?"

She pushed back just enough to look up at me. She was shaking her head back and forth frantically, and her jade gaze overflowed. "I had a miscarriage. The night of the fire. I don't know when it happened. Sara noticed the back of my pants were soaked in blood when she found us."

Sobs escaped her, and I was speechless. How the fuck didn't I know? I swiped at the two tears that trailed down my cheeks. The act so foreign that I couldn't remember the last time I cried. Maybe the night my brother almost died? I could count on one hand the number of times I'd cried in my life.

"I'm sorry. I'm so sorry. I wish I'd been there for you. Why didn't you tell me?" I dropped back down to sit on my bed and pulled her onto my lap.

"I don't know," she said through her sobs. "I was ashamed that it happened. I couldn't believe it happened to me. We were safe. I couldn't face you. I didn't want you to look at me differently."

"I could never look at you differently. This is not your fault, baby. It happens. But we're in this together. I could have been there for you. Have you been checked? Is everything okay? Did you see a doctor?" I asked.

She uses her sleeve to catch her tears. "I saw Sara's father that night at the hospital, and I went to a gynecologist yesterday. She said it most likely would have happened regardless of the fire. She said miscarriages are actually very common, and I wasn't very far along."

I studied her face, and all I saw was devastation. "I'm so fucking sorry. How do you feel?"

She shook her head and the tears started to fall again. "That's the worst part. I don't know how I feel. I'm sad that it happened, and disappointed in myself for being in this situation. I should have taken more precautions. But a part of me is relieved that I'm not pregnant, and I'm disgusted with myself for feeling that way. So many people want to have children, and I'm relieved that I don't? I want to be a mom someday, but not right now."

Her entire body shook in my arms and I hugged her tighter. Jade was carrying the weight of the world on her shoulders. "You're being too hard on yourself. It's normal to be relieved, Jade. You're human. You're nineteen years old and you have big dreams to chase first. There's nothing wrong with that."

"Well, I've started birth control. But I need you to know something moving forward, and it's probably something we should have discussed before we took this step in our relationship."

"Okay."

"If I hadn't lost the baby, I would have kept it. Even though the timing would have been wrong, Cruz, I would have kept it. It would have changed our lives drastically. That's why I think I'm relieved I didn't have to make the decision for us," she said, her gaze locking with mine.

"I understand that. If I'm being completely honest with you, I would have wanted to keep it too. I'm in a different position than you though. First off, it's your body, and I respect that. Second, I'm twenty-one and only have a year left of school. Financially we'd be good, but I know that it would interfere with your goals and dreams and that you aren't ready."

Her head fell back, and she smiled. Her gaze glistened. "You're a rock star. What would you do with a baby? What about your dreams?"

I thought about her question before speaking, "I don't know what my dreams are yet. But I know they include you and having a family with you is the first thing in my life that feels right. But not until you're ready. So, if you think telling me that you want to keep the baby if you get pregnant again while using two forms of birth control, is going to scare me off—you missed the fucking mark on that one. I'm not going anywhere."

She sighed. "It feels good to talk about it with you."

"Does your father know?" The thought of her dad knowing made my chest tighten. I liked him. It would suck for him to hate me, and he most likely would.

"Oh my god, no. Cruz, no one knows. I don't want them to. Only Sara." Her face was so serious, and I tucked her hair behind her ears.

"I'm not telling anyone. It's no one's business. But I'm glad you had Sara to help you."

"Me too. I missed you so much," she said, and she hugged me. Her cheek rested against mine, and I made a silent promise to make sure she never hurt like this again.

"I've been fucking miserable without you, *More Jade*," I whispered against her ear.

"I love the song you wrote for me, by the way. We haven't talked about it yet with everything that happened."

"Glad you like it. The label thinks it's our best song," I said, taking her in. I couldn't believe how much I'd missed her. The idea of being away from her again did not sit well.

"It was so beautiful. I want you to sing it to me again. Just you and me."

"I'll sing it to you every day if you want." I leaned forward and covered her mouth with mine. Her fingers tangled in my hair and it felt so fucking good to be with her again.

"So, what happens now? When do you leave?" she asked when she pulled away. Her pouty lips were swollen, her eyes puffy, and her nose was red. Fucking beautiful.

"Not until school is out, so a month. I wanted to talk to you about that. You seemed upset the day we met after the fire. You said I'd never asked you to go with me, but I need you to know why—I don't want to be an asshole. You have a plan. One you've had for a long time. I don't want to take that from you. If you come with me, it would solve all my problems, but I'm thinking of you, not me," I said.

She shifted her legs and straddled me before placing a hand on each side of my face. "I appreciate that. Maybe I can put things off for a year? You only have to commit to a year, right?"

"I hope so. That's the plan. Would you lose your scholarship?"

"Yes, probably." She searched my gaze for answers.

"I would be happy to pay for your schooling, Jade. But you'd have to agree to that."

"No. I couldn't do that. And I've earned my scholarship. I'd hate to give it up. I'll go talk to my counselor this week and find out my options. Maybe they'll hold it for me?"

"No one knows this yet, but I met with Luke today and asked him to inquire about having auditions for a lead singer now. I just want him to ask. The rest of the band would be intact. Maybe the label knows someone. I said I'd still be willing to write all their music, but it would be a way for me to stay here. We'll see what they say."

She moved off my lap and stretched out on the bed, and I rolled on my side to face her.

"People survive the long-distance thing, too. We could make it work if we had to," she said.

"Dex is an asshole and I'm not looking forward to being trapped on a bus with him. My brother's been really shady since the fire. He's always in his room. Never seems to go to class. He gets mad when I ask about it. He'll have his associate's degree before we leave, and I want him to see it through. Just because we're going on tour does not mean we've made it. If we don't keep our shit together, it can all still blow up. I wouldn't mind if it did, but I don't want it to be at Lennon's expense."

"You're such a good brother," she said and moved closer to me.

Her head settled under my chin, and she smelled like sunshine. Her hand found mine and she interlinked our fingers, and we both dozed off. And just like that, everything was better.

"Why are you here?" I said to my father as he flailed around in my living room.

"You know damn well why I'm here. You think you can change the terms of this contract now? You had Luke ask about your replacement in the middle of this deal. So much for your big, fancy education. You're not as smart as you think you are. They aren't happy, Cruz. They want a commitment from you, or they're out. Sorry, boys, but they think he's the talent," my father said.

I hate this man even more than usual right now. I watched my brother crumble, and Adam's gaze didn't leave the ground. Dex jumped to his feet and joined my father in his tirade.

"What the fuck, Cruz. Are you trying to kill this deal for us? I can't even believe Luke agreed to speak with them. We're lucky they aren't walking," Dex said.

"Shut up, Dex. He never wanted this, and you know it." Adam rarely got involved, but his face is red and angry.

"Surprise, surprise. Adam's on team Cruz. Shocker. If this deal dies, it's on him." Dex was in Adam's face now, and I jumped between them.

"Calm the fuck down. I just inquired. I didn't say I'd walk. I offered to write the music which we all know is the only thing I'm decent at. Anyone could replace me as lead singer, and you know it," I said.

"They don't agree. They said if you walk, they walk," my dad said. He's so smug and happy to shatter everyone's hopes today. Force me to do something I didn't want to do and make the other guys feel unimportant.

"Jesus, Cruz. This is all for some girl-next-door fucked-up fantasy. Cut this chick loose, man. I'm over it." Dex stared at me and it took all the self-control I had not to drop his ass. Again.

"Dude, I've warned you to stop talking about her," I said as the door flew open.

Luke walked in looking like a disheveled mess. He was always so put together and polished that it surprised me to see him like this. His sandy brown hair was sticking up, like he'd been tugging at it for hours. His T-shirt was dirty and untucked, and he was wearing sweatpants. I'd never seen Luke in anything other than cargo pants and a collared shirt. He was a preppy son of a bitch, but not today.

"Okay. We're good as long as you agree to stay, Cruz. They are pulling the offer if you walk. I assured them you were in, so tell me I didn't just put my reputation on the line for nothing," Luke said.

"Oh, you're not walking, because if you do, I swear on everything I have, I will disown you. I'll freeze your trust so fast your head will spin. You won't be able to pay for school on your own, nor will you be able to afford to buy your girlfriend a house to live in. Don't think I don't hear about your large purchases, son. You don't want to fuck with me. You can't make it on your own," my father said.

His veins were bulging on the side of his neck and his face was dark red. He'd never threatened my trust fund before. I didn't think he had the power to freeze it, but I didn't have a fucking clue. He most likely set everything up to work in his favor, so maybe he was right. I didn't know if I cared anymore. Being free of this man would be worth it.

"Steven, you need to relax. Give the kid a chance to answer before you threaten him," Luke said, and he gave me an apologetic shrug.

"You'd never risk everyone knowing you disowned me. It wouldn't look good on you, old man. But I'll keep you posted."

I walked out of the room and down the hall, slamming my door and dropping on my bed. Fuck my life. How did I get here? Trapped into doing something I didn't want to do when I finally had a reason to stay.

There's a quiet knock and my door creaked open. My brother was hesitant and nervous. He knew better than to push me right now. He shut the door, but he didn't attempt to sit.

"If you want to walk, I'll understand. I'm sorry you feel all this pressure because of me."

I sat up and ran a hand over my face. "You know, we could just stay a local band and finish school. Have a little normalcy in our lives."

"It's not an option for me," Lennon said, and he met my gaze and I knew he was going to drop a bomb.

"Why is that?"

"I failed out of school a few weeks ago. I didn't know how to tell you," he said, covering his eyes with his hand.

"Jesus, dude. That was your out. You would have had your associate's degree next month. It was a step in the right direction."

"Maybe for you, Cruz. Not for me."

"Fuck." It's all I could say. He'd taken everything else off the table. Exiled was literally all he had. All he wanted.

"We're so close. I really think once we start touring and we grow in popularity, you will be able to step away. Maybe you just give it a year? I'll help you get out," he said.

He wouldn't. Lennon had never been someone I could depend on. It was always my job to take care of him, and maybe it would be that way forever. But I needed him to grow up. Man the fuck up. Take care of himself.

"I'm not going to walk if they're going to terminate the deal."

Luke and Adam knocked on the door before barging in. They informed us that my dad and Dex both left. Lennon told them that I agreed to commit to one year. My chest tightened. I knew I was making a deal with the devil. The devil being my father.

"Thank you, Cruz. I will do everything in my power to help find a replacement for you in a year. Let's just not talk about it with the guys at AF Records right now. We can work behind the scenes," Luke said.

"Did you tell them I need my own room on the bus because I'm going to finish my degree online? I'll be studying while these assholes are getting drunk. I can still graduate on time. And did you talk to them about October thirty-first?"

"I did. It's been added to your contract. No shows will take place on Halloween."

Lennon looked over at me and nodded. He and Adam were the only ones that knew it was the day Jade's mom died. I may not be able to control where I lived for the next twelve months, but I could make sure I was there for her on the anniversary. I'll be there for her on the day that she needs me most, regardless of what she decides to do. My choice was now out of my hands.

"Okay. Thanks for trying," I said, reaching for my backpack. Regardless of the shit show that was my life—I had finals to study for. And most importantly, my hot study partner was waiting for me.

JADE

"I'M GLAD WE CAME TO THE BEACH. IT ALWAYS CALMS ME DOWN BEFORE exams," I said, lying on my stomach and looking up at Cruz.

He was sitting up, smoking a cigarette. He hadn't smoked in a while, but his nerves were rattled since his visit from his father today. I wasn't surprised the label wouldn't let him walk. We both knew it was a long shot. Cruz was way more talented than he gave himself credit for, and AF Records wasn't signing anyone unless he was on board. My concern was that they would never let him go. Why would they be okay with him leaving in a year?

"There's something I need to tell you," Cruz said.

"Is it bad?" I sat up on the purple Northwestern blanket beneath us and crossed my legs.

There was a light breeze coming off the water, and I was thankful for the warm spring weather.

"It's not bad, but I wasn't completely honest with you about something." He snubbed out his cigarette and dropped the butt in his empty water bottle.

"What?"

"The house you and Ariana are moving into on Grove Street? It doesn't belong to a friend of mine. I bought it a few months ago," he said.

He was watching me. Assessing my reaction. The old me would be more upset. But after all we'd been through these last few weeks with the fire and the miscarriage, nothing seemed all that tragic anymore. The one thing that came from all the bad—Cruz and I were more solid than ever. And I wanted to be with him even if it meant making sacrifices.

"Why didn't you tell me?"

"Same reason you don't tell me shit. I didn't want to upset you," he said, reaching for my hand.

"So why now?"

"Because my asshole father knows, and I don't want him to throw it in your face." He kissed my hand and pulled me onto his lap.

I understood what my father meant about Mom being his other half now. Cruz was mine. I couldn't imagine my life without him. I loved him so much it scared me sometimes.

"Well, it certainly makes sense why the rent is so cheap," I said with a laugh. "So, what happens to the rental house if I go on tour with you for the year?"

He nuzzled my neck. We hadn't had sex since I told him about the miscarriage, and I was glad because I wasn't ready. Yes, I was taking birth control, but emotionally I just hadn't been in a hurry. And Cruz would never push me. We were both content just sleeping together, kissing and cuddling. To say we had a lot on our minds was an understatement, and just being with him made everything easier.

"Nothing. It's yours. I want you to have a place regardless of what you decide. If you come on tour and you hate it, you'll always have a place here that's yours. But I don't want to make you feel pressured. We can make this work, you know. The long-distance thing. We have access to a plane, and you can fly out to wherever I am as often as you want."

"You don't think I should go with you?"

"Of course, I want you to come with me. But you'd be giving up a lot for me. What if it derails your path and you resent me later?"

"Maybe you're my path?" I said and his lips turned up on the sides.

"You didn't tell me what your counselor said today. Didn't you meet with her this morning?" he asked.

I didn't bring it up because I knew he wouldn't like it. "Yeah. It's what we thought. I'll lose my scholarship if I leave. I can reapply, but she said it would be unlikely. She said I could take some courses online while we were traveling, but with my major, it would be tricky because there are so many labs. She said med schools won't be impressed if my science courses are taken online, so I would need to postpone those until I returned."

"Fuck. You know I'd stay for you if I could. Honestly, I don't give a fuck about my dad's threats. He'd get over it, or he wouldn't—I'd survive either way. But Lennon. I feel like he'll spiral if I don't go. If this all dies right now. It sucks choosing between my brother and my girlfriend. The truth is—I'd choose you, Jade. But the reality is that you will survive for a year without me, and Lennon might not. If I walked away right now, and the deal fell through, I think he'd shut down," Cruz says. His hair blew in the wind and I ran my fingers over the scruff on his jaw.

"You shouldn't have to choose. I don't feel like you're choosing anyone over me. You're just doing what you have to right now. That's why I feel like I should go. Everything in my life will still be there when I get back."

The more I thought about it, the more I leaned toward following my heart. Cruz wasn't leaving me to chase his dream—he was leaving me because he was afraid of what would happen to Lennon if he didn't go. He didn't have the option of chasing his own dream, because he'd been living someone else's for so long.

"You still need to talk to your dad, and I don't think he will support it. So, let's just focus on finals, and get you moved into the new house this weekend. You're coming with me for the summer regardless, so there's no rush to make a decision."

Finals. The bane of my existence. I couldn't believe I was almost done with my freshman year. In some ways, it felt like years had passed since I moved away from Bucktown and met Cruz. In other ways, it felt like just yesterday I moved into my dorm room and met him. So much had changed. But the good news—I finished my first year exactly how I'd hoped. My grades were great, I'd made new friends, and I'd found the love of my life. And yeah, there had been some bad times. But when the smoke cleared, Cruz and I were still standing. And that's what mattered most to me now.

◠℞◞

"How much is this place?" my dad asked as he carried in the laundry baskets of clothing. The man had an actual issue with buying boxes.

"Five hundred a month," I say. Cruz asked me not to tell my dad he bought the place unless he specifically asked who owned it, because he didn't want it to make Dad uncomfortable.

"How is that possible?" He stood in the living room and took in the amazing space.

Natural light poured in through the plantation shutters on the windows. It wasn't large, but it was quaint. The original wood floors had been refurbished, and the kitchen was white and bright. It wasn't something a college kid typically lived in. Ari and I were expecting a dingy apartment, so we were thrilled.

"The guy wanted to rent it to two brainy college girls who wouldn't throw parties, so we were in luck," Ariana said with a chuckle. She knew Cruz owned the place, but she'd been sworn to secrecy.

Jace carried in a huge stack of her clothes on hangers and she guided him to her room.

"It's amazing, Jady bug. And it came furnished? This stuff is nicer than our furniture at home," Dad said.

I dropped down on the couch and decided to broach the subject with him.

"So, I told you Cruz is going on tour, right? He tried to get out of it, but they won't sign the rest of the band if he walks."

Dad sat down beside me. "He's in a tough situation. He thinks he can get out in a year? Will he finish his courses while he's on the road?"

"Yes. There's so much you can do online now, so he can still graduate on time," I said, planting the seed of positivity.

"Oh yeah? That's good."

"So, he asked me to go on tour with him this summer. I wanted to see what your thoughts were."

He sat a little straighter. "I figured this was coming. Well, I think it's been a tough year and you've worked hard. I'm not against you having some fun, but you had plans this summer to work and take classes too."

"I know. I've already signed up for my summer session. I'm going to take two courses online, and Cruz said I could do some work for the band. They need people to manage their merchandising and Tory's going to do it too."

"Who the hell is Tory?" Dad rubbed his temples and I knew this was a lot for him to digest. We'd never not lived in the same city at the same time.

"Oh, sorry. She's Adam's girlfriend."

"I just don't know how I feel about you living in a tour bus with a bunch of guys," he said, and his dark gaze landed on mine.

"Cruz has his own room on the bus, and I'll stay in there."

He pushed to his feet. "Not helping, Jade. That is an image I don't need."

"Oh, sorry. I just meant I'd have a space to go to get away from everyone. Think of the experience. I'd be traveling all over the U.S. You know that's something I've always wanted to do. It's just happening sooner than I planned."

He studied me, pushing his hands in his pockets. "Are we talking about a summer here? Why do I feel like there's more to this?"

"Well, Cruz has to go for a year. I'm thinking about going with him and taking a leave from school for a year," I whispered.

My dad was not a hothead. He'd always been calm in stressful situations, but I could tell he was struggling with this. He moved to sit beside me again.

"That's a lot to sacrifice, Jade. You'd probably lose your scholarship, and you'd be putting your education on hold."

"I would. I've looked into it. I could reapply, but it's unlikely I'd get it back. But Dad, sometimes life happens, and you need to follow your gut, right? My path will just change a little, but I will still get there. I know I will," I said.

"Wow. You've already looked into this? What does Cruz say?" He watched me intently now.

"He thinks I should go for the summer and come back to school. He's afraid I'll resent him later. He said we could do the long-distance thing and he isn't worried about us making it work."

"Then what's the problem. Why make a sacrifice if you don't have to? I think he's right."

"Because I don't want to be away from him. He needs someone to support him. He's never had that, Dad. His parents have never been there for him, and he's always taking care of everyone. I want to be there for him," I said, and tears streamed down my face.

"God, you remind me so much of your mother sometimes. She was a stubborn pain in the ass too, most of the time." He took his thumbs and swiped beneath my eyes. "No more tears. You're a smart girl and I trust you, always have. But really think about this, Jade. This is real life and these decisions will affect you for the rest of your life."

"I promise you, I will. Nothing's set in stone yet," I said, but I'd already made up my mind.

I was going with him.

～ℛ～

Cruz stopped by the new house after his final.

"Wow. The place looks great. Did your dad leave already?" he asked.

"Yep. There wasn't all that much to move. I talked to him about taking the year off from school."

He looked up at me, and I saw the panic in his honey-brown gaze. He didn't want my father to dislike him, and I understood that. But my dad wasn't like that. He wouldn't hold my decisions against Cruz.

"What did he say? Is he pissed?"

"Surprisingly, no. He listened. He thinks there's still a lot to think about. He supports me going for the summer, but he wants me to work, because that was the plan. I promised I'd take my two summer courses online while we travel."

"You know you don't have to work. I can happily pay your bills," he said, wrapping his arms around my middle.

"You're missing the point. It's about being responsible." I laughed and turned around to face him. He flinches and I pulled back. "What's wrong?"

"Nothing. I have a surprise for you." He tugged his T-shirt over his head.

There was a bandage over the left side of his chest. "What happened?"

He lifted the tape to show me a new tattoo beneath the bandage. It was a shimmery jade color and the script read: *More Jade.*

"Now you'll always be with me, whether we are together or apart."

I couldn't believe he'd permanently written my name on his body. My heart swelled.

"It's beautiful."

"You like it?" he asked.

"I love it. But we're not going to be apart because I'm coming with you. I just have to meet with Holly, my counselor, to figure out the new plan. So, it might take me four or five years, and I might have to take out student loans if they don't choose to renew my scholarship, but none of that is the end of the world."

"It's not the money I'm worried about. Hell, I'd pay for your schooling now. My dad won't fight that. But I don't like you changing your life for me. I don't want to derail you." He pulled me close and whispered against my ear.

"You derailed me the day we met," I said with a chuckle before he captured my mouth with his.

I reached for his hand and started walking backward while he continued to kiss me. He laughed against my mouth.

"Where are you taking me?"

"You haven't seen my room yet," I said, and my voice was all tease.

My legs hit the back of the bed and I fell on the mattress, pulling him on top of me. He braced himself so he didn't crush me beneath him.

"We don't need to rush things. I know you've been through a lot," he said, pushing the hair back from my face.

"No more waiting. I'm all in." I pulled him back down and captured his mouth.

No more holding back.

JADE

FINALS WERE BEHIND ME AND I HAD OFFICIALLY COMPLETED MY FRESH-man year. Dad and I stayed up talking until two o'clock in the morning, and I needed to get some sleep. He didn't pressure me about my decision, and I appreciated it. I was really doing this. I was leaving school to go on tour with my rock star boyfriend. I was anxious to get everything organized with Holly in the morning. These were the times I missed my mom most. With Dad, I just felt like I needed to convince him I was doing the right thing. I imagined my mom would be the one convincing me what she thought I should do. But being with Cruz was the right thing to do for me.

I packed up a few of Mom's journals and slipped the one I was currently reading in my purse. This was the last night I'd spend in my childhood bed for several months. I reached for my phone before slipping into bed. There was a text from Cruz.

Cruz ~ Miss you, More Jade. I can't believe we're leaving in the morning. So, fucking glad you will be by my side.

Me ~ Miss you too. Nowhere else I'd rather be. I'll see you right after my meeting with Holly. Love you.

He didn't reply. He was probably already asleep. I tucked into bed and pulled the covers up to my chin, closed my eyes and drifted away.

I woke up feeling off. *Really off.* I dreamed of my mother last night. This had only happened one other time in my life when I'd been really sick and spent a few days in the hospital when I was younger. She'd come to me one night and stopped my shivering. She'd hugged me and held me tight. I could still see her vividly from that night. I always figured it was a hallucination from the high fever I had at the time. But last night—she was there. She wore the same white gown she'd been in last time. She kept saying the same thing over and over. *Don't lose yourself.*

Maybe my subconscious was struggling with my decision. I wasn't following the rule book according to Jade like I always had before. I flipped through my phone to check my emails. There was an email from Professor Peters.

Dear Jade,

I wanted to drop you a note to let you know you received the highest score in the class on your final. It was a near-perfect score, and I am impressed with your hard work and dedication this semester. You are an extremely talented student and it has been my pleasure teaching you this year. I look forward to seeing what you achieve in the future.

Best, Robert Peters

I read the email twice and my heart squeezed with pride. I'd studied so much for that final and I was thrilled that I did so well. The doorbell rang and Dad called me from downstairs.

"Sam's here," he said.

"Be right down." I closed my laptop and tossed it in my backpack before bounding down the stairs.

Sam wanted to say goodbye, so he agreed to drop me off at my counselor's office. Cruz had my other two suitcases already loaded on the tour bus.

"Are you ready, rock star?" Sam asked.

He didn't agree with my decision to leave school, but he understood why I wanted to go. He liked Cruz. They'd actually become friends. But Sam's instinct would always be to look out for me, and I understood that. But who was looking out for Cruz?

Sara had spent the night, and she and Dad were officially dating. I was so happy they were together because it made leaving a whole lot easier.

"I'm ready. We aren't saying goodbye, Daddy-O. I told you I'll be back at the end of summer for a visit," I said, pushing up on my tiptoes and kissing his cheek.

"Yep. And if you need me, I can come to you." His voice cracked, and a piece of my heart splintered at his words. Sara rubbed his back and gave me a sad smile.

"You're going to get on a plane and come see me?" I teased. I didn't want this to get heavy.

"If you need me, yes, I'll get on a plane."

Sam and I exchanged a look because Dad didn't fly. I threw my arms around him. Everything I didn't want to happen was happening now. He hugged me so tight that tears pricked my eyes. I'd never been far from him, and I couldn't hold back the emotions and a sob escaped as the floodgates opened. Tears streamed down my face.

"I love you, Dad."

"Love you too, Jady bug. Be safe. Don't get lost out there," he said with a chuckle, an attempt to lighten the situation. Why was everyone talking about me getting lost? I'd be on a gigantic bus with the love of my life.

"I promise I won't."

I turned and hugged Sara. "I love you, Sara."

"Love you more, sweetie. I'm going to miss you so much."

"Call me tonight and let me know where you are," Dad said.

Sam grabbed my duffle and led me out the door. We remained silent until we were on the freeway.

"You okay?" he asked.

"Yep. I'm good. Just hate saying goodbye to him."

"You sure that's it? You aren't having second thoughts?"

I rolled my eyes. "Nope. But thanks for the vote of confidence."

"I'm going to miss you, J-bird."

I'd never been far from Sam either. But we were growing up. There were things Sam didn't know about me now. Things I'd only shared with Cruz.

"I'm going to miss you too."

We pulled in front of the admissions building and I gathered my things.

"No weepy goodbyes, okay?" I said.

"Nope. Text me tonight from the road."

I leaned over and hugged him goodbye. "Love you."

"Love you, too," he said.

I jumped out of the truck and I didn't look back. No more looking back. Only forward. I was ready for this new adventure. I walked into the quiet building. Everyone was out for summer break, and the place was pretty desolate.

"Hi. I'm Jade Moore. I'm here to see Holly Green."

"Oh yes. She just phoned me and asked me to apologize. She's caught in a bit of good ol' Chicago traffic, and she'll be here in ten minutes. You can take a seat over here if you'd like," she said, motioning to the chairs in the waiting area.

"No problem."

I sent Cruz a quick text to let him know I'd be a few minutes late and I pulled out Mom's journal. I loved reading her daily entries more than ever now. Her life had gotten more exciting since she entered college, and in a way, I was sharing in her journey too. She was starting her first summer break after her freshman year in college as well. But I guessed she wasn't going on tour with a rock band.

May 9th

Dear Journal,

What a day it's been. I got all the information for my semester abroad in Australia. I've dreamed of this my entire life and it's finally happening. Mom and Dad wouldn't let me go my first year in college, but now they are on board. What I didn't expect was to be fighting with my boyfriend all week. Jack and I never fight. Well, never say never. He doesn't want me to go. And guess what? I thought about not going because I love him.

God, I love him so much it's silly, really. But he's a stubborn ass. I understand that being apart will be hard, but if we love each other, what's the problem? I'm planning on growing old with this man. Why can't I pursue the things I've always dreamed of and love him at the same time? I can. And if he can't, then maybe we weren't meant to be together.

I've struggled with my choice this week, and I'm hoping I didn't make a mistake because Mom and Dad just paid the deposit. I'm young and there's so much I want to do. I don't want to be forty and resenting him because I gave things up when I shouldn't have. I don't want to be old before I have to be. And right now, I'm young and curious and ready for some adventure. I want to see how other cultures live. I want to see what the rest of the world looks like. I want to pursue my passions. And I want to come home to the boy I love, and I hope he's waiting for me. It's not a long time, and in the big picture of life, this will be a little piece of our time together. He's pursuing his dreams to become a fireman, and I need to pursue mine.

I read Jack one of my favorite sayings this morning: The most painful thing is losing yourself in the process of loving someone too much. It was written by the brilliant Ernest Hemingway.

I think he gets it. I love Jack Moore more than I ever thought possible. I'll come back to him and we'll be together. But I love me too. And I'm going to spread my wings and go to Australia like I always planned. Hopefully Jack will support me. I think he will. We don't have to want the same things right now, or experience everything together—all we have to do is love one another enough and trust in that. Hopefully that's enough for him too.

Ciao for now,
J.E.

I stare at the journal entry for a minute before slipping the book back in my bag. I knew my mom had studied abroad. I had no idea it had been an issue for them. I think about how difficult it must have been to make that choice. I can't believe Dad gave her a hard time. I'm grateful Cruz supports my dream. Heck, I think it's part of what drew him to me. That determined side of myself. The part of me that wants to change the world any way I can. Save someone else from the pain of losing their loved ones. Make a difference as a physician.

"Jade, I'm so sorry. Come in," Holly said as she barreled through the door. Literally. Her briefcase opened and papers spilled out on the floor. She reached for them and tipped her coffee cup and the lid fell off, allowing the liquid to pour on the floor. The woman was a flustered mess.

"It's no problem at all," I said, bending down to help her gather her papers.

I replay the words from my dream last night as I pushed to my feet. *Don't lose yourself.* Have I done that? Did all the stress from the fire and the miscarriage cause me to lose sight of my own dreams? I pushed the thought away and followed Holly into her office.

"Okay, I have all your paperwork and I just want to go over all of your options one last time, but I know you have your mind made up," she said, laying out several papers in front of me.

My mind raced. I thought of Professor Peter's email, and I was overcome with pride. I listened as Holly went over all the pros and cons to taking a year off. There are more cons than pros because loving Cruz wasn't something she counted as a pro. But it was the most important reason for me. But I listened as she laid my future out before me.

I took an Uber to meet Cruz at the tour bus, feeling terrible for holding them up. He met me outside and reached for my duffle.

"Everything go okay?"

"Yep. All done. Wow, look at this thing," I said, taking in the enormous monstrosity parked in front of us.

"It's our new home for the next twelve months, baby. Have I told you how much I love you yet today?" He took my hand and led me inside.

Tory hurried over and hugged me. "Can you believe we're doing this? You and me on the road with our rock star boyfriends."

The day had been a whirlwind and it wasn't even lunchtime yet. The bus was enormous and spacious, and the guys were spread all around. Dark wood flooring and black leather couches ran along both sides of the space. Lennon and Adam were playing a video game on a big screen television and they both waved to me. Tory settled back on the couch beside her boyfriend. Dex looked up from his laptop and tugged out his earbuds.

"I can't believe you went through with it, Princess," Dex said.

I didn't react to him. At least he wasn't calling me Yoko Ono anymore, but he still found a way to insult me with his sarcasm.

"Jesus dude, really? Is this how it's going to be?" Cruz said.

"Relax. It was a joke. Lighten the fuck up."

"Hey Jade, glad you're coming along with us," Luke said. He was a nice guy and I appreciated that he always seemed to be looking out for my boyfriend.

"Me too."

Cruz tugged me down the hallway toward the bedroom and my phone rang. I saw Holly's number and my stomach twisted. I was exhausted from our meeting, and I couldn't imagine what else she would possibly need to tell me. It was done. I'd made my decision.

"It's Holly, my counselor, I better get it," I said, and Cruz dropped to sit on the large bed. He tossed my duffle bag on the window seat and patted the spot beside him for me to sit.

The bus started to move, and I answered the call, holding the phone to my ear.

"Hey, Holly," I said, sitting down on the bed.

"Hi, there. I just wanted to let you know I filed all the papers, and everything is done."

I turned my back to my boyfriend and let out a long breath. "Okay. Thank you for everything. I appreciate your help."

"Of course. It's my job. I've actually really enjoyed working with you. You had an incredible first year and I'm really glad you changed your mind about next year, Jade. I submitted all of your courses and it looks like if you complete the two summer school classes online, you'll remain on track to graduate in three years. Your scholarship is intact, and I look forward to seeing you in the fall. Have a nice summer and I'll see you in a few weeks."

"Okay. Thank you." A deep lump formed in my throat as I disconnected the call.

Cruz wrapped his arms around me, and the bus jolted a little as it pulled out of the parking lot.

"I'm so glad you're here with me," he said, and his lips grazed my ear. Chill bumps covered my arms at his nearness, and I squeezed my eyes closed.

"Me too. But there's something I need to tell you."

I took a deep breath as the bus merged onto the freeway.

What I was going to tell him would change everything.

I just hoped he loved me as much as I loved him—because it was the only way we were going to get through this next year.

THE END

A Love You More Rock Star Romance Series...

*When good goes bad in this star-crossed lovers trilogy,
you'll want to be there every step of the way.*

BOOK 2
MORE OF YOU

*Bereft, betrayed, and broken, the healing begins in the last
installment of Laura Pavlov's star-crossed lovers trilogy.*

BOOK 3
MORE OF US

Book 2:

More of You

Chapter One

JADE

MUSIC BOOMED BEHIND THE STAGE WHERE I STOOD. THE WALLS VIBRATED from the loud cheers coming from the audience. It was still hard to wrap my head around—how quickly Exiled's fanbase had grown. "*More of Me*," the song Cruz wrote, had skyrocketed to number one on multiple charts. Their tour sold out within an hour of tickets going on sale, and we'd spent the summer traveling across the U.S. from venue to venue. I kept a journal of our travels, and Cruz and I tried to do one touristy thing in each new location we visited depending on time. He always made a point to find a library in each city for me to see.

The music for "*More of Me*" started to play, and my stomach dipped. It always did when he performed my song. Cruz liked me to sit on the side of the stage where he could see me during his shows, so I sat in a chair and wrote in my journal as I listened.

Things had changed dramatically in the last two weeks, and the tension was palpable when the band wasn't on stage. They did their best to hide the turmoil when they performed, but I had a front row seat to what was going on. Tory used to sit with me during the shows, and I missed my partner in crime. Now I sat solo. She'd been gone for more than a week, and nothing was the same. Adam was miserable, even if he was too stubborn to admit it. The day she'd left was horrible. Adam told her to leave and she'd been inconsolable. We'd spent two nights at a hotel in Nashville, and Tory had stayed up late drinking with a few friends from high school who attended college not far from the venue. Cruz and I usually went to our room after the shows. Adam had been exhausted and turned in before Tory was ready to say goodnight to her friends. He woke up early in the morning and realized she hadn't come to bed. He found her in Dex's room with all her friends and a pile of white powder on the table, and apparently some on her face—and he'd lost it. Tory had never done drugs in front of me. I think she had too much to drink and got caught up in the moment. But Adam was not okay with it. He and Dex didn't get along before this happened, so things had gone from bad to worse.

The roar of the crowd pulled me from my thoughts, and I realized the music had stopped. I looked out onto the stage to see Cruz smiling at me. He motioned for me to come out there, and panic surged through my veins.

"Come on, baby. They want me to sing to you," he said, his voice sexy and raspy through the microphone.

I shook my head. My legs froze in place. The thought of going out there in front of all those people terrified me. The lights were flashing, creating all sorts of designs in my peripheral vision, and I heard my boyfriend say something to his fans about giving him a minute. There was laughter and whistling as he jogged toward me. He pulled his headset off and a wide grin spread across his beautiful face.

"Everyone wants *more Jade*," he said, melting my heart just like he always did.

I laughed. He was ridiculous but in the best way. Cruz Winslow made me feel like the most important person on the planet every time he looked at me. And it would all come to an end soon. This was the last show I'd be at for a while, as I was going back to school in a week.

"What are you doing? I can't go out there. I like watching you from here."

"Do you trust me?" he asked, his head cocked to the side, and his honey-brown gaze locked with mine.

"Always."

"Come on." He took my hand and led me onto the stage. I wasn't sure how my legs were moving, but they were.

I bit down hard on my bottom lip and used my free hand to grip the back of his T-shirt, tucking myself behind him. The cheers from the audience were deafening and I glanced over at Lennon. His gaze locked with mine and he winked. He really was a different person on stage. It's where he came alive. I'd grown so close to him, and he'd become more like a brother to me over the last few months.

"My girl's a little shy, but I told her you wanted a little more Jade, am I right?" he said, and the crowd went crazy in response.

"Yeah, trust me. I fucking get it. I can't get enough myself." He teased his fans, and the cheers and screams only grew louder. Luke came out of nowhere with a stool and Cruz helped me to sit down. I covered my face with my hands and tried to remain seated, but I wanted to sprint off the stage.

The music started again, just as it had when I'd been in my little cocoon just moments ago when he'd halted the show to come and get me. The audience quieted, and my boyfriend started to sing. He looked only at me, and for a moment, I forgot where I was. He sang to me often in the quiet confines of his room, and for the next few minutes, that's exactly where I convinced myself I was. Just he and I. He moved closer, stepping between my legs, and his hand caressed the back of my neck while he sang the last part of the song to me.

And she asks me…
Why would you want more of me?
She doesn't know just what I see.
Beautiful girl with eyes of jade.
Shines so bright can't find the shade.
Heart so pure even in her pain.
In the drought she is the rain.

When he finished, his eyes remained locked with mine. I wrapped my arms around his neck and settled my head against his chest, hugging him tightly. He pulled me from the chair and my legs came around his waist, just like they always did. We just didn't usually have an audience whistling and screaming when we did so. He carried me back to my hideaway beside the stage and set me down on the stool.

"You okay?" he whispered against my ear.

I nodded and pushed up to kiss him before he ran back on stage. Cruz had come into his own these last few months. As much as he was convinced this wasn't his passion, he was a natural. He'd written so many new songs as we traveled on the bus, and whether he believed it or not, he was an amazing singer and songwriter. We spent as much time together as possible, as we both knew things were going to change when I went back to school.

Telling Cruz that I'd chosen to return to Northwestern in the fall was one of the hardest things I'd ever done. I'd chosen myself over him. And it certainly wasn't because I loved myself more than I loved him. I didn't. I loved him more than anything. More than I'd ever known possible. But I knew I was doing the right thing, even if my heart didn't agree. I needed to stay true to myself for *us*. For our future. But the thought of not seeing him every day—it did something to me.

He hadn't been fazed when I told him. He said he thought I was doing the right thing, and we'd make the most of the time we had together. He was hoping to walk away from Exiled next year and he'd move back to Chicago until I finished school. I didn't know how it would all work, and I wondered if him leaving the band would be more challenging than he thought. Exiled was an international sensation now, and AF Records was scheduling a worldwide tour for them. How would they just suddenly replace Cruz as the lead singer without it being a problem? He didn't seem worried, so I tried to do the same.

I'd been home to visit Dad twice. I talked to him, Sam, and Ari every single day. They loved seeing photos of our travels, and I was enjoying this time away from the regular stresses in life. Luke hired me to handle all the social media for the band this summer, as it was an actual position they needed, and it allowed me to fulfill my promise to my father to work. Cruz didn't want me handling the merchandise during the shows, because he didn't think it was safe. He was as overprotective as my dad.

I pushed to my feet when they ran off the stage. It would only be for a few minutes and they'd go back out and perform another song or two. Dex walked by, giving me one of his creepy smiles. He was a predator. In every sense of the word. He exploited others for his own benefit. He knew exactly what he was doing when he came between Tory and Adam. It was premeditated and malicious. He hated that I didn't give him an opening to mess with me and Cruz. He was the worst kind of narcissist, and his sudden taste of success and fame didn't help the situation. Adam ruffled the top of my head as he moved past me, and Lennon paused and kissed me on the cheek.

"Good job out there tonight, girl. You did it," he said with a laugh.

"I didn't have much of a choice," I teased.

"Move," Cruz snarled at his brother before he pushed me up against the wall and kissed me.

Lennon chuckled as he walked away, and my hands tangled in my boyfriend's hair.

"Hey," I said, trying to catch my breath when he pulled away.

"You mad at me for making you go out there?" he asked, nipping at my ear.

"No. You're impossible to be mad at."

"Love you," he said, leaning down to kiss me one more time before he ran back out on stage.

I stood and watched Cruz sing the last song in his dark skinny jeans, a ripped tee, and combat boots. His hair was a disheveled mess, and he was the most beautiful boy I'd ever seen. His chiseled jaw and full lips made him all the more appealing. But it was his honey-brown eyes that always did me in. He glanced over his shoulder and I gave him a small wave. He chuckled as he sang because, for some reason, Cruz seemed to think I was funny even when I wasn't trying to be.

"Hey," Luke said, coming up behind me.

"Hi. Great show tonight." I turned to face him. I liked Luke. He was more than just a manager, and he always looked out for Cruz, which I appreciated.

"Yeah, they killed it. You gonna miss all this?" he asked.

"I am. I wish I didn't have to leave."

"Nah, you'll be fine. You're doing the right thing, Jade."

"You think so?" I asked as cheers and screams filled the space around us. The band was wrapping things up.

"I do. You two will be fine. I took care of that little favor you asked me for, and he's here. He set up in one of the spare rooms in back. He's supposed to be the best in town, and I checked his references and saw his work. Seems like a talented dude. But when Cruz loses his shit, don't blame me," Luke said with a laugh.

I leaned forward and hugged him. "I won't, I promise. Thanks for doing this. I'll meet him after the show."

"Anything for you," Luke said as Dex came running toward him and picked their manager up off his feet.

"Put me down, asshole." Luke pushed back and almost fell on his way down.

"I'd love to pick you up, Princess, but I think it would piss off your broody ass boyfriend. What do you think?" Dex invaded my space.

"If you touch me, you'll be very sorry," I said, glaring at him.

"Oh yeah. What are you going to do to me, Jade? You like it rough, huh?"

I stomped my foot hard on the top of his and he stepped back with a laugh.

Cruz walked up and looked between us. "What's going on? Is he bothering you?"

"So protective. How are you going to watch her when she's gone?" Dex's smile resembled the Joker's. It made the hair on the back of my neck stand up.

"Shut the fuck up," Cruz said, taking my hand and leading me down the hall.

"Just ignore him. He wants to get a rise out of you," I said.

"He's such an asshole. I don't like him messing with you."

"I can handle myself. Dex doesn't scare me," I said.

He stopped in the back room and grabbed two water bottles. The guys no longer chugged a celebratory beer after shows because Adam wasn't speaking to Dex. Cruz didn't mind because he'd cut way back this summer. I think he learned that he couldn't beat me at a single card game when he was drunk, but he claimed it was because he wanted to set a good example for his brother. I loved how much he cared for Lennon.

"You shouldn't have to handle anything when it comes to Dex. I swear to Christ I'm going to kick that kid's ass someday. And I'm going to enjoy the hell out of it."

I laughed. "Hey, I have a little surprise for you. Will you come with me?"

"*More Jade*, I'd go anywhere with you. You need a little something right now?" He pushed me up against the wall and kissed me hard.

"Oh my god, no." It was difficult not to laugh through my words as I forced him to look at me. "I don't need a little *something*, I get plenty of that."

"Then where are you taking me?" he asked.

I took his hand and led him into the room at the end of the hall. "I have a surprise for you."

"And clearly it's not sex. Just for future reference, baby—that's all I ever need."

I laughed as I pushed the door open. "Hi, you must be Skully?"

"I'm not into threesomes. I don't share," Cruz whispered against my ear.

The large tatted man stood and offered me a hand. "Yeah, you must be Jade."

Cruz glared at him. He was ridiculously jealous, even when there was no reason to be. I rolled my eyes. "This is my boyfriend, Cruz."

"Nice to meet you, man. Great show. Luke gave me the best seat in the house."

"Cool. Who are you and how do you know my girl?"

Skully laughed. He was much older than Cruz and me, probably in his mid-forties. He put his hands up and smiled. "Easy tiger. I'm a married man with three little hellions that my wife insists we keep. I don't have time for anything more."

"You do know you're ridiculous, right?" I said to my boyfriend. "Skully is a talented tattoo artist and I'm getting a tattoo."

"The fuck you are," Cruz said.

"Excuse me?" I crossed my arms over my chest and Skully chuckled before walking away to give us a minute.

"Tattoos are painful, baby. I'm not watching someone hurt you."

Me and Skully both laughed at the same time. Cruz had gotten a few tattoos while we'd been traveling this summer, and his arm was fairly covered in ink. And he was telling me not to get one?

"I'm not a child, nor am I afraid of a little pain. I'm getting a small one," I said, taking his hand and leading him over to see Skully's work.

"Dude, I've been doing this for a long time. She's going to be fine. It's a small tat. If you think you can't watch though, you should step outside. I don't want you making her nervous."

I tried to cover my smile. Skully was not taking Cruz's shit, which I'd come to learn he actually liked.

"Fuck that. I'm not letting her do it alone. What do you want to get?"

"A small music note, on the inside of my wrist. A little something to remind me of you," I said, dropping down to sit in the chair next to Skully.

"That's sweet. And how did you find *Skully*? No offense dude, just want to make sure you know what you're doing before you touch her."

"I hear you, brother. Trust me, Luke researched the shit out of me, but here's some of my work." Skully handed him a binder full of the art he'd inked on people over the years.

"This is impressive." Cruz studied each page.

"Thanks. Mind if I check yours out?" Skully asked, quirking a brow as he glanced at Cruz's arm.

"Not at all." My boyfriend tugged his shirt over his head, and my cheeks heated as I took him in. He was stunning. Chiseled abs and strong muscles covered in beautiful colors with meaningful sayings and drawings.

"Nice work. Who did them?"

"I had them done at Dark Angel back home," he said.

"Yeah? I worked with the owner, Chris, for years. We trained together before I moved out west. Did he do this one? More Jade?"

"Yep. I drew it and he inked it." Cruz looked over at me and winked.

"Incredible work. The color is insane," Skully said, handing Cruz his notebook with the drawing of the music note.

"Yeah, I'm happy with it. All right, I'm being an asshole. You've got this. Sorry."

"I get it, brother." Skully winked at me.

Cruz bent down and took my free hand. Skully got to work and once the design was ready to go, he tested out the area on my wrist and asked if it hurt.

"Not at all. I'm good," I said with a laugh, looking over at my boyfriend who squeezed my hand and studied my every move.

We talked as he inked the tiny music note on my left wrist, and Cruz started to relax. "That's sick, baby. I love it."

"I do too." I like that I'd have something to remind me of him forever now.

"Okay, let me just clean you up. You're a champ, Jade. This one's a different story." Skully jabbed his thumb at Cruz and we all laughed.

"I'm sorry for being a dick. Just can't handle seeing her hurt."

"Nah, man. I'm the same way with my lady. She makes you human," he said.

"She does." He kissed my wrist over the bandage and fought me when I paid for the tattoo.

"Let her win this one. She just tatted herself for you," Skully said.

Cruz put his hands up. "Okay, okay, I got it."

We jumped on the bus to head back to the hotel. Cruz never let go of my hand. Everything was about to change, and we were both feeling it.

Like a dark cloud that loomed above—we were preparing for the storm.

Thank you for reading More Jade, *book 1 in the Love You More Series. I hope you enjoyed your journey with Jade and Cruz! Please consider leaving a review on Amazon/Goodreads!! They help authors SO MUCH!!*

Acknowledgements

Pathi, Natalie, Hannah, Abi, Annette, Nicole and Doo, thank you for being the BEST beta readers EVER! Your feedback means the world to me. I would be lost without you!

Thank you, Jena Brignola for bringing this cover to life. I am so thankful that you worked your magic on this cover!

Sue (Edits by Sue), thank you for sharing your expertise, encouraging me and believing in this story!! Your support means the world to me. I appreciate you more than you know!!

Ellie (My Brother's Editor), thank you for being the most fabulous copy editor, working around my schedule and inviting me to my first book event!! I am so thankful for you!

Rosa (My Brother's Editor) thank you for polishing this book and being an amazing proofreader!

Tamara Cribley (The Deliberate Page), thank you for sharing your talent and turning my words into an actual book!!

A huge Thank you to Jo and Kylie at Give Me Books Promotions! I am truly so thankful for you!! Love working with you all so much!!

Nazarea (Inkslinger PR), thank you for all the support while promoting More Jade! You are the best!

Ashlee (Ashes & Vellichor) there are not enough words to tell you how much I love your book trailers! Thank you for capturing Jade and Cruz and bringing them to life!!

Huge thank you to Krista Thompson for making the CUTEST swag EVER!! Love you!

Dad, thank you for teaching me to never give up! Semper Fi. 10-4. LU.

Mom, Thank you for reading everything I write, and supporting me through it all. Love you!

Sandy, Thank you for ALWAYS supporting me. I know the *sexy-parts* and the F-bombs are torture for you, yet you keep on reading!! Love you!

Lisa, Eric, Julie, Jen and Jim, thank you for being the best siblings on the planet, and always encouraging and supporting me!! Love you!

Big thank you to Natalie Burtner (Head in the Clouds, Nose in a Book), for putting my newsletter together every month!! I am BEYOND thankful for you and our friendship! Love you!

Kathleen Pathi, thank you for always being my biggest cheerleader! Your friendship means THE WORLD to me! Thank you for believing in me! Love you!

Steph, Nicole, Sue, Thompson, Pathi, Bell, Natalie, Annette, Margy, Mindy, Kristin, Laura, Anne, Abi, Dina, Kelly, Maggie, Leigh Anne, Julie, Nancy, Bev, Leslie, Florence, Tina, Renae, Cindy, Darleen, Althea, Carol, Jess, Ariel, Heather, Shannon and Krisi (and all the girls at d'annata boutique), Johana, Kayla, and UNLV Rebel reads, Bridget (and the sweet ladies at Bloom), and all of my friends who have supported me along this journey…thank you so much!!

Other books by Laura Pavlov

Laura Pavlov

The G.D. Taylors Series with Willow Aster
Wanted Wed or Alive
The Bold and the Bullheaded
Another Motherfaker
Don't Cry Spilled MILF
Friends with Benefactors

KEEP UP ON NEW RELEASES…
Linktree
Newsletter

FOLLOW ME…
Website laurapavlov.com
Goodreads @laurapavlov
Instagram @laurapavlovauthor
Facebook @laurapavlovauthor
Pav-Love's Readers @pav-love's readers
Amazon @laurapavlov
BookBub @laurapavlov
TikTok @laurapavlovauthor

Made in United States
Orlando, FL
15 February 2024

43695586R00155